GW01471576

Sean Wilson is a writer, playwright and communications professional from Perth, Western Australia. His short stories have been published in Australian and international journals, anthologies and literary magazines including *Island* and *Narrative*, and he was previously shortlisted for the Patrick White Playwrights Award by Sydney Theatre Company. He now lives in Melbourne with his fiancée. *Gemini Falls* is his first book.

GEMINI FALLS

Sean Wilson

affirm
press

affirm
press

First published by Affirm Press in 2022
Boon Wurrung Country
28 Thistlethwaite Street
South Melbourne VIC 3205
affirmpress.com.au

10 9 8 7 6 5 4 3 2 1

Text copyright © Sean Wilson, 2022
All rights reserved. No part of this publication may be reproduced without prior written permission from the publisher.

A catalogue record for this
book is available from the
National Library of Australia

ISBN: 9781922806390 (paperback)

Cover design by Lisa White © Affirm Press
Cover image credit © Mark Owen / Trevillion Images
Typeset in Granjon by J&M Typesetting
Proudly printed and bound in Australia by McPherson's Printing Group

MIX
Paper | Supporting
responsible forestry
FSC® C001695

For Kat

'Sometimes a sad man can talk the sadness right out through his mouth. Sometimes a killin' man can talk the murder right out of his mouth.'

— John Steinbeck, *The Grapes of Wrath*

1

The night Catherine Fletcher died, Capricornus was high in the northern sky. I know because I'm listening to Father talk about her on the telephone. I can see the grey hairs mixed in with the black of his beard, lit by the faint glow of the kerosene lamp. He's standing in the hall, speaking in his quiet voice. His hand is cupped over his mouth but from where I am, crouched on the stairs, I can hear most of what he's saying. If there's one thing I've learned about men like Father, it's that they can't, for the life of them, speak quietly on the telephone.

They found Catherine Fletcher in a mine tunnel in Gemini. Out near mountain country, underneath the bright stars of the Southern Cross, more than halfway along the road to New South Wales and some miles south of that. A long way from Melbourne, from our house in Hawthorn. I've seen Gemini marked on a map in Father's library. A little dot on paper, wrapped by tight, curved lines. It's a small coal town in a valley between hills, barely eight hundred people to call it home. That's all Father has said about it, in the few times he's talked about the town. It's where he grew up, where his whole family is from, but he hasn't been back in a long time. Something happened, something Father won't talk about, and the town and everyone in it are off-limits for us.

Her body was lying in Long Tunnel East, down along the sloping, narrow rail tracks they use to cart coal up from the depths. She was a few feet past the tunnel entrance, before you get to the locked gate. She had some clothes on but not many, less than a young woman would wear outside her home. There were dark marks around her neck, marks that shouldn't have been there. She had two wounds in her back. Stabbed from behind, Father repeated through the telephone. Stabbed while she was walking away.

She was on her back in the tunnel when they found her. No blood around, nothing soaked into the dirt. It was as if her blood had been drawn from her body and carried to the heavens. Her face was covered by long brown hair, laid down like a shroud. That's the word Father used. I repeat the word in my head. *A shroud, a shroud, a shroud.* I try to see her in my mind's eye. It makes me sick and sad at the same time.

It had rained that night in Gemini. A big storm, the kind they often get there. That's what I know about Gemini, what I've put together from the newspapers and weather reports on the radio. A place of storms. A place where the clouds gather and settle. It had rained from midnight on. Catherine Fletcher was last seen by her mother at eight that evening. She must have stolen out of her room after that, but her body was dry. She didn't get wet in the storm. That means she died between eight and midnight, before the first rain fell.

Between the hours of eight and midnight. Capricornus shining in the northern sky.

People say the stars shine brighter in the country. The darkness makes them stand out. The furthest from here I've gone is some dairy farms and market gardens a horse ride away. I try to imagine them, the stars above Gemini, laid out like a quilt from one end of the sky to the other.

I never knew Catherine Fletcher, never saw her in my life. Even so, I wish I could turn back the clock and stop that happening to her. I think about my sister and how I would feel if it was her lying in a tunnel, hair covering her face, rain falling outside. Father must be thinking the same. I see the way his shoulders slump, the way his head rolls to the side, as if weighed down by these thoughts. Something tells me he's thinking what it would be like to be Catherine Fletcher's folks, losing a daughter that way.

My name is Morris Turner. I'm thirteen years old. The man down there on the telephone is my father, Jude Turner. Detective Turner. My older sister is Charlotte, but everyone calls her Lottie. We used to be close. We used to tell each other everything. When we were younger, I would go to her room in the middle of the night when bad dreams haunted me. She would turn down the sheet, wrap an arm around me and hold me close. I'd feel her heart beating against my back and my breathing would slow, my eyelids would droop and close. I can't remember ever feeling better than that, taken from fear to comfort so fast, the speed of it making the good feeling stronger. These days she hardly talks to me.

It's late. From my place on the landing of the stairs I can see dust floating in the air above me and around me, lit by the warm glow of the lamp. It's pleasant, the way it moves, the way each speck shifts like a star making its way across the night sky. Making constellations in the air and then falling apart.

Anyone keen on stars knows that at this time of year Capricornus is highest in the middle of the evening, this time of year being late spring. Lottie told me Mother used to say you could see all of time in the stars. She said that in the sky, the same lights have shone down on every person who's ever lived. I wish I had the same memories of Mother, but I was too young. If I try to imagine it, I can almost feel her arm around me, her finger lifting my chin to the sky. I can almost be with her, looking up at the stars, our eyes taking in light from the galaxies.

I've seen Gemini and Capricornus in the night sky, along with Sagittarius, Scorpius and most of the rest. We've got an old telescope on the balcony, and some nights, when I've done my chores and the clouds have blown out of the sky, Father will let me use it. We'll stand there for hours looking at Orion and Centaurus and Hydra, calling out the names of the stars we see, old names that feel strange on my tongue.

Father says people called Capricornus 'the Gate of the Gods'. When you run a line between the stars in the constellation, it makes a shape that looks like an opening. People thought it was the gate where our souls pass after we die. The Gate of the Gods. I wonder if that was where Mother passed. I want to ask Father, but whenever I talk about Mother, a shadow passes over his face and he turns away or leaves the room. I feel the words forming on my tongue, but I swallow them down. They go deep inside my body where they join together, packed tight into bricks made of the words I can't say. He can't talk about her and so I don't talk about her.

Out in the hall, Father's voice gets louder. It's a storm cloud rising above me. One word is louder than all the others. It stays in the air, thunder rolling around the hall. *Pregnant.* Catherine Fletcher was pregnant when she died. She was little more than a child herself, Father says on the telephone, and she was almost a mother.

Father says goodbye and drops the handset on the base. He sighs and runs his fingers through his hair. I can see the outline of his nose, the places where it has broken and healed. A crooked line, a constellation all his own. His back is hunched. His shirt hangs loose around him.

I know I should be back in my room. I know I should lift one leg after the other, lift them up step after step. I can't do it. This isn't like me. I want to know more. I want to know more about Catherine Fletcher. I want to know more about Gemini.

Father told me wherever a star forms in a galaxy, a ring of gas and dust fills the space around it. The pull of the star makes those bits and pieces fall into orbit. It becomes a system, he said. The system pulls toward the star and, over time, the bits and pieces join together. Year after year, they get bigger and bigger until they become planets. That's how our planet came to be.

The way I figure it, a murder is like a planetary system forming. People get pulled into orbit around it. They circle the crime, side by side, everyone moving around and around that terrible thing. They can't help it.

We're about to fall into orbit around Catherine Fletcher, I know it.

2

When I wake, Father is gone. Rain is falling and I wait out the storm indoors. It's Melbourne Cup Day, a holiday for most. Father has left four shillings on the table and a message for Lottie to buy some bread and eggs from the corner store.

I leave the coins where they are and go back to my room. Money is sacred to me. Other boys waste what coins they can gather on sweets and marbles. I keep whatever comes my way in a jar under my bed. Money is what keeps the wolf from the door. That's a saying Father told me. In the evenings, when me and Father stand on the balcony and look at the stars, I watch for the weak lights of Richmond. Those streets on the other side of the river, with factories and houses like rubble patched together. I imagine what our lives would be like if we lived there. The grime that would cover everything, the holes in our clothes, the light shining off muddy puddles. I watch the smoke that drifts over the river, over the dirty brown water they call the Yarra, and I see it settle around the trees in our street.

Lottie walks into my room, rubbing sleep from her eyes. I keep my head down and lace my boots. I don't want to see the way her pyjamas pull tight below her shoulders, the way her hips reach out, pushing her legs to strange angles. The way her brown hair hangs loose, strands falling over her face. I shake my head to move away the thoughts from last night. The shroud made of hair.

'Where are you going?'

'Off with George. Father left a note in the kitchen,' I say.

'Where is he?'

'Working, I suppose.'

'He left before breakfast,' Lottie says. 'What's going on?'

'He's got a new case,' I say. 'It's a murder.'

'How do you know? Did he tell you?'

My mind takes me back to last night, to the phone call, to the feel of the rug between my toes as I crouched on the landing. I wasn't supposed to be listening.

'I'm only guessing,' I say and yawn, as if I dreamed the murder. 'Why else would he leave before breakfast?'

I put on my wool cap and pull it down over my forehead. Lottie watches me.

'Where are you off to exactly?'

'To town.'

Lottie lays her hands on her hips.

'And who'll be left to do the chores around here?'

'It's Cup Day. We're off to see a concert in town,' I say. 'George's cousin is meeting us. Hugh. You know him.'

Colour floods Lottie's cheeks at the mention of Hugh. She watches me. I'm dressed in the best clothes I have other than my Sunday clothes. I move past Lottie and I'm at the stairs, already down the first step, when I call over my shoulder.

'I'll let Hugh know you've been thinking of him.'

I hear Lottie wail and tell me I better not dare if I know what's good for me. She's still yelling when I open the front door and step into the light.

'Master Turner, where are you off to so early?'

It's Mrs Clayton from next door. She's kneeling in her front garden, surrounded by the whites and reds and yellows of her roses. The tangled, thorny bushes line the iron fence between our gardens. Mrs Clayton's terriers, Fish and Chips, come running to the fence, tails wagging, and I reach through the iron bars and let the dogs lick my hand.

'I'm off to town with George. We're meeting his cousin.'

'Are you indeed? Isn't it a lovely day to be out?'

Mrs Clayton often speaks in questions. It's something grown people do. They ask a lot of questions that don't need answers. I've heard the Prime Minister, Mr Scullin, talk in questions on the newsreels. Father says he's a good working man, Mr Scullin. It's not his fault the crash happened. He'd only been sworn in as prime minister two days before. Mrs Clayton rises from her garden and walks over to the fence. Her back has a hunch, holding her barely higher than the roses. Her eyes are a dim blue and her white hair bends in the breeze.

'Will you watch the race today?' I ask.

'Not me, no. I'll be here in the garden. That'll do me.'

Mrs Clayton had a son who died in the war and a husband who took to the influenza not long after. I once asked Father how Mrs Clayton gets money now there are no wages coming in. He said she gets by with the help of family and I should never ask her a question like that. Not ever.

I make for the gate and Mrs Clayton holds up a hand, waves me over.

'Do me one favour, will you, before you go?'

I nod, watching Mrs Clayton's eyes, the edges ringed with a red as bright as her roses.

'Promise me you'll be careful on your way,' she says. 'I've heard some awful stories since we got into this trouble. People aren't themselves in hard times. Promise me, will you?'

'I promise.'

Mrs Clayton lets me go on my way. It's quiet in the street. I look at the houses I pass, all perfectly still from the outside. The people who live on our street are civil servants, estate agents, building contractors. There's a surgeon and a lawyer. A couple of the houses are empty, the lawns like crops ready for harvest. People in the street talk about the families after they've left. They say words like 'destitute' and 'insolvent'. People say the families got in too much debt or they lent money they can't get back. No matter how it happens, this is what's left behind. Empty houses, long grass.

I walk past Mr and Mrs Elliot's house, where they live with their daughter, Iris. They have the oldest house on the street. Made of dark bluestone, wider than it is tall. There are ritzy plants growing around the house, and a straight tree standing above it all. It's a foreign tree, something brought over from Europe. It looks nothing like the twisted gum trees that grow beside the river, the ones that drop thick boughs in the heat or crack in two during storms. This tree looks made to last any trouble.

Across the street and a few houses down is the Greene family. I knock on the front door and George answers. He's dressed in his usual clothes but there's something strange around his neck. Below his red cheeks, around his pale neck, there are woven leaves and flowers.

'Come on,' George says, pushing me back from the door. 'Let's get going.'

'What is that, a Christmas wreath? Did someone mistake you for the front door?'

'All right. Keep moving.'

We're twenty yards down the street when we hear Mrs Greene calling out behind us.

'You boys be careful,' she says. 'Remember what I told you, Georgie.'

George waves back to her, keeps on rushing away from the house. I'm a head taller than him but I have to break into a run to keep up.

'What's going on? You joined a new religion or something?'

George has a pained look on his face. Eyes narrow, lips parted, showing teeth that are too big for his mouth.

'You never have a clue what's going on, Turner,' he says. 'You ought to get your head out of the stars now and then.'

George turns and looks back the way we came. His house is out of view now, lost behind the line of trees. He pulls the wreath over his neck and drops his arm, letting it drag along the street. 'It's camphor and some other nonsense,' he says. 'If you knew anything, you'd know there's some polio going around again. Mother thinks this is going to stop me catching it.'

I feel a heat in my neck. *Polio*. The word makes me think of twisted feet, knees bending backwards, shiny leg braces that clatter like chains. I saw a picture once of children in hospital beds. The boys were lying bolt-straight in bed, legs strapped and bandaged. Each one staring at the ceiling, not one looking at the camera.

'She thinks I'm going to walk around with this on my neck, she's got another thing coming. I smell like a roast chicken. And does my father say anything? He lets her do it.' George shakes his head. 'Why'd I have to get a mother who's always in my business?'

I think of that warm feeling on my cheek, of my mother holding my chin, her hand pointing my eyes to the sky. And then it goes. The warmth falls away. I don't feel her anymore.

We get to the line of gum trees near the river. George bends down and lays the wreath against one of the trees, the way they do with flowers when there's a motor car accident.

'You know she'll want to see you wearing that when you get home.'

'I know it,' George says, kicking dirt at the wreath. 'We'll pick it up on the way back. Nobody's going to steal a stinking bunch of leaves.'

We make our way south. When we get to the bridge, the one that crosses over to Richmond for the short way to town, George turns and starts walking over.

'Where are you going? You know we're not allowed over there,' I say.

George looks over his shoulder and shrugs. 'I've been over plenty,' he says. 'Nothing to it.'

George keeps walking over the bridge. I think about the smoke that rises over Richmond. I think about the stories I've heard. People boiling horse bones for soup. Men so thin their clothes flap like flags in the wind.

I get a feeling inside, standing at the bridge, watching George cross over. My body is still but the insides of me move around and bubble like they're on the boil. It's a feeling I can't shake. Whenever there's anything to worry about, my nerves start to go. Some days it's all I can think of, this problem with me. The detective's son who can't hold his nerve.

George looks back from the other side of the river. 'What're you waiting for? You forget how to walk?'

I cross the bridge and follow George, watching my feet as the steps take me further from home.

It's not long until there's a change in the air. There's a gloom that sets in the further we go. We pass under the awnings of shops selling cheap goods and staples. We see the worst cuts of meat, old clothing, limp flowers. Many shops are empty, newspaper tacked up on the windows. I see a headline about the crash on Wall Street.

We cross side streets and see rubbish in the gutters. We see sullen people, their faces in need of a wash. Children with torn shirts or dresses made out of sacks. We pass a motor and coach works near Church Street. Men move around, inside and out, dragging tools from place to place. They're breaking down cars and coaches. There are piles of metal around the outside of the shop, mounds and mounds of scrap shining in the morning light.

We make our way back down to the river and follow it toward town. The sun shines on the surface of the brown water, turning it golden. Ducks wade out from the banks. People crowd the path that runs along the Yarra. Some look to be out for a stroll. The men wear new hats and waistcoats and smoke cigars. The women wear hats with flowers. They carry parasols the colours of spring.

There are other people too, men who look like they've been beside the river a long time. Their faces are low, hidden under the brims of hats dotted with holes. Their collars hang limp around their necks, white cotton turned the colour of the river's banks. There are no women with these men. They stand in small groups, talking quietly.

'They must be on the susso,' George says, tilting his head toward the men.

'What's the susso?'

George sighs. He looks me up and down. 'You're hopeless, you are. It's a wonder you can work the front door of your house and make it outside.'

'Are you going to tell me or not?'

George looks at the sky, thinks it over. 'The susso is what they give men who can't work,' he says. 'My father told me about it. It's short for "sustenance". There aren't enough jobs to go around so they give some men the susso.'

'How much is it?'

'I don't know if it's money. It might be flour and tea and sugar, things like that. Mother says it's not enough to live on. She says people give more than that to a dog.'

We pass men playing chess on a bench. The pieces look hand-carved, rough and jagged like the wood that washes up in the river. It's hard to tell the white from the black on the board. I stare at the faces of the men as we pass and I wonder if they've cheated or stolen. If they've done something to wind up here. I look at their eyes, trying to find some difference in them.

'My father says there are settlements upriver, with people on the susso,' George says, pointing upstream. 'He won't usually talk about that but one night after the horse races he got so wild on gin that he threw up in the kitchen sink.'

'That's disgusting.'

'You're telling me. The kitchen smelled like an outhouse covered in acid. Anyway, he got so wild he told me about the people living in little towns made of wooden crates and tar paper. He said they sleep under newspapers and that the ink stains their skin and they have to glue hessian on the soles of their shoes to stop the wet getting in.'

It sometimes floods there, further upriver. I try to imagine it, the houses made of crates, the people huddled together as the water rises. The thought makes me remember the telephone call. What Father said about the storm and the rain falling outside the tunnel. I think of water pooling near the feet of Catherine Fletcher, of her pale skin, of the hair laid down over her face.

'I heard Father talking on the telephone last night,' I say.

'What about?' George says as he picks up a stone and throws it into the river.

'There's been a murder. A woman found in the coal tunnels in Gemini, out where Father's from.'

'He taking the case?'

'Don't know yet,' I say.

We move into town, to the wide streets and tall buildings. Trams roll by carrying men and women dressed for the races. Shoe leather polished to shining, rouge on cheeks, gloves white as bone. I can smell the perfume as the cars pass.

We walk down the hill and the people ahead of us start turning down side streets. They cross over to the other footpath. At one of the churches up ahead is a queue of men stretching away down the hill, longer than you see at weekend football matches. We get closer and I can see them. Some look like the men down by the river. There are others who look like they've come from offices and factories and shops, collars starched.

Outside the church, a dozen people dip ladles into vats and drop soup into tin mugs. They hand out bread and boiled potatoes. The men shuffle forward and take the food, bowing and nodding. They walk away from the line and turn down the street that leads to the river.

'Makes you wonder where they all come from,' George says.

We pass the end of the line and weave through the trams and cars and horses near the town hall. On the footpath, there's a man with a sign hanging over his neck. The sign runs from his shoulders to his knees. It reads, *I am for sale. Give me work or I starve.* He paces back and forth near the road. There are other men selling apples from crates. The apples are half rancid, soft and wrinkled.

'That night my father drank the gin, he told me how all this happened,' George says. 'He said the stock exchanges went south and that's the reason it's all a mess.'

'Went south? Did they move to Tasmania?'

George goes on, shaking his head, ignoring me. 'He said it's all greed. A lot of greedy people at the exchange and the banks put on bets. Just like the races. They even borrowed money for the bets and it worked as long as the price went up. He said there has to be someone next in line to buy it or it doesn't work, and when people stop lining up, when you can't sell it to them, it all comes tumbling down.'

We pass another man with a sign, held out in front of his chest. It reads, *Skilled CARPENTER of 15 years. I need a JOB not a HANDOUT.*

'My father said ordinary people weren't to blame for the crash so we should go easy on them,' George says. 'They're caught up in something bigger like fish in a net. You wouldn't say the fish are to blame, swimming into the net and getting caught. They're only swimming. They'd be fine without the net. He said there are people in the world who make the nets and there are people who swim into them, and we ought to remember who is who.'

George's cousin Hugh is standing outside the bank on the corner of Elizabeth Street, the flat stone of the building rising around him. He waves when he sees us crossing the street. Hugh and George are the same kind of build. Low to the ground. Thick legs and arms filling out their clothes. They look like a matching tea set, cups and saucers on a shelf, looking for all the world like they belong together. A family.

We follow Hugh across Elizabeth Street and climb the hill on the other side. We're near the Western Market when I hear it. A sound beside the engines of the motor cars and shouts of policemen directing traffic. I hear brass instruments and percussion. There's the thrum of a double bass. Above it all, I hear the sweet sounds of women singing.

15

'They've been holding these concerts in the hope people come to town and buy something,' Hugh says, hands clasped behind his back, ear pointed to the wind. 'This should be a good one.'

We turn at Market Street and see a crowd of people gathered near a bandstand made of wooden slats and canvas. The street is blocked off and people are hanging from streetlamps to get a look at the musicians, each player dressed in matching suits and bowties. The musicians dab their foreheads with handkerchiefs every chance they get. Two policemen on horses are watching on. One of them is tapping on his thigh, keeping time.

Hugh takes off his cap and waves it above his head. George sways to the music. I look around at the faces of the men and women and children. They're smiling, leaning forward as if their bodies want to get closer to the good feeling. There's something odd about the people around us. There's a well inside them, a deep hole that's run dry. A place they need to fill. People puff on cigarettes and blow the smoke high into the air. Smoke and music gather around the onlookers, joining them together.

3

The news gets around in the afternoon. Phar Lap has won the Cup. We get back to our street and the neighbours are out of their houses. Men are in their shirtsleeves, despite the chill in the wind. Women are passing out drinks. Mrs Clayton stands in the street, holding her hat to her head.

'Master Turner and Master Greene,' she says. 'I expect you've heard the wonderful news.'

'We sure have,' George says. 'We've come straight from Flemington ourselves. Saw it with my own eyes. Incredible, it was.'

George makes like he's riding a horse, whipping with one arm and moving his legs like he's in a gallop. Mrs Clayton rolls her eyes.

'He's telling fibs,' I say.

Mrs Greene looks over from their gate. 'George Greene,' she says, calling over the sound in the street. 'Stop fooling around and give your mother a kiss.'

George acts like he doesn't hear.

'You better go kiss her cheek, Georgie boy,' I say. 'You don't want to break your poor mother's heart.'

'I'd rather kiss the hand of sweet Lady Luck. Me and Phar Lap here are going to win every race in the world.'

He neighs and kicks his legs high in the air. Mrs Greene is smiling. She seems to have forgotten about the camphor.

I look out at the street, at the people talking and toasting. I can't remember the last time there were this many neighbours out in the street. Someone switches on a record player and a handful of people form couples. Others link arms and sway. The cool wind picks up but nobody seems to feel it. They go on dancing and talking. The sun starts to fall, drawing long shadows across the street. I see Lottie in the crowd. She's standing apart, talking to a young man I've seen around the neighbourhood. He stands close to her, hands in his pockets. She smiles and touches her hair.

A car pulls into the street, inching along, parting the crowd. It turns onto the driveway at the grand old Elliot house. Mrs Elliot gets out, followed by Mr Elliot. She moves fast, legs tumbling forward. Her hair is down. I've never seen Mrs Elliot's hair down. She raises one arm and points a finger at me. 'You!'

I feel my face flush, hot as an oven.

Mrs Elliot swings her arm as she walks. Her finger points at George. 'And you,' she says. 'It's all your fault!'

People step aside as Mrs Elliot rushes through the street. Mr Elliot follows behind, trying to reach his wife.

'Missus Elliot,' I say. 'What's wrong?'

'It's your fault she caught it.'

Mrs Clayton wraps an arm around me and moves between me and Mrs Elliot. George falls in behind us. I see Lottie looking in our direction. Mrs Greene moves past neighbours, neck craning for a view.

'Ida, what's all this about? Why are you shouting at the boys?' It's Mrs Clayton talking. She raises a hand as Mrs Elliot gets near.

'I wouldn't get any closer to these two,' Mrs Elliot says. 'It's not safe.'

The whites of her eyes are a mess of tangled red lines. There's hardly any white to see.

'What are you talking about, dear? You don't seem well.'

I look around Mrs Clayton's shoulder at the people gathering closer. Someone calls out for Mrs Elliot to explain herself. I can see Mrs Greene trying to get to us through the crowd.

Mr Elliot lays a hand on his wife's shoulder. She flinches, her whole body shaking the way people do when they're in a fit. I once saw a boy in my class have a fit on a hot summer day. It looked as though his soul was trying to shake out of his body.

'I'll tell you what I'm talking about,' Mrs Elliot says. 'She's caught polio and it's their fault.'

'Who's caught polio, dear?'

'My Iris. She's in the hospital and it's their fault. Paige Mitchell saw them go into Richmond, over there in those dirty streets. You ask Paige. They've been in before and they've brought this back. They've carried it back into the street only they haven't got sick, my Iris has.'

Mrs Elliot looks down her nose at George and me. Her eyes dart back and forth. Mr Elliot takes hold of one of her arms.

'Come home,' he says. 'There's no good in this.'

'I'm not leaving until these boys admit what they've done,' Mrs Elliot says, raising a finger. It's a picket running through me, burrowing into the soft earth of me. 'Admit it, you dirty little boys.'

Mrs Elliot's anger seems to lift me and turn me. I feel like I'm floating. I am floating. Someone is holding me. I can feel the arms circling me, the force moving me around. I turn my head and see the side of Father's beard, the dark and twisted hairs. He drops me and then he's standing there between me and Mrs Elliot.

'You go on home now, Ida,' Father says.

19

Mrs Greene reaches us and takes hold of George's hand. She starts to lead him back home.

'They have to know,' Mrs Elliot says.

There's less feeling in her voice now. It starts to waver, the way singers' voices do on the records, the pitch of her voice trembling along with her body.

'They have to know what they've done.'

'Come on, dear,' Mr Elliot says. 'Let's go home.'

He leads Mrs Elliot by the elbow. Tears fall down her cheeks. Mr Elliot speaks to Father, to Mrs Clayton, to me, to everyone gathered around.

'I'm sorry,' he says. 'Forgive us.'

Father nods, his body square on Mr Elliot, keeping me behind him.

'Sorry about your girl,' Father says.

People move back to their houses. Mothers and fathers guide their children away toward gates and front doors. I see George and Mrs Greene up ahead. George turns and looks at me before he's out of sight, lost in the moving mass of people. Everyone leaving at once like the birds we learned about in school. All those birds moving across the sky, drawn back to their nests.

'Thank you, Ethel,' Father says.

He's talking to Mrs Clayton. She looks like she needs to lie down. She puts on a weak smile.

'It was nothing,' she says.

Lottie reaches us, lays a hand on my shoulder. It feels light and heavy at the same time. It feels like the pull of a star, the gravity that keeps the planets spinning around and around in space. She hasn't put her hand on my shoulder in a long time. I try to remember the last time, but I can't. There's no memory, only the thought of moving water. River water washing downstream in a current. I start to wonder what the thought means and I feel Father's hand on my other shoulder, pushing me gently toward our house.

'Back home,' he says. 'We need to stay out of the street.'

4

We don't speak at tea. It's not until after he's finished his mash and the last of his pie that Father sets down his knife and fork.

'There's been a murder,' he says. 'Over in Gemini, where I'm from. We're leaving tomorrow.'

The room seems to shift, one side dropping.

'It was a girl.' He shifts his weight, moving in his chair as if trying to fix an ache. 'A young woman, not much older than Lottie. We have to go.'

'Did you know her?' I ask.

'I knew her father, but not well.'

I think back to the night of the telephone call. Father's head weighed down by thoughts.

'What about school? We can't miss our classes,' Lottie says.

'There's not much school left,' Father says. 'It's almost summer.'

The planet tilts. We've strayed, cut loose from what held us, moved to the orbit of something else. Catherine Fletcher.

'We'll stay with your uncle and aunt and cousin. Out on the farm.'

There's something in Father's face, in the way his brow comes together, in the way the skin around his eyes goes tight. Lottie told me once that Father's mother died when he was young, died giving birth to his younger brother. It was only Father, his brother and our grandfather for many years, until Father left Gemini. Our grandfather died some time after he left.

'It's safer there, with the polio. There's open country and the air's good.'

'I don't care if there's an ocean of country,' Lottie says. 'I'm not going.'

'When we leave,' I say, 'can we bring the telescope?'

Lottie turns to me. I can almost feel the heat coming from her. She rises from the table, knocking her chair to the ground, and leaves the room.

'She'll come around,' Father says.

He lifts Lottie's chair, puts it back on its legs. We spend the next few minutes tidying without talking. After all the plates are washed and the glasses are rinsed, Father leaves to speak to the Greenes about looking after our house when we're gone.

A light rain begins to fall outside. I hear it tapping on the tin roof. In the distance, below the sound of the rain, I hear cars passing along a nearby street and the odd horse clipping by.

I pace around the house, moving from room to room. My eyes are open but my mind is elsewhere. I walk past Father's library. The door is slightly open. I can see a shard of light between it and the frame.

The library is small and crowded. There's a leather armchair, a small rug, a globe on a side table. One wall is a bookcase, stacked high with leather spines. There are papers tacked up on the walls. Names and numbers. I can't make sense of them. The room is mostly taken up by Father's desk. Plum-coloured wood and heavy. On the desk, out in the open, I see photographs that I shouldn't be seeing.

There are five photographs. A woman's body, bright against the soil and rocks. Hair where her face should be. I see her shoulder and neck, dark patches on the skin. One photograph shows her bare feet covered in mud. Another shows her legs, the skin scratched. Scrapes up and down the pale skin. Another shows two wounds, marks no longer than a finger. Cracks in the place between life and death.

My heart starts to race. This is Catherine Fletcher, I know it. I can't get my breath. The walls of the library seem close, the leather spines on the bookcase long and large. I can see the names on the spines. *Aristotle. Seneca. Plato. Homer.* They are witness to me being here. They see me standing over her body. I look down and see something in the dirt next to Catherine Fletcher. It's in one of the photographs, almost hidden in the pile. It's hard to make out. I pick up the photograph. There, in the background beside Catherine Fletcher's body, is a single flower. A lily.

'Morris. What are you doing in here?'

Father rushes to me and takes the photograph from my hand. He gathers the other photographs and pushes them into a folder. He turns on me, eyes wild. My heart is racing and I feel a burning at the base of my throat.

'Why do you do this? Why do you test me?' He steps back, breathing fast. 'How am I supposed to do this on my own?'

I want to melt into the floor. Father holds the folder tight. His eyes scan the walls and the desk, and his movements slow down. He takes a deep breath and holds it inside.

'I'm sorry,' I say.

Father steps over to me and puts a hand on my shoulder.

'It's all right,' he says. 'I shouldn't have left this out.'

I look at the folder in his hands.

'Who is she?'

Father doesn't know that I heard him on the telephone. He doesn't know I watched him lean against the wall in the hallway, how he stayed there after the call.

'Come with me,' he says.

We walk in silence. I follow Father up the stairs, through his bedroom and onto the balcony. On one side of the balcony is the telescope. It's a long black tube with shiny rings around each end, resting on thin, straight legs. There's an eyepiece attached to the top of the tube, pushing out like a growth. Father leans over and looks through the eyepiece. He turns the telescope around on its mount like a captain moving a ship. He stands back.

'Tell me what you see,' he says.

The stars rush to fill my vision. I can't find a place to rest my eyes. They're so bright. There's so much to see.

'I don't know,' I say.

'Keep looking.'

I can hear him behind me, his breath slow and steady now. Father says looking at the stars is like looking into the past. Light takes time to reach us. The stars as they look to us now are actually the stars as they were a long time ago, when the light left them to travel to us. If the stars change, we won't know about it for a long time. There are many things we don't know until later.

'I don't know what it is,' I say.

'Yes, you do. Find one pattern and the rest will come.'

All I see is light. I can't make out any shapes, any patterns. And then I see it. Three stars close together.

'I see Orion's belt.'

'Good. You've got it now. Let the rest fall into place.'

The constellation comes to me, as if lines are being drawn in the sky. I see Orion's shield. I see his sword, raised above his body. I see it all, as if it was always clear to me.

'We have to take our time,' Father says. 'When we're ready, we'll see what we need to see. Be patient and wait until you're ready to see the world how it is. That goes for the stars and everything else, Morris.'

I know what Father is saying. He has a way of talking about what matters without talking about it. It's the same in the books he has in his library, with stories that stand in place for something else. Father says that sometimes talking like that is the best way to get across your meaning.

'Have I told you the story of Orion?'

'Tell me again,' I say.

Father clears his throat. 'Orion was a hunter,' he says. 'To the Greeks, he was the son of Poseidon, god of the sea. He was strong, the most feared hunter in Greece, and he thought that meant he could do as he pleased. So he hurt people. He promised to kill every animal on Earth and he angered Gaia, the mother of all life. She sent Scorpius to kill him.'

The Orion I see in my head, the one I'm imagining over these stars, changes. Now he's looking over his shoulder.

'That's why you never see Orion and Scorpius in the sky together,' Father says. 'When one rises, the other one falls. They're on opposite sides. Scorpius is always chasing Orion.'

Even in the stars there are stories about the awful parts of the world, about what can happen down here on the ground. These are the stories that stand in for something else. Stories about the ones who hurt and the ones who hunt them.

'There are always two sides,' Father says. 'One against another. Opposing forces in us and all around us. The trick to life is working out how to hold on to the good side, holding on to what you believe is right, and not letting the other side take over.'

I think about the men down by the river. I think about Catherine Fletcher lying in the dirt. I move away from the telescope and look at Father. He's resting against the window, looking off toward Richmond.

'How do I do that?' I ask. 'How do I know what to do?'

Father smiles, musses my hair with his hand. 'There's plenty of time to work that out. That's what growing up is for.'

Father lifts the telescope. He moves it near the wall and steadies it on the boards of the balcony.

'What happened to that girl, is that because of someone like Orion?'

'I don't know,' Father says. 'That's what I need to work out.'

I look down at the balcony floor, at the raw wooden boards. 'The photograph in your library, is there one like that of Mother in someone else's library?'

I can feel Father looking at me. I keep my eyes on the boards, roughing them with my heel.

'No, son,' he says.

I can sense him turning away from me. In the distance, a whistle rings out from one of the factories. A fruit bat lets off a shrill call. I look out over the street and see clouds coming in from the south, blue-grey in the dim light, dye dropped in water. They leak over the stars, one by one.

What I know about Mother, what I've gathered together, is that she was from a place near Gemini. An even smaller part of the country, one that's hard to find even when you're looking. When Father and Mother were young something happened, something he won't talk about. They came here to the city where me and Lottie were born and that was it. They never went back.

'Come on,' Father says. 'Off to bed now. We've got a lot on tomorrow.'

I follow him through the door and into the house. I look over my shoulder as I leave the balcony and see the clouds swallow up the last of the stars in the sky. A thought stays with me as I move into the light. The photographs I saw, the body by the tunnel. The hair, the arms, the legs. If I didn't know it was Catherine Fletcher, I could have sworn it was Lottie.

5

Father is out by the car, warming the engine. The back seat is loaded high with bags and hats and coats. On top of the pile, shining in the light, is the telescope. On one side of the seat there's a space wide enough for my body.

The street looks different somehow. Everything seems more important. I watch the blooms on the trees shake in the breeze. I see flies moving in the air, the shadows of passing clouds shifting over the road and rooftops. This must be what it feels like to leave somewhere.

Lottie walks out of the house and passes through the gate without looking back. She climbs onto the front seat, face blank and empty.

Mrs Clayton opens her front door and walks out to her yard, Fish and Chips running circles around her legs. 'Come say goodbye to the dogs,' she says. 'They'll miss you.'

I walk to the fence. Lottie stays in the car, arms folded.

'Oh dear,' Mrs Clayton says in a whisper. 'It's that bad, is it?'

Fish and Chips press their snouts through the gaps in the fence and sniff. Their tails are metronomes, keeping time. I lean down and scratch each of them under their snouts, staring into their weepy eyes.

'I'll miss you two,' I say. I stand and notice something in Mrs Clayton's hand. It's a chain, thin as a few strands of hair, dangling from her fingers. There's some kind of pendant at the end of the chain.

'This is for you, Master Turner. I've had it for a long time.'

I take the pendant and lift it to my eyes. It's a small circle, a kind of plate, with a plant on its face.

'It's white heather,' Mrs Clayton says. 'It's for good luck, for men and women alike. It used to belong to my boy, Neil. He left it behind when he went to the front.' Mrs Clayton's breathing gets faster. Colour floods her cheeks. 'Wear this every day and it'll give you luck and protect you,' she says.

'I will,' I say, staring at the pendant, a white glow in the morning light.

'Be careful out there,' she says. 'Life is different in the country. There are dangers you can't always see.'

Father walks out of the house, pulling the front door behind him. He closes it and shakes it on its latch, testing the lock.

'Don't you worry,' Mrs Clayton says to Father. 'I'll keep an eye on the house.'

'I know you will, Ethel,' he says, walking to the fence, 'and those savage beasts there will tear any thieves apart, I'm sure. Good morning, Fillet and Potato.' He reaches through the fence and pats the dogs around the ears. 'Keep an eye on the street, you two.'

George comes rushing down the street, waving his arms above his head.

'Go on, then,' Father says. 'Don't be long.'

I cross the street and wait for George under one of the trees. He's wearing the wreath of camphor around his neck. He stops ten feet away.

'Is it time for Sunday roast already?'

George rolls his eyes. 'Funny,' he says. 'Try coming up with your own jokes, Turner.'

'Why are you standing over there?'

'Mother says I can't come any further. She says it's not safe, with the polio and all. She'd like to lock me in a cupboard and feed me meals through a slot.'

I watch George's face. He's smiling but there's something behind his smile, something I can't make sense of.

'At least the world would be spared your ugly face,' I say.

'Very funny. Is that one of my jokes too?'

A breeze rolls leaves over the soil and grass. Wattlebirds call from the trees.

'You almost left without saying goodbye,' George says.

'It all happened fast,' I say. 'I don't know what it's like to go away somewhere.'

'Well, don't go turning into a country hick out there. I don't know if they'll let you back in the city if you're covered in coal dust. You're not going to miss much, you know. Mother won't be letting me out at all this summer. Not with polio in the street. It's going to be a dull time, Turner. Just make sure you solve the case. You're always getting your poor old man to do the work. Time you helped out.'

'I'll do that,' I say. 'Shouldn't take long and then I'll have the rest of the summer off.'

We stand there a while longer, ten feet of air between us. I don't know much about polio, how it's catching. I've heard you shouldn't get close to other people. The sickness gets into someone and makes them pass it on. They become the enemy.

We say our goodbyes and I take my seat in the back of the car. Father lets the engine turn a while and then we're moving, the tyres crunching over loose stones in the street. Our neighbours wave, then they're behind us. I look back, watching our house get smaller and smaller and the people we know get further and further away. We turn the corner and it all disappears.

Father holds tight to the steering wheel like it's money in his hands. The muscles in his arms push against his shirtsleeves. They wrap around him like coils, storing some kind of power, something I worry we'll need out where we're going, for whatever is in store for us.

6

Offices and factories give way to windmills and fences. The houses space out, gaps filled with thick bush. There are gum trees anchored to the ground on wide trunks. Great boughs reach over the streets, shading the road with their leaves. Light flickers as we pass under them. Crops stretch out in paddocks cut by lines of trees. We pass sheep, heads bent to the grass. Cows stand in the shade of wattle trees.

I look over my shoulder and I can't see the buildings of the city. All I see are trees and dirt and the odd house by the road or out near a paddock. There are other buildings too, away from the houses, over where the rivers and creeks pass near the road. Crowded together near the water or in clearings left behind by old bushfires, black poles of trees standing around them. These buildings are made of boards, tarred hessian and scrap. They look as though they've been pulled whole from the water or they've grown from the ground, sprouted from seeds that fell in the wind. These are the shacks George was talking about, the buildings that go along with the soup and bread lines, the crowds outside the banks, the rows of people waiting for a job. They go together, the same suit in a deck of cards.

There are people near the shacks. Men hunching over fires, women holding babies to their chests. A set of legs poking out from under a rusted car. A hand swinging a hammer, a back turned, a head tilted away. Children crouch in the dirt, their mouths slack and open, watching us pass. We don't talk about the people or the shacks.

Father has to stop and look at a map. He unfolds it on the bonnet of the car, paper crackling as he runs a hand over it, flattening it. He's looking for the town where he grew up. I wonder why he needs a map to get there. He runs a finger over the curved lines on the paper and I lean against the warm metal of the car, looking out at the bush.

In the distance, out past some fields and a line of gum trees, is a group of thirty or forty buildings, white walls shining in the sun. Some of the walls have cracks running up from the ground to the roof. It looks like another camp, but these are proper buildings, not shacks. I see fences and what looks like porches outside some of the buildings.

'What's that place?'

Father looks up from the map. He squints and holds a hand over his eyes.

'That's the old reserve,' he says.

'What's a reserve?'

Father turns and starts to fold the map, end over end.

'It's where they sent the people who lived here long before people like us came along.'

'You mean the darkeys?'

Father rubs the skin between his eyes.

'Don't use that word, Morris,' he says. 'That's not a good word.'

I stare at the buildings. They look empty. No smoke coming from the chimneys, no dust rising from the ground. No noise.

'Where are they?'

Lottie walks past me and out to the edge of the bush. She stands in front of a short tree that's starting to bud with small white flowers. 'You think they're going to be standing out front waving at you?' she says.

Father tucks the folded map into his breast pocket.

'The government moved most of the people further east. Out to another place like it.'

I stare at the fields in front of the houses, overgrown with grass and small bushes.

'Was it a farm?'

'Not exactly,' Father says. 'Not the way we think of a farm.'

'What was it?'

'It's hard to say,' he says. 'It's a place where people lived and worked but they weren't free.'

'Why did they live out here?'

Father clears his throat.

'I don't know,' he says.

I watch Father as he stares out past the trees. He runs his tongue along the back of his teeth. Sometimes Father says he doesn't know when he does.

We climb back into the car and Father starts the engine. We set off again on the dusty road, the trees leaning over, cutting out the light, and the odd car and horse-drawn buggy passing on the other side.

The road starts to pitch up, moving toward the clouds. The trees get thicker the higher we climb. The air seems to thin out, as if it's making room for us. The engine wheezes and clacks and shudders with the effort. I've never been in a car this long. My shoulders ache and my backside is numb. A few minutes up the road, we reach a town. Father tells us we're going to stop for food. My stomach makes a noise and my mouth gets wet.

This town is bigger than any of the other towns we've passed. We drive along the main street, past couples and small groups of people. Ahead, some boys throw a ball against the wall of the hotel. Their trousers end above their ankles and their wool caps are covered in holes. Father pulls the car over near the boys. They stop their game and stare at us as we leave the car and walk into the hotel.

The name of the hotel is The Grand. I've seen pictures of the grand hotels they have in London and New York and Paris and India. Places with marble stairs, silk curtains, ceilings so high they look like a second sky and lights that drip like honey from above. This place has none of that. There's a bar shaped like a horseshoe with a few old men leaning against it. There are wooden tables with chips in the legs, and chairs with cracked leather cushions. There are no ritzy lights hanging from the ceiling, only a few lamps in the walls that show the dust circling in the air.

We take our seats at the counter, Lottie and me on each side of Father. A thin woman with curly hair walks over to us, sniffing as she goes. She wipes her nose on the back of her hand. Her teeth are blotchy and brown, sprinkled with filth.

'What can I get you?'

'I'll have the stew with a lager, please,' Father says. 'These children won't have anything. They're not hungry.'

Lottie digs a hand into Father's ribs. I shake his arm. The woman looks as though she's smelled something sour.

'Only kidding,' Father says, winking at the woman. 'You might need to bring in an extra cook. They're ravenous, these two.'

The woman sighs and shakes her head. We give her our orders and she walks off to tell the cook. When she comes back to the bar, she's sniffing again. It sounds like she's trying to drain a lake with her nose. She puts a glass under the tap and pulls the handle. She looks at

Father, at Lottie and me, and narrows her eyes. 'Just passing through? On your way somewhere?'

'To Gemini,' Father says. 'Left Melbourne this morning.'

The woman's eyes get wide. She places the lager in front of Father. 'You hear about that girl?' she asks. 'The one they found in the mine?'

Father looks at Lottie and me. He flattens his beard with one hand. 'Yes. I know about her.'

'I hear she was known around town, if you know what I mean. Had a few men down at the mine knew her quite well.'

Father shifts in his seat.

Lottie leans in close to the woman. 'What happened to her? I don't know,' she says. 'Father won't tell me.'

The woman looks over her shoulder at the old men down the bar. She leans in close to Lottie. 'Heard they found her right after a storm, and not a stitch covering her most delicate skin, if you know what I mean.' The woman raises her eyebrows. 'Makes you wonder what kind of girl leaves home like that, in the middle of a storm, not covering the parts of her the world shouldn't be seeing.'

Father reaches over and puts a hand on Lottie's arm. The woman stands up straight.

'We'll find out the details soon enough,' Father says. 'Put an end to the speculation and rumours.'

The woman's chin sinks in close to her neck. 'Oh, and what makes you so sure?'

Father taps a finger on his chest. 'I'm going up there to investigate.'

The woman takes a step back. 'You're police?'

'Yes,' Father says. 'I'm police.'

The woman looks like she's been caught taking something from a store without paying. People often look that way when they find out about Father.

'Oh, that's good news,' she says, forcing a smile. 'Make sure you catch the devil who did it. Last thing we need is some evil pest wandering around. Enough going on as it is.'

The woman smiles and turns away. She picks up a glass and a rag. I see her put another rag over a thick, leather-bound book on the bench behind her. She turns back and smiles again, polishing the glass. A man wearing a dirty white apron carries our food out from the kitchen. He sneers as he drops our plates. We dip our heads and eat in silence.

I've just taken in the last mouthful when I hear a ball bouncing on the floorboards. I turn to see the three boys from outside.

'Oh, no, you don't. I've told you, you're not to come in here,' the woman says, rounding the bar and marching over to the boys. 'How many times do I have to tell you? Get out, you little dogs. Nothing here for you. What we have you need money to buy. This isn't a charity. Now, go on. Get going.'

She takes two of the boys by the collar and leads them through the door. The other boy, the smallest one, hurries on ahead. The meal feels heavy in my belly.

The woman strides back into the hotel. Her face is as red as a pool of blood. She walks back around the bar, shaking her head and muttering as she goes. When she gets near, she picks up the rag and a glass and goes back to polishing, harder than before. 'It's too much,' she says. 'Far too much for one life. I can't get over the way some people live. Did you hear there are people out there living in caves? Can you believe that? Living in caves like beasts. They have no respect, these people. Living rough, begging off good, working folk. Why can't they earn some money instead of begging off the rest of us? As if I haven't got enough to worry about. I keep my house in order. That's enough. I don't need beggars coming around here for a handout.'

Father finishes the last of his meal and drains the rest of his beer. He reaches into his pocket and takes out some notes and coins, lays them flat on the counter. The woman watches and rushes forward to take the money. Father places a few more coins on the counter and points at a dish on the bench behind the woman.

'We'll take those scones there,' he says. 'To go, please. Half a dozen of them.'

The woman looks at the coins on the counter and smiles. 'You're a ha'penny short, I'm afraid.'

Father places a halfpenny on the counter. The woman scoops up the coin. She bows her head a little, lifts a paper bag from behind the counter and fills it with the scones. She hands the bag to Father.

'Wishing you luck in finding the evil out there, out in Gemini,' she says. 'Remember what I told you about those beggars. I'd look there first, if I was you. I'd round those people up first.'

She smiles again. Father doesn't smile back.

'Thank you for the meal,' he says.

We follow Father out the doors of The Grand and onto the stairs out front. The three boys are standing nearby, bouncing the ball and scuffing the dirt with their shoes. Father waves them over. They look at each other.

'It's all right,' Father says, holding up the paper bag. 'This here is for you.'

The boys walk slow and careful like they're moving near a sleeping animal. Father hands the bag to one of them. He reaches in and takes a scone, then passes the bag to the next boy. They stand there, sniffing the scones and whispering to each other.

'Thank you, sir,' says the boy closest to us.

'You're most welcome. Each of you, very welcome,' Father says. 'I want you to do one small favour for me in return.'

The boys glance at each other.

'Don't worry, it's nothing hard. You know the landlady who runs the hotel?'

The boys nod.

'I want you to stand by the window, hold up a scone and wave at her.'

The boys look at each other. The biggest one blinks quickly and squints at Father. 'You want us to wave at her?'

'That's right,' Father says. 'All you have to do is wave. We'll go with you. We'll all wave together.'

We follow the three boys to the window. Past the grime on the glass, I can see the woman standing at the bar, near the old men. Father taps on the window, and they turn to face us. The boys hold up their scones and wave. Father lifts his hand and starts to wave too. He glances at Lottie and me, and we each raise a hand and wave. Even from here, I can tell that the woman's face has turned red again. I can see her mouth moving. Her lips are going fast but I can't hear any of the words she's saying.

'Come on, lads,' Father says. 'Time to go, I think. She got the message.'

Me and Lottie stand next to Father and watch as the boys race off into the street, past shops and other buildings, past men and horses and women in hats, and down a dirt track, into the bush.

7

We're driving past trees with trunks as wide as boats. The car draws the sweat from us, the steel on the doors like branding irons. The road gets rough, stones blown into ridges that make the car shudder. We drop into a valley, tall hills on both sides. Behind the hills, in the distance, are taller peaks, their slopes covered in cloud. We're falling into an abyss. That's a word Father told me about. It's a place you don't want to go, a place that's hard to come back from. The wheels keep spinning, dropping us into the valley. This is Gemini.

Gemini gets its name from these hills, the twin hills. They're called Castor and Pollux by the people of the town. They're the names of the two brightest stars in the constellation Gemini. I don't know what came first, the name of the town or the names of the hills. I guess you could say that about almost anything. Father told me 'Gemini' comes from the Latin word for 'twin'. Castor and Pollux were twin brothers, one the son of a god and the other the son of a king. You can trace their shapes in the northern sky in summer.

I smell the town before I see it, a thick scent of burned coal. It catches at the back of my throat and won't shift. I lift my shirt over my nose, but it's no use. Lottie has a hand over her mouth. Father doesn't seem bothered by it. I think about what he told me about priming engines. You run some fuel through the engine before you start it, to get it ready. Father has been primed with this smell.

'You'll get used to it soon enough,' he says. 'It's worse up here. Better down below.'

Now and then, the wheels slip on the dirt. On one side of the narrow road, the land drops away, a steep slope dark with bark and leaves. I can see something shining far below, at the bottom of the slope. The shine comes and goes. We move around a horseshoe bend and I see the shine is coming from water. Far below us, a river carves through the slopes, heading the same way we are.

There's a break in the bush and I see a town spread out in the valley. There is a thick group of buildings in the middle, surrounded by a scattering of houses like buckshot from a rifle, some climbing up Castor, partly hidden by trees. Pollux is mostly wild. There are bigger buildings in the distance ringed by smokestacks.

There are few people in the main street, some women and older men. They watch as we pass, heads turning like telescopes. The women with young children hold them close and then move them away, inside shops or down side streets. We pass a stone fountain, an old man cupping his hands to drink the water. We pass a bandstand on a patch of grass and a wooden structure built near the river, a hose running down from the building to the water and the word *FIRE* written on the wall. We pass a double-fronted building made of bluestone. There are bars on the windows, the ends chiselled into the dark stone, and a white plaque above the door with a word I know well. This is the police station. This is where Father will be working.

Father stops the car by the river, at a bend overlooking a hotel with wide balconies covered in iron lattice. There are people at the river's edge, a few men, an old woman and a little girl not more than seven years old. They look different to the people we passed earlier. The old woman is rinsing a dress in the water. She pulls it from the river and swings it onto a flat grey boulder, slapping the water free. A man fills his hat and tips it over his head. The water streams down his face, past eyes set deep in their sockets.

'Let's stretch our legs a while,' Father says.

We follow Father down to the river, the grass going from parched yellow to a rich green. Rivergums bend over the water, and kookaburras perch in the branches, their feathers the colours of bark and stones.

'G'day,' Father says, waving at the people. 'How do you do?'

The old woman glances at Father and then rolls up the wet dress, walks downstream. The men shuffle away after her. I can see the ankles of one man, younger than the others, and the holes in the hems of each of their shirts. Their collars are dark, same as the men down by the river in the city. The little girl skips over to us. She has a purple flower in one hand and a yellow one in the other. She holds them up for Father and me, and we take them from her. She stares at Lottie's dress. I can see streaks of mud on the girl's chin and neck and in her hair. Father smiles and pats the girl on the head. He does it soft, his hand barely touching her, the way you'd pat a kitten. Father once told me that you always have to be gentle with what's smaller than you. That's the mark of a man, how gentle he can be. You have to know your own power, he said, know it as well as you know that the sun rises in the east and sets in the west. I look down at my flower. It's dirty, covered in the dust thrown out by passing traffic, but I can see the yellow petals shining under the dirt.

'Come on, Nettie,' the old woman says, her body half turned back to us. 'Come along now.'

The girl runs over and takes the old woman's hand. They walk slowly downstream, away from the town and out toward the bush.

We follow Father back to the car and keep driving past the main part of town. The buildings begin to thin out, giving way to grass and crops in long, wide paddocks. Animals dip their heads to feed. After a couple of miles, Father turns down a dusty path. I see a sign made of rusted car parts, an axle staked into the hard ground. There's a name scratched into the metal, a name I've known my whole life. Turner.

We stop at the end of the path, in front of a plain farmhouse. It's covered in long wooden boards, painted white but faded. There are two short chimneys. A vine creeps over one side of the house, and there's a scattering of wildflowers beside the boards. Two sheepdogs leave the shade and run over to the car, tails swinging left and right.

Outside the house, a man stands on the tray of a truck, running a broom back and forth. The tray has wooden slats and wire on each side. He stops sweeping and holds a hand over his eyes. 'The big brother,' he says. The man drops the broom and jumps off the tray, landing in the dirt. Dust rises around his legs. 'Better late than never.'

Father turns in his seat and looks between Lottie and me. 'That man there,' Father says, 'that's your uncle Jimmy.'

The man is around the same height as Father, with the same broad shoulders and heavy arms. He's missing the beard and his hair is different, longer and slicked back. His skin is darkened from the sun. We get out of the car and walk over. There's a smell in the air, one that gets stronger the closer we get to the truck. It smells like the lavatories at school on a hot day. My eyes start to water. I take short breaths.

'What's that?' Lottie asks, holding a hand to her nose.

Uncle Jimmy laughs, pointing at the tray. 'That's what's left of the lambs I took to market out in Wodonga,' he says. 'It's pretty ripe now. Don't smell it myself after a while.'

'How did you do?' Father asks.

Uncle Jimmy sniffs and scratches behind his ear. 'Not nearly what I wanted for them. Times are hard.' He takes a rag from his trouser pocket and wipes his hands. 'Then I get back and all hell has broken loose. Only gone a week and everything's different in town. Awful what happened to that girl.'

He shakes his head and looks at the ground. We stand there a moment, trying not to think about the murder, trying not to breathe. After a while, Uncle Jimmy points a finger at Father.

'Still, good to have the cavalry here to catch who did it.' He stares at Father's face. 'Strange to let your beard grow like that. You look like an old man.'

Father smiles, the lines around his eyes like rays coming from the sun. I've seen him smile this way before, when people come to the house and he's tired but doesn't want to show it. 'James, this is Charlotte and Morris.'

'Pleased to meet you both,' Uncle Jimmy says. He reaches out to shake our hands but changes his mind, pulls back his hand. 'Best I wash up before I do that. Come on inside. There're a couple people want to see you.'

Inside the house, it's warm and it smells sweet. There are flowers in vases in the hall. There's light coming in from every room. The smell and the light, it gives me the feeling that this was what our house back in Melbourne used to be, before everything changed.

Uncle Jimmy is up ahead, leading us through the hall. 'You're quite the young lady, Charlotte,' he says. 'Few years we missed along the way.' He looks past Lottie toward me. 'And you, Morris. You've grown up. You're a long way from shitting in cloth.' He stares at Father for a moment before looking ahead again. I don't know what to make of him, this man I'm related to. It's like meeting a stranger in the street, and somehow he knows everything about you, more than you know yourself.

'They've grown up well, that's for sure,' Father says.

'That they have,' Uncle Jimmy says. 'That they have. Nothing like good fortune for that. It'll make the road easy for anyone, a bit of good fortune. We've been all right here though.'

'Right,' Father says.

'Well,' Uncle Jimmy says, 'here they are, then.'

The hall opens to a long room with a kitchen and a dining table. There's wood panelling on the ceiling and copper pots hanging from hooks in the wall. A woman and a girl about my age are standing by the table. The girl is dressed in overalls and a cloth shirt. Her hair is tied up tight to her head, making her long hair seem short. She looks like she just came in from milking something. The woman is smiling. She's younger than Uncle Jimmy, her features smoother, her skin softer. She wears powder on her face.

'Morris. Charlotte. This is your aunt Beth and your cousin Flo,' Father says.

Aunt Beth rushes forward. 'Welcome. Welcome,' she says. She hugs me, squeezing so hard some air leaks out of my mouth. She lets go and takes hold of Lottie's shoulders, leaning back to look at her. 'You're a fine-looking thing, you are,' she says. 'So pretty.'

'Thank you,' Lottie says.

'Don't you just look like your ma? The spitting image.'

Lottie's face flushes red. Father takes a step back and looks down at the floor. Uncle Jimmy walks over and takes hold of Aunt Beth, pulling her away from Lottie.

'Don't fuss,' he says. 'Let them take a breath.'

Aunt Beth blinks once, long and hard, and then looks back at us, smiling quickly.

'She doesn't see many girls in dresses,' Uncle Jimmy says, nodding in the direction of Flo.

Flo is staring at Father, her hands in the pockets of her overalls. Her lips are a straight line, a dash in her face.

'It's good to see you again, Jude,' Aunt Beth says.

'And you,' Father says, looking up from the floor. 'I hardly recognised you. You were only a girl last I saw you.'

'We all got older,' Aunt Beth says. She wraps her arms around her waist. 'I got thin too. Nothing burns off weight faster than worry and rumination.' She laughs and looks around at our faces, but nobody joins in.

'Well, thank you for having us,' Father says.

'This is yours as much as anyone's,' she says.

Uncle Jimmy clears his throat, pushes his shirtsleeves back from his wrists.

'Hope you don't mind, James?' Father says. 'Bit of a surprise when you got back, hearing we were coming?'

Uncle Jimmy smiles but his jaw is set tight. 'It's no bother,' he says. 'Good to have another set of hands around. It's not easy looking after a farm, especially since the old man died. That made some things easier though.'

'How long have you been a detective? How many criminals have you caught? Did you lock them up yourself?' The questions come from Flo. They pour out fast, one after another, as if she's practised them.

'A long time, a lot and not exactly,' Father says.

'You'll have to excuse her,' Aunt Beth says. 'She's a little hooked on detective stories. Reads them all day, every day. She must have dog-eared the pages on dozens of them. We don't often get those kinds of tales in real life around here. Not until lately, that is. Awful. Just awful what happened.'

Father rolls his shoulders and looks at the ceiling, the walls. He seems to be taking in every crack, every splinter in the wood.

'Will you be wanting your old room?' Uncle Jimmy asks.

Father shakes his head, slowly.

'Didn't think so. Beth fixed up the cottage for you. Figured you'd be happier set up in there, away from the big house.'

'Right,' Father says, no rise and fall to his voice, only a steady, hollow sound.

'Well, that's the introductions done,' Uncle Jimmy says. 'I guess you'll want to get unpacked and all after the drive.'

Father bows his head and we file out into the hall. Behind us, Uncle Jimmy is whispering to Aunt Beth and Flo. I can't make out the words, but I have a feeling they're about us. I imagine Uncle Jimmy running his hand through his hair, whispering at our backs. Lottie, me and the brother he hasn't seen in a long time.

There's a space between them, my father and my uncle. A space where something grows, trapped under the surface like a boil.

8

We carry our bags down a narrow path beside the house. There's a low fence on one side, weathered old posts linked by tangled wire. Up ahead is a wattle tree heavy with bright golden flowers. Father pushes the branches aside and waves Lottie and me through. I'm just past the wattle when I see the cottage that we'll call home for the summer.

It's made of stone, odd-shaped bits stacked into walls. A rusted tin roof that slopes down to a lean-to made of wood. Weeds grow in the cracks between stones. This cottage is held together by a spell. It looks as though it could scatter into pieces at any moment.

'She's not much,' Father says. 'This is the old cottage, the first our family built. Many, many years ago.'

Inside there are two bedrooms and a sitting room up front. One of the bedrooms has a large bed. In the other, two small ones.

'You'll have to share,' Father says.

The skin above Lottie's nose wrinkles like she's smelled something rotten. 'This gets better and better,' she says.

We keep walking through the cottage. Out back is the kitchen, and past that, in the lean-to, are the laundry and bath. Past a kitchen door, off to one side and down a thin gravel path is another building, narrow and small.

'That's the outhouse,' Father says. 'Make sure you need to use that before you step inside. It's not a place to pass the time.'

Lottie's face gets tighter, all the parts bunched together. 'What a dream come true,' she says.

We walk back inside, and Father tells us to unpack our bags and get clean. Me and Lottie rush to the bedroom. She beats me there, shuts the door and turns the latch. I hear her move inside the room. She opens the door and points at one of the beds.

'That's your one,' she says.

I sit on my bed and it sings like a bird. Lottie smiles, takes a small case from her bag and turns for the door.

'Wish me luck with the bath,' she says and leaves the room.

I lie on the bed, my bag beside me, telescope at my feet. I think about what our family must have looked like, the ones who built this cottage. I imagine people wearing old-time hats and coats. I imagine them cutting down trees with axes, stripping back grass and ferns. Chipping stones and stacking them one on another, building each wall higher and higher. I look at the ceiling, tracing the cracks with my eyes, seeing how they move apart, reaching off in new directions, only to come back together again.

9

'Wake up, Morris. Come on, son.'

Father is kneeling by the bed, wearing a suit and necktie. My mouth is dry. I rub my face and yawn.

'We've got to go,' Father says. 'There's a town meeting tonight. Bring your coat. It gets cold after dark.'

As we drive into town behind Uncle Jimmy's truck, I see people on the main street all moving in one direction. There are a few cars on the road but most people are walking or being pulled by horses. Steam rises from the nostrils of the horses we pass. Veins show beneath the hair on their flanks, muscles twitch. We park our cars and then we move with the crowd. There are men with stained black faces, women carrying babies or dragging children by the hand.

'Stay close,' Father says, tense as cornered prey.

We're headed toward the tallest building on the street. There are a dozen white columns out front. We climb the steps and enter a foyer with doors at the far side and stairs to the left and right. Men and women take off their hats and split up, some climbing stairs, some moving straight ahead. I see Uncle Jimmy lead Aunt Beth and Flo up one set of stairs. Me and Lottie follow Father as he pushes through the crowd to the doors at the far end, past rows and rows of seats, all the way to the edge of a stage. On stage there's a man in a fine suit standing next to a lectern, a deep red curtain reaching to the ceiling behind him. On one side of the man are some chairs, a few empty and the others taken up by a man and a woman. Next to them is a boy in a wheelchair, pale skin, legs covered by a dark blanket. He looks as though he could be my age. I get a feeling when I see him. It makes me think of holding a hand over a flame, feeling the warmth from somewhere dangerous.

'You two sit there,' Father says. 'Be on your best behaviour.'

We take our seats and watch Father walk onto the stage and shake the hand of the man at the lectern. He whispers something in the man's ear then walks over to talk to the other man seated on the chair. Father leans down, shakes the woman's hand, kneels next to the boy in the wheelchair. The boy nods as Father talks to him.

'They must be the family,' Lottie says.

The man in the fine suit raises his hands and taps on the microphone. Father takes a seat with the family.

'For those of you who don't know me, I'm Art Napier, Mayor of Gemini. For those of you who wish you don't know me, I can't help you with that.'

Mr Napier smiles, two rows of pearly white teeth. He touches the hair at his temples and runs a hand over the bald top of his head. There are a few sniggers from people in the balcony and then there's silence again. Mr Napier glances at the family next to him, pulls at the knot in his necktie.

'Enough of that. We're here for an important reason,' he says, his voice dropping deeper. 'A solemn reason. As you well know, young Catherine Fletcher was tragically taken from us. We've been reeling ever since, shocked that this could happen in our small, safe town. I know many of you have been praying for answers, looking to our Lord for guidance. We've been coming together, all of us here in Gemini, trying to heal. And we've been remembering Catherine Fletcher. A young woman only starting her life in our town. An innocent. A lamb.'

I hear whispering in one of the rows behind me. Someone coughs, a laugh barely hidden beneath.

'Did you hear that?' I ask Lottie, whispering. 'What did they say?'

Lottie shakes her head. She raises a finger to her lips.

'While we ought to remember the life of poor Catherine, celebrate who she was, we must also understand how she left us,' Mr Napier says, tapping a finger on the lectern. 'We must find those responsible and bring them to trial. They must be held to account, whoever they are, so that they may atone for their crimes before they meet the judgement of our Lord. We will not rest until we find them. There'll be no peace for Catherine's family until the perpetrators are brought out into the light.'

There are murmurs around us. Some people in the balcony clap their hands. Mr Napier bows his head until the townspeople fall silent.

'To help us find those responsible, one of Gemini's sons has returned.' Mr Napier points at Father. 'Mister Jude Turner from Victoria Police has brought his family all the way from the city. He'll be here until those responsible are in shackles. Now, he'll be leading a small group of police from nearby towns, asking the questions that need to be asked, and I know, people of Gemini, that you'll give him your full cooperation.'

Mr Napier steps to the side. Father stands and walks slowly to the lectern.

'Thank you, Mayor Napier,' he says. 'Some of you know me. Some may not. My family have lived in Gemini for generations. My brother, James, and his family live out on our land. I grew up here, alongside many of you.'

I hear people talking, low and quiet. It goes on for a few seconds. Then there's a silence that makes me feel strange, as if my muscles want to move out of my body. I look at the crowd, at the people watching Father.

'We're like kin, you and me. Even if some don't feel that way, we are like kin, and kin don't let something like this go unpunished. Someone in this room knows what happened to Catherine Fletcher on the night of the storm. Someone here has information that can help us find who did this. I urge you to come to the station. Don't let this weigh on your conscience. Speak and let Gemini heal.'

Father steps away from the microphone and takes his seat. Mr Napier moves over to the lectern.

'Thank you, Mister Turner,' he says. 'Now, Will Fletcher would like to say a few words.'

The man in the chair stands. Tall and thin, shadows around his eyes like burns on his face. He walks across the stage and his feet seem to drag through the boards like ploughs through sunbaked dirt. He reaches the microphone and clears his throat. The sound echoes around the hall.

'My Catherine was a good girl,' he says. 'She didn't deserve none of this. Didn't deserve to be left at the mine. Dumped like a dog at the tunnel where we work, where we sweat and labour to bring home enough to feed our children. And then for this to happen to that child. It's not right. It's not right.'

He hangs his head and I see others hang theirs too, as if in prayer. Will Fletcher looks up and his voice has changed. Now it's steady and strong, a boulder rolling downhill, picking up speed.

'We don't need to look far and wide for who done this. We all know what's next to the mine, out there in a clearing in the bush not five hundred yards away. It's that camp of dirty beggars. We never had any problems until they showed up.'

There are murmurs in the crowd. Someone in the balcony shouts something I can't make out.

'Take a walk out to the camp. Go on. See how they're living. I seen it with my own eyes. Fighting over scraps, they are. Cooking out in all weather like savages. Children screaming for food all day long. Why'd they come here? Ask yourself that. Why'd they camp next to the mine? What have they got in mind? They soak up the kindness of others. How many of you have brought food out to those beggars? Out of the goodness of your heart, when they first came. What have they done? They never left. That's the problem with charity. They figured they were on a good ticket, they did. Next, they'll be holding up their hands for our jobs. Why else would they camp next to a mine? Ask yourselves, do you want that? You want them to take away our lives, bit by bit? You mark my words, if we don't do something, if someone don't take a stand with these beggars, they'll take everything from us until this town is nothing.'

Will Fletcher backs away from the microphone. A few people call out. I hear words like 'gutter' and 'disgrace'. I get that feeling in my body again, the one where my heart races and my legs start to tingle. I feel a pain above my eyes. Will Fletcher returns to his seat next to his family. I watch Mr Napier whisper something to Father then step over to the microphone.

'Please,' Mr Napier says, his hands above his head. 'Please. Let's not come to our own conclusions. As much as our minds wander, and that's only natural, the police are here. They'll ask their questions and find those responsible. We mustn't let our anger get the better of us.'

55

'And why shouldn't we? I say anger's the only way for this town right now.' A man is standing in the audience, out in the middle of the stalls. He's short and stocky, shoulders round under his shirt. The hair on his head is dark, but the whiskers that colour the skin above his lips are ginger, making his face a poor match.

'All right, Hayden,' Mr Napier says.

'That's *Mister Cornwell*, thank you. I got a right to speak. As one of the leading men in this good town, I think I speak for many of us when I say we've had enough of the pandering, Mister Napier. We've had enough of the charity and the sweet talk. These are desperate people and there's nothing desperate people won't do. When a man drops as low as the people in that camp have, there's nowhere further to fall. He's capable of anything.'

Mr Cornwell looks out over the people. He points to the far side of the stalls. 'Missus Wade, tell them what you said to me this morning. Tell the good people what you think about the camp. Tell them how you fear for your daughter.'

A woman rises slowly from her seat. Her face is wide and round, her eyes small. She holds her hat out in front of her body like a shield.

'It's only, I don't trust them,' she says. 'The young men that come into town to drink from the fountain, I've seen the way they look at my daughter. The way they look at Carla. They watch her the way a fox does sheep.' Mrs Wade covers her mouth with her hand. She blinks a few times and then she drops her hand. 'I'm not one to speak ill of folks but I'm a mother first. That's my warrant, above all else. We don't know these people that come in and out all the time. They could be anyone, straight from the gaol to our town, for all we know. I don't want them here, that's all. That's all I can say about that.'

Mr Cornwell claps his hands. A few people around him join in, but the clapping dies out.

'Thank you, Missus Wade. I think many of us share your sentiments,' Mr Cornwell says. 'I want you all to know, I'll be running for mayor when we have our election next year. I want you to know that a vote for Hayden Cornwell is a vote for the people of Gemini, not a vote for these outsiders. We have to take our town back, get our safety back. We're good people here in Gemini but good people have their limits.'

'All right, Mister Cornwell,' Mr Napier says. 'You've said your piece. This isn't a campaign. This is about Catherine Fletcher and her family.'

Mr Cornwell stays standing for a moment, chin up, watching Mr Napier. After a time, he drops slowly to his seat. There are whispers in the crowd and then the noise begins to drift away, a tide going out to sea.

'Thank you all,' Mr Napier says. 'I thank you for being here this evening. I think we can fairly say that there's one notion that unites us all and that's justice for the Fletcher family. We'll get it, don't you worry. We will get justice, but we have to do it the right way. God's way.'

People around me start nodding. Mr Napier worries at his necktie. He shows his rows of white teeth.

'Now, the ladies from the association have put on a spread. It's all out in the foyer. Don't be shy about taking your fill. There's no shame in it. There's plenty for everyone.'

We file out of the hall. I hear some conversation from two men ahead of me. I watch the backs of their heads as they put on their hats.

'How can he show his face around here?'

'Who?'

'You know who. After what he did, what he caused. He's no right coming back after all this time.'

10

Out on the street, a woman hands me a plate with steamed vegetables and mashed potato. I find a place to sit, out on a patch of grass by the road. Light from the hall shines on the heads of the people gathered outside. I watch them walk over to Father, one after another. He clasps his hands behind his back and listens to each of them. Lottie is off talking to Uncle Jimmy and Aunt Beth. Art Napier is talking to a group of young women. He's leaning in close to one of them, whispering something in her ear.

I finish eating, lean back and look at the night sky. There are clouds above me, low clouds that glow a faint grey in the dim light from the town. The clouds part, and the brightest stars I've ever seen shine through the dark. They're everywhere, scattered like salt spilled across a black sheet.

'What you looking at?'

Flo is standing in front of me. She's squinting, arms folded across her overalls. There's a boy standing next to her. He's dressed in a fine wool suit. He looks like a shrunken-down man, without the thinning hair or the strong limbs.

'I was looking at the stars,' I say.

'The stars? Don't they have stars in the city?'

'Not like this. You don't get to see as many as this.'

Flo unfolds her arms and takes a seat across from me. The boy sits down beside her.

'That's one thing Gemini's got, I guess,' Flo says. 'Nothing much else here. As soon as I can, I'm getting out and heading to the city. Isn't that right?'

She looks over at the boy and he nods.

'This is Sam. His dad's the mayor, the one who did all the talking tonight.'

Sam pulls at some grass, twirls it around a finger. He's got faint lines in his forehead, the kind you get from thinking and worrying. In that suit, with those lines on his face, he looks ready to follow in his father's footsteps. He looks like someone getting set for a life of standing in front of crowds, of telling them he's the one to take on their problems.

'Sam is heading to the city too, aren't you?'

He nods, his hands moving the grass around his fingers.

'Sam's going to be on stage,' Flo says. 'Moving pictures too. Isn't that right? Just like Charlie Chaplin. Tell him.'

'Just like Charlie Chaplin,' Sam says.

He drops the grass and stands beside us. He stays still for a moment and then his face changes. His eyelids droop, his mouth curls into a sly grin. His arms and legs go limp. Sam starts stumbling left and right, as if he's spent the evening at a pub. He tips his cap at us and pretends to be sick inside it. He straightens, puts on his cap, goes to lean on a post that's not there. He tumbles to the ground and picks himself up, acting angry at the missing post. Me and Flo are laughing. My sides start to hurt.

'See what I mean? Just like Charlie Chaplin,' Flo says.

Sam takes a bow, still acting like he's on liquor. There's a shout from behind Sam, off in the distance. Someone is calling out his name. Sam whirls around, in character. He sees who called him and his face changes. He stands straight and lowers his head. It's Mr Napier who called out to him, Sam's father, standing over by the lights of the hall with the group of young women. They're all staring our way. Mr Napier shakes his head and turns his back on us.

Sam tumbles to the ground. He goes back to twirling the grass over his fingers. It's quiet for a moment before he speaks. 'He doesn't like me doing that,' he says.

'Mister Napier doesn't like him acting,' Flo says. 'Says it's not manly. Can't have Sam not be a little copy of him, suit and tie and all.'

'All right,' Sam says. 'No need for a biography.' He shakes his head and drops the blades of grass, wipes his fingers on his pants. He sits there a moment, looking at the grass, and then looks up at me. 'You're a Turner too?'

I nod. The way he says it, it's as if there's some hidden meaning behind the name. Sam and Flo share a look between them.

'What?' I ask.

'Nothing,' Sam says.

Mr Cornwell comes out the doors of the hall, Mrs Wade beside him. He walks her out into the light, over near Mr Napier, his hand on the small of her back. Mr Napier glances over at them and turns a shoulder, moving in closer to the young women. I notice the way Mr Cornwell's chin lifts when he sees that. He pushes his hands down into the pockets of his trousers, looking past Mrs Wade while she talks, over at Mr Napier.

'Who is he?' I ask, pointing over Sam's shoulder.

'Oh, Mister Cornwell,' Sam says. 'He owns a few farms across the high country. Started with one paddock and built it up from there,

60

he likes to say. Doesn't like that my dad got his money from family. Dad says he's been keen on becoming mayor for a long time.'

'Why's he want to be mayor?'

Sam shrugs. 'Likes the idea of it, I suppose. Maybe likes the idea of taking it from Dad. I overheard him saying Mister Cornwell might use the murder to get it.'

That word, 'murder', seems to run a chill through Sam. I feel it too.

'What about your dad?' Sam asks. 'You think he'll solve the case?'

'I know he will,' I say.

'I would've solved it already, if it was me on the case,' Flo says.

Sam scoffs and throws some grass at Flo. 'He just got here,' he says. 'How could he solve it already?'

'I'm only saying,' Flo says. 'I have the skills to solve it faster than anyone. I've trained for this my whole life. If it was me, I'd come up with a suspect and have them followed until they let their guard down. I'd find witnesses and get them to talk. I'd walk in the footsteps of the victim and get to know their life so I could know how they met their end. It's simple. It's like the recipe for a cake. You've got to get all the ingredients, put them all together in the right order and follow the steps to make sure it comes out right.'

Sam looks at me and points a thumb at Flo. 'She thinks she's going to be a detective. Doesn't get that they only give those jobs to men.'

Flo punches Sam on the arm. He screws up his face, rubbing the part she hit.

'I'll be more man than you,' she says. 'Besides, I'll be so good they won't be able to say no.'

Flo and Sam shake their heads at each other. I look past them to the people near the hall. There are small groups of men standing together, talking quietly and spooning mouthfuls of food. Some in suits and hats, others in shirtsleeves marked by the dark stains of things brought up from below. I watch them all, wondering if one of these people killed Catherine Fletcher.

'You think it's someone from the camp? What Mister Fletcher said? We saw camps like that between the city and here,' I say.

Flo shakes her head. Sam pulls at more of the grass, ripping it up, roots and all.

'Could be,' Flo says. 'Can't rule it out yet. It's a process of elimination.'

'You just read that in a book,' Sam says. 'You don't know how to do it.'

'Sure I do. You come up with your list of suspects and mark them off one by one. You work out what they get from the murder, where they were when it happened and how well they knew the victim.' She hooks her thumbs under the straps of her overalls, as if she's giving a speech. 'The most important part of any murder investigation is keeping an open mind and letting the facts lead you to the killer. You've got to gather up the facts like you're harvesting a crop. One by one each of your suspects will be cleared by the facts until there's one left. That's your killer.'

Sam laughs, the collar of his shirt bouncing up and down with his body. 'Is it a recipe or a crop?' he asks.

'Both,' says Flo. 'They're called metaphors, Sam.'

Sam laughs again. 'Makes it sound like she's in charge of the police, doesn't it?'

'I can be in charge of our little police force,' Flo says.

'What do you mean?' I ask.

'I mean, why don't we try to solve the murder? They've cancelled the rest of the school term because of the murder. We'll have time.'

'That's not a good idea,' Sam says. 'I'm not letting you drag me into trouble again. Remember last summer?'

'What happened last summer?' I ask.

'Nothing,' Flo says. 'Don't listen to him. No harm done.'

'Tell that to Missus Watson.' Sam leans in closer to me. 'Flo got everyone thinking Missus Watson from the bakery had used her dog Kittens as meat in her pies. Turned out Kittens had just taken off somewhere and came back one day with a litter of puppies.'

'Wait,' I say. 'She had a dog named Kittens that had puppies?'

Flo lets out a loud shushing sound. She waves her hands in front of her. 'None of that matters,' she says. 'The fact is, we're the best team to solve this murder. I know everything there is to know about investigating. Sam here knows everyone in town because his dad knows everyone in town, and Morris has fresh eyes.'

'Fresh eyes?' I ask. 'What does that mean?'

'I mean, you don't know anyone here. You can see them for what they are.'

Me and Sam look at each other. Those faint lines in his forehead get heavier and wider.

'What do you say?' Flo asks. 'Do you want to be the ones who find Catherine Fletcher's killer?'

Sam bites his lower lip, shakes his head.

'There's nothing to be worried about,' Flo says. 'Come on, Sam.'

He chews on his lip. He keeps chewing until the lines on his forehead start to fade. 'I suppose so,' he says.

They turn and look at me. I think about the photographs of Catherine Fletcher, about her body near the tunnel. I get a feeling inside, one that gets my guts churning. It makes me want to run away, to go back home to the city, to hide under the blankets in my bed.

'I don't know,' I say. 'I don't know if that's a good idea. Father will solve the case.'

'He won't know where to start,' Flo says. 'He's been away too long, doesn't know the town like Sam and me. Come on, Morris. We need you. You've got the fresh eyes.'

I feel their eyes drilling into me. I don't want them to know about the feeling deep within me, roots as strong as the trees on the hills around here. I don't want them to see my nerves. I think back to what I said to George, before we left for Gemini. About how sure I was I could find out who killed Catherine Fletcher. I need to do this, need to make this right.

I lift my chin and let it fall again. One nod. 'All right,' I say. 'Where do we start?'

'We can start with you telling us what you know,' Flo says. 'You must have heard something, found out something.'

'I don't know. I listened in on Father's telephone call and I saw some photographs in his study. I'm not supposed to know what I know.'

'Those are the best things to know,' Flo says, slapping her leg. 'You have to tell us now.'

I close my eyes and take a deep breath and I'm back on the landing at home. Back in the city, watching Father in the light from the kerosene lamp, watching him talk about Catherine Fletcher for the first time.

'Well, she went to bed at eight in the evening, at least that's what her mother said. She must have snuck out of her room. They found her in a place called Long Tunnel East and her body was dry, which means she was there before the storm. She was missing her shoes and what she was wearing under her clothes. She had cuts in her back and marks on her neck and there were scratches on her legs. Where they found her, there were lilies near her body, flowers there in the dirt. She was on her back, arms by her side, legs together, the way you would lay someone out in a coffin. Her hair, it was laid down over her face like a shroud. That's it. That's all I know.'

My body shakes as I finish. Flo takes in a deep breath and sighs. I can almost see what I told her moving around in her head, filling the spaces.

'Where was Will Fletcher when this happened?'

'I don't know,' I say. 'That's all I know.'

Sam and Flo share a look.

'Not much to go on,' Sam says. 'How do we find out the rest?'

Flo drums her fingers on her cheek. We wait for her to speak, listening to the sounds of the people talking in front of the hall and nearby horses scratching at the dirt.

'We need to work from the inside out,' Flo says. 'The most likely suspect is the one closest to the victim. Look at him.'

Flo points to where Will Fletcher stands. He leans against an iron column under a shop awning. His family, his wife and the boy in the wheelchair, they're off to one side. People walk up to them, shake hands with Mrs Fletcher, touch the hair of the boy. Will Fletcher doesn't look at them. He smokes a cigarette, pushing the smoke out in bursts, down toward the ground.

'What did you make of his act tonight? You buying what he's selling?' Flo asks.

'What do you mean?' Sam asks. 'His daughter died. He's angry.'

'Maybe,' Flo says. 'Or maybe he's trying to get everyone to look the other way.'

Will Fletcher drops his cigarette and grinds it into the ground with his boot. He takes hold of the wheelchair and pushes the boy away from the hall. His wife follows and they disappear into the dark.

'What about his family?' I ask. 'Wouldn't they know if he did it?'

'Missus Fletcher? She's so deep under him she can't see the sun,' Flo says. 'Ollie can't go anywhere they don't want him to be. They won't know much, those two.'

'What happened to him? Why's he in a wheelchair?'

'Polio,' Sam says. 'Mister Fletcher is from here but they were living up in New South Wales. Ollie caught it when it spread through their old town and they came back here.'

I think of George with his wreath of camphor, standing ten feet away in the shade of a tree. I think of Iris and of Mrs Elliot walking through the street, finger pointed at me.

'Morris. Come on, now. We're leaving.'

Father is standing in the dim light of the street. Lottie is next to him. She has her arms wrapped tight around her body. I realise now that I'm cold. I get to my feet, shivering as I rise. Flo grabs hold of my wrist.

'Remember the plan,' she says. 'We're going to find out who did this.'

She lets go. I nod at Flo and Sam, and they nod back. We've started something here tonight. I wonder if this is how everything starts, moving through words until they lead you somewhere. Creeks flowing together, forming a river. We're rushing with the current now, me and Flo and Sam. We're together on this.

I walk over to Father and Lottie, and I follow them back to the car, looking up now and then at the stars above us, a million lights shining down on this town that holds a killer inside.

11

We're dressing in our best clothes. The three of us are buttoning and pinning and tying to make ourselves proper. This is what people do before something important. Today is Catherine Fletcher's funeral.

Father says a pathologist had her body until now. I don't know what that means. Why did they need her body? Where did they keep her? What were they doing with her? I don't ask these questions. I only nod and say I understand. Flo will know.

I try to get the knot in my tie straight and even. I do it four times, each time undoing and unwinding the length of it. It's a black tie to match my black coat and pants, and my black shoes polished by Father last night. On the fifth try, my tie looks halfway decent and I pull it close to my neck, smooth out my coat and pants, and walk into the hall. Father and Lottie are out there, leaning against the walls. Lottie yawns, opening her mouth wide, laying it on thick.

'About time,' she says. 'Can we go now?'

Father looks me up and down. He smiles and winks at me. 'It's an important occasion,' he says. 'He wants to look his best to show respect. Isn't that right?'

Lottie breathes out slow and loud and rolls her eyes.

'I couldn't get the tie straight,' I say.

'Let me see.' Father moves my tie around. He pulls down the collar on my shirt.

'Looking a million quid,' he says. 'Let's get on the road.'

The church is at the base of Castor. White all over, every brick and board painted, shining in the mid-morning sun. People are filing into the building, shaking hands as they meet. We make our way into the church and I see people glancing at us out of the corners of their eyes. They don't come near. It's always like this at funerals, people moving away, watching from a distance. Everybody wants to know about the man who's hunting the killer, but nobody wants to get close.

There's organ music inside the church. My eyes find the coffin. It's up front, a crucifix hanging high on the wall behind it. The coffin is closed and covered in white cloth. Next to it, there are flowers and a candle resting on a table.

We find a spot in the pews. I see Flo sitting with Uncle Jimmy and Aunt Beth. Flo is wearing a dress, the first I've seen on her. Uncle Jimmy and Aunt Beth are talking quietly, but Flo is looking around. She sees me and nods, then gestures across the room with her chin. I see Sam. He's dressed like a little politician in a three-piece suit with silver buttons. He sees us and we pass some meaning with our eyes, right as the reverend steps to the altar and the lady playing the organ lifts her fingers from the keys. We all stand.

'"I am the resurrection and the life," says the Lord. "Those who believe in me, even though they die, yet will they live. And whoever lives and believes in me shall never die."'

I hear someone crying. Mrs Fletcher, Catherine's mother. She's in the front row near the aisle, holding a handkerchief to her eyes. It looks like a shroud, the way she's holding it, and I have to work to stop the pictures of Catherine Fletcher from flooding my mind. I don't want to see that. Not here, around these people who knew her.

Next to Mrs Fletcher is the only person sitting in the church. Ollie Fletcher is in his wheelchair near his parents. He wipes away tears. I can see his pale skin, the way it seems to glow in the light shining through the stained-glass windows. The way you get skin that pale is from being indoors most hours, away from the sun, away from people.

I look around the room. The person who did this, who took Catherine Fletcher's life that night, might be in this room. They might be standing here with us, hearing the same words as us. I keep looking around, staring at the faces, and then I see Flo. She points with her eyes, over to the front of the church. I follow her eyes to Will Fletcher. She wants me to see him, standing there next to his family. Will Fletcher's not crying. He's not shaking. He's not doing any of that. The man, the father, is standing straight as a post, staring at the coffin.

I turn to face Flo and she mouths three words at me, slowly so that I can see each one.

He. Did. It.

The cemetery is on the hill behind the church, halfway up Castor, at the end of a steep stone path flanked by old gum trees. The pallbearers place the coffin on a cart led by two horses, hair dark as charcoal, and we fall in line. It's a hard climb. People slip and lose some skin from their hands. They gasp and fan themselves. The horses strain on the stones, hooves grinding down the rock. I see Ollie Fletcher ahead. He's being carried by two men, one on each side, lifting him above the mourners.

We're quiet as we climb to the graves. Many of the women carry flowers. They stare down at them as they walk, straining to reach this high, sad place. We pass through the gates of the cemetery and weave through the headstones. The men leading the team stop the horses at an open hole in the ground. This is the place where Catherine Fletcher will rest. I look out past the grave and see why they made the cemetery here, high on the hill behind the church. All of Gemini is laid out below us, the river, the main street, the houses dotted around. Over there is the mine with its smokestacks, the blue hills beyond. They want the people they bury, the people they love, to watch over them. They want to spend their lives under the view of their loved ones, before they join them here on Castor.

We stand around the grave while the final words are said. Four men lower the coffin into the ground on ropes. Mrs Fletcher sobs into her hands. I see tears falling down Ollie's cheeks, but Will Fletcher's eyes are as dry as the stones around us. Not even when the ropes are pulled away, when the dirt is dropped on his daughter's grave, not even then does Will Fletcher cry.

My eyes wander and I see two people staring at me. They're not staring at the coffin or the ground or the sky above. They're staring at me. Two old people, a man and a woman. The man has a round, red nose. White hair that curls at his ears. The woman's hair is also white. She wears eyeglasses that shine in the light. As they stare, the reverend finishes his words, then we move away from the grave and make our way down the hill. I lose sight of the old couple.

'Did you see that?' Sam asks. I'm standing with him and Flo, down by the church. Sam is pulling at his necktie, trying to free himself. 'Did you see Will Fletcher? You'd never know it was his daughter's funeral.'

I look around at the people milling about the church. Miners and farmers in small groups, hands in the pockets of their trousers. Women herding children away from the men. They look far from comfortable, under all that clothing. The heavy fabrics, the starch. The weight of clothes people wear only when someone passes over. I see Father standing with Mr Napier and Uncle Jimmy. Father is looking past them, over to where Will Fletcher is standing. He's watching as Will Fletcher shakes hands with the other mourners.

'I saw it, all right,' Flo says. 'He didn't flinch. You could eat dinner off his face, it was so still.'

'So what if he didn't cry?' I say. 'The men never cry. I've been to other funerals and it's always like that. The women cry and the men look like they're falling inside themselves.'

I see that Father has moved away, following after two people. He talks to them, to their backs as they walk away. One of them turns and I see that it's the old man, the one from the cemetery, the one who was staring at me. He says something to Father, something mean by the look on his face. He holds up an arm, a finger pointed at Father. And then he turns. The old couple disappear behind some buildings. I watch Father walk slowly back to the church. He's looking down at the ground as he goes, as if searching for answers in the dirt.

Flo snaps her fingers in front of my eyes.

'Falling inside themselves? You don't know what you're talking about. Take it from me, he's the one who did this. All we have to do is prove it.'

'How are we supposed to do that?' I ask.

We hear a whistle and we turn. It's Uncle Jimmy, waving Flo over. She backs away from Sam and me, talking as she goes.

'It's old-fashioned detective work, Morris,' she says. 'We have to find the motive.'

12

Men down by the river. I see their faces, blank as stone. There's something missing in them. I stare into each of their eyes. No blues or greens or ambers. Each eye is the colour of river water. Dirty brown. Man after man, standing near the river, the muddy water framing their faces. The men start to join together on the banks, drawn in as if with magnets. There are hundreds of them, shoulder to shoulder, perfectly still, heads turned upriver. They're waiting for the river to give them something, for anything to float by. Nothing comes. The river flows on and on without end.

I wake, sweating under bedclothes. The chill of the night is gone, the room is bright. The sun must be over the hills and bearing down on Gemini. Heat like a blanket thrown over the valley. Lottie is gone, her bed empty. I dress, tie on my boots and leave the bedroom. There's no sign of Father or Lottie anywhere in the cottage, only a note on the table in the kitchen, telling me to come to the big house for breakfast. Father is always leaving them. Making records, taking down statements.

I follow the stone path, listening to the sounds of insects, to the buzzing and chirping. It's a symphony hidden in the ground and grass and ferns and trees. I walk through the hum toward the big house.

Uncle Jimmy is out back. He's shirtless, sitting on the back step, head over a bucket. Rubbing something on his hair, black liquid marking trails down his hands and arms. A smell like smoke from a car engine drifting over from the bucket. The two sheepdogs stand a few feet away, sniffing.

'Morning,' he says. He winks, rubbing his scalp. 'Fresh eggs from the chickens inside. Get yourself some.'

One of the dogs, the blue heeler, edges closer and gets his snout near the bucket. The red heeler stays well clear.

'Get out of it,' Uncle Jimmy says, elbowing the blue heeler away. 'Pain in the neck, you are.'

The dog backs away and then sits on the patchy grass and licks its paw.

'What are their names?' I ask.

'That bugger is Blue,' Uncle Jimmy says, nodding at the blue heeler. 'The other one is Red. No prizes for guessing how they got their names. They're good dogs. Hard workers. We need all the help we can get around here.'

He wipes his hands on a rag, turning the beige fabric black.

'You better get on inside before all the eggs get gobbled up,' he says.

Father, Lottie and Flo are at the table. They're finishing the last of their breakfast. Aunt Beth is at the stove, steam rising around her.

'Good morning, sunshine,' Father says. 'Glad you decided to join the living. I thought we might have lost you there.'

'He was snoring like an old dog,' Lottie says. 'No mistaking the fact he's alive.'

I point back over my shoulder, back the way I've come.

'I saw Uncle Jimmy out there,' I say. 'He was doing something to his hair.'

'He's colouring it,' Flo says.

'Made some awful concoction with leftovers from the farm,' Aunt Beth says, scratching a pan with a wooden spoon. 'Doesn't want anyone to see his grey hairs.'

I take a seat at the table and Father stands. He scrapes his plate and rinses it in the basin.

'I've got to go into town,' he says. 'You children spend some time with your cousin.'

Me and Flo look at each other. She leans back in her chair, hooks her thumbs under the straps of her overalls. 'Got a lead on the case?' she asks Father.

'Something like that,' he says.

'Why you think she was murdered? You got a motive?'

Father wipes the back of his hand across his mouth. He stares at Flo, breathing loud through his nose. 'We don't know that yet,' he says.

'You going to round up people from the camp?'

Aunt Beth turns and points the wooden spoon at Flo. 'You mind your own, young lady,' she says. 'Don't go sticking your nose in where it's not needed, and don't go talking about that camp.'

Flo reaches a hand to her lips and mimes sewing them shut. Aunt Beth watches her for a moment and turns back to the stove.

Father heads for the door. 'I'll be back later,' he says, over his shoulder. 'Be good.'

We cut through the paddocks, me and Flo and Lottie. The yellow grass is half dry, half wet under our boots, morning dew clinging to the blades wherever there's shadow. In the distance, under a gum tree, a few sheep lean over the grass. We walk in silence, listening to the calls of birds and the rush of wind that moves across the land, picking up dust. Red and Blue follow us out near the edge of the paddocks, panting near our heels, before they break off and make for some shade under a stand of trees. We've got our swimming clothes on and we're carrying our lunch in paper bags, sandwiches packed by Aunt Beth. Flo is taking us somewhere special, somewhere that makes this town bearable. We're going to Gemini Falls.

Flo leads us to a track that cuts through the bush bordering the farm, a shortcut upriver. The track is as wide as a cricket bat is long, no more. We duck branches and move past ferns. We get the sweet scent of myrtle on our skin. It's cooler in the bush, away from the heat of the sun. We keep walking, on and on through the bush, sticks leaving scrapes on our skin, and then the path starts to swell. I hear the sounds of rushing water and laughter and we reach a clearing at a wide part of the river, calm enough for swimming.

The waterfall is a thread of silver running from a rocky ledge down to the pool where the land flattens out. Boulders line the edge of the pool, cut here and there by thin beaches made of pebbles. Past the pool, the river runs on, bending down toward town.

'There he is,' Flo says. 'The little politician with a different suit on.'

Sam is standing by the water, wearing a matching blue swimming vest and shorts. There are a couple dozen other people here, our age and a little older. There are boys and young men using a swing made of rope and wire, looping out under the bough of a gum tree and falling into the water. They seem to float in the air when they let go, only for a moment, before crashing into the river. There are girls standing by the water's edge, talking quietly.

'This is Sam,' I say to Lottie, when we reach him. 'His father is the mayor. This is my sister, Lottie.'

'Pleased to meet you, Sam,' Lottie says. She winks at Sam and he smiles, blushing.

'You been in yet?' Flo asks.

'I was waiting for you,' Sam says.

'Well, I wait for no one.'

Flo drops her towel and lunch on the bank. She climbs a boulder and leaps into the water. The splash sends ripples out to meet the ones coming from the falls.

'I suppose we ought to join her,' Lottie says.

We lay our towels on the bank and walk to the pool. The water is clear at the edge, so clear I can see weeds bending in the currents. We wade in, letting our breath out in short bursts. Flo is floating on her back when we reach her.

'It's so cold,' Lottie says. 'My bones are aching.'

'You'll get used to it,' Flo says. 'Give it a few minutes, you won't ever want to get out.'

I swim into the pool and the bottom drops out below me. It's deep in the middle, currents rising from below, colder water reaching my toes. On the bank, three girls are throwing flower petals onto the water. They look around Lottie's age, their legs thin and pale below their swimming costumes. The petals float on the surface, reds and yellows and whites mixing together.

'What are you doing?'

The question comes from the falls. A young man, sitting on a boulder with some companions, out where the river drops down to the pool. He has dark hair, the strands pulled away from his forehead. His face is tanned and there's a scattering of freckles around his nose.

'Why are you throwing those flowers in the pool?'

The girls turn their bodies away from him. They go on throwing petals, colours sailing through the air.

'You doing that for Catherine?'

'If you must know,' the tallest girl says, looking down her nose at the man. 'We're having a memorial for her.'

The man laughs. He looks at his companions and back at the girls.

'You lot were too good for her a few weeks ago. What's changed now?'

One of the girls starts to cry. She moans as she sobs, a sound so loud it carries over the water.

'You didn't know her. Don't act like her friend now.'

Another girl throws a petal in the direction of the man. It drops short and spins on the surface. 'And I suppose you knew her, Eamon Slater?'

'I'm only saying she didn't have a friend in life, other than her little brother. Seems strange to have so many in death.'

The tallest girl throws the last of her petals, all at once. She rubs her hands and walks from the bank, over to some towels at the edge of the bush. The other girls throw their petals and follow. The man watches them as they go, shaking his head. Water runs in streams from his hair, moving down his face.

We swim until the skin on our fingers gets loose and wrinkled. I follow the others out of the water and we dry off on the bank. Lottie hands Flo and me our sandwiches. Sam takes out a lunchbox and a knife and fork. He cuts into some cold roast beef. There are potatoes and peas and carrots. There's even a Yorkshire pudding, tucked away next to the peas.

Flo laughs, the sound muffled by a mouth filled with bread. 'Did you bring a three-course meal?' she asks, pointing at Sam's food.

'My mother packed it,' Sam says, shrugging. 'I don't choose what she makes.'

'You need a maid to come here and serve you that.'

Flo laughs again. Sam looks down at his food, blinking fast.

'Flo,' I say. 'Did you know they were going to do that?'

Flo stops laughing and looks my way. 'What?'

'The flowers. Did you know those girls were having a memorial?'

Flo raises her eyebrows. 'I might've heard something,' she says. 'We've got to gather all the evidence, you know. Be there when it's happening, anything to do with Catherine Fletcher.'

'I wouldn't call that evidence,' Sam says.

Lottie's eyes narrow. She swallows the last of her sandwich. 'What evidence?' she asks. 'What are you up to?'

'We need to start following Will Fletcher,' Flo says. 'That's what we need to do.'

'The father? What are you talking about?'

Flo mimes sewing her lips. Lottie looks my way. I get that feeling, the one that gets my insides moving and turning. I should say something. Father would say if he's on the hunt. This is the family business.

'We're going to solve the case,' I say, lifting my chin.

'You? Don't make me laugh.'

'We will, you'll see,' I say. 'Flo says we've got the best chance, with her detective skills, my fresh eyes and Sam, who knows everyone in town.'

'Wait, I don't want to know,' Lottie says. She points a finger at me and then waves it over Flo and Sam. 'You need to let the police do their work. Don't get mixed up in this.'

Flo looks at me and smiles. It's a toothless smile, her lips sewn shut with the fake thread. I feel my ears getting hot, a flame held near the skin.

'You'll see,' I say. 'We'll solve it and the whole town will thank us. There'll probably be a parade. You can stand in the crowd and watch as everyone cheers.'

'You've really got your head in the stars if you think that'll happen,' Lottie says. She looks up at the trees and shakes her head. 'Why am I wasting my time? I'm not getting caught up in child's play. I'm going to find some sane people to talk to. There must be a few in this town.'

She rises from her towel and walks away, over to the water. A wind passes through the trees and over the clearing, picking up dirt, pushing it into my eyes.

'We don't need you,' I say, rubbing my eyes.

When I open them again, Lottie is in the pool, swimming away from the bank. Flo is watching her.

'She looks an awful lot like Catherine, you know,' she says. 'Same hair, same eyes. Even the same height, give or take. They could be sisters.'

The sun shines on Lottie as she moves through the water. I remember the pictures of Catherine Fletcher, lying in the darkness near the tunnel. The cuts opening her skin to the world.

Flo finishes her sandwich and claps her hands. 'Well, what do you say? Should we follow some leads?'

'I can't,' Sam says, standing and wiping the clay from his legs. 'I have to get home. I have a piano lesson.'

'Tomorrow, then,' Flo says. 'We'll start on the case tomorrow.'

Sam nods and says goodbye. He walks away to the trees and moves along another path that cuts through the bush. I chew on the last of my bread and watch the water. The surface shines gold in the light. I see Lottie swim over to the falls, turning over and floating on her back when she reaches the boulder. The young man, Eamon Slater, the one with the freckles, watches.

13

We leave after breakfast, only me and Flo this time. We ride bicycles from the farm, following the road that leads into town. When we reach the main street, we see storekeepers sweeping the path outside their shops. We see horses tied to posts, tails flicking at flies. There are a few people walking in the street. Some watch us as we pass.

Flo leads us to a house off the main street, and we drop our bicycles near the fence. Outside the house, in the well-watered garden, there are marigolds and poppies and petunias. There's a bottlebrush tree, looming over it all. Flo strides to the front door and knocks three times. A stout woman in a white apron opens the door.

'Florence,' she says. 'How did I know it was you?'

'Must be my confident knock, Missus Napier,' Flo says.

'That must be it,' Mrs Napier says. 'Will you be needing my Sam, will you?'

'I will be,' Flo says. 'We will be. This here is my cousin, Morris. His dad is here to solve the murder.'

Mrs Napier squints in my direction. She holds a hand over her brow as if she's looking into the distance. I'm only out by the fence, hardly more than five paces away. It's as if I've shrunk in Flo's shadow.

She's sure of herself and I'm hardly here. I wish I could be like her, stride up to the doors of the world and make them open for me.

'I'm in need of my glasses but I'll take your word for it,' Mrs Napier says. 'I'll get Sam. Promise me you'll not get up to any mischief this time.'

Flo brings a hand up to her chest, covering her denim overalls.

'I promise,' she says.

Mrs Napier walks off and we stand there near the entrance to the house, listening to the crickets chirping and the wind pushing through the flowers. Sam walks out of the door.

'Hello, Flo. Hello, Morris. Ma's only letting me out for a few hours. Where we off to?'

'We're going to find out about Catherine Fletcher,' Flo says. 'We need to know more about her. It's the obvious first step in any investigation.'

Flo turns and walks past me. Sam looks at me and I shrug. She's out the gate and making her way down the street before me and Sam turn to follow her.

'Where are we going, Flo?'

Sam scuffs his boots in the dusty street as we walk. I'm beside him, walking in Flo's shadow. She's ahead of us, turning her head left and right as we pass shops and houses.

'I'll know when I know,' Flo says. 'I've got to get my bearings first. Detective work is about sniffing out a clue. It's not always easy.'

'All we're doing is sniffing the dirt we kicked up last time we came up this road,' Sam says. 'This isn't detective work. This is boredom.'

Flo stops and turns on her heel.

'You're welcome to go on home and hang on to your ma's apron,' she says.

Sam shakes his head and looks at the sky, as if searching for strength in the heavens.

'Sam's right,' I say. 'We're not doing much of anything. We ought to come up with a plan.'

Since we left Sam's house, Flo has led us down to the river, along the main street, around the streets that twist up Castor. The sun has been climbing higher in the sky. Heat rises from the ground beneath us, meeting the heat falling from the sun. We're being grilled and roasted at the same time. I feel sweat running from the back of my neck down my spine.

'I don't hear the two of you coming up with many plans,' Flo says. 'Why is it on me to do all the thinking?'

It's been a long time since breakfast. My insides feel tight and empty.

'We should go somewhere cool and get something to eat,' I say. 'Won't get much done if we die of starvation.'

'There's a plan,' Sam says. 'The first sensible plan I've heard.'

Flo sends a look my way. She scratches her nose and takes a few deep breaths.

'Good one,' she says, finally. 'We'll go to the pub. We can ask some questions while we're there.'

The Union Hotel spans a turn on the main street, looking out at the approach into Gemini. On the other side of the turn are more shops and, further on, farms and the mine that gives Gemini its money and its people. Flo opens the door and we make our way inside. I feel the cool air inside the pub rush to me. It's like passing through a barrier, an invisible line in the world.

There are a handful of people in the pub, mostly older men, the ones who can no longer swing a pick or hold a plough. They hunch over beers, eyes as shiny as the glasses in front of them. Flo strides over to the bar.

'We're after a few counter meals, please,' she says.

A tall young man with closely cropped hair walks through a door behind the bar. He's thin but his head is wide and heavy like something carved from marble. His shirtsleeves are rolled to the elbows. 'Florence,' he says. 'How many times do I have to tell you not to come in here without your dad?'

'Liam,' Flo says, matching his tone. 'We're not looking for a lecture, although some information to go with our meals would be fine.'

Liam's eyes move past Flo and settle on Sam and me. He looks me up and down.

'You know Sam, and this is Morris, my cousin from the city,' Flo says. 'His dad, my uncle, he's here because of Catherine Fletcher.'

'I know. Not much happens in town without it being talked about over this bar. Nice to meet you.'

'Nice to meet you too,' I say.

'Come on, Flo,' Sam says. 'Let's get a meal somewhere else.'

Flo waves a hand at Sam. 'That's why I said we ought to come here,' Flo says. 'Not much happens without you hearing, Liam, and we're looking into what happened to Catherine. Helping out the case.'

'How would you help the case, Flo?' Liam asks. 'Remember what happened with Missus Watson? I don't think she's got over those rumours.'

Flo takes a half step back, as if hit by a wind. 'Everyone makes mistakes,' she says. 'You can't live a life without making a mistake, but this time we've got Morris. His dad's a detective so some of that must have rubbed off on him. We're only trying to help. No harm can come to a girl who's already gone, can it?'

'Plenty of harm can come to the family that's left behind. Just think about that when you're out and about asking questions.'

Flo goes quiet for a moment. It looks as though she's working herself up, steam moving around inside her.

'Come on, Flo,' Sam says.

Flo waves at Sam again.

'Just this once, please,' Flo says. 'We only want to ask you a few questions, same as anyone else who comes in here. Just once and then I'll never ask you for anything again.'

Liam is quiet for a time before he speaks. 'I do this and you'll stay out of here when you're not with your dad? I have your word on that?'

Flo looks at me and Sam. She seems to be passing something around in her head, weighing up the odds in her gamble. She looks back at Liam. 'That's right,' she says. 'Do this and I'll keep out for good.'

Liam nods and then disappears through the door behind the bar.

'Di,' he says. 'Diane. Come down here a minute, will you? Mind the bar for a bit.'

Liam returns, followed by a short woman. She's young in her face but old in the way she moves, back hunched, limbs heavy and slow. She nods at us and then walks over to the other end of the bar.

Liam points to the front door. 'Go on out there and around the back. I'll get the cook to work something up for you. The shift at the mine's changed and we'll be full before long. Best you're not here when the men get back.'

I follow Flo and Sam out the front door. We walk into the light and the heat hits me. It's like walking into a wall. We turn down a laneway beside the hotel, stepping over weeds and broken glass. It smells of stale urine. At the end of the laneway, we see Liam standing on the back steps. He waves us over.

'Come on,' he says. 'Let's get this over with.'

We make our way over and find a place to sit on the steps. Liam leans against the stone wall of the hotel, waiting.

'We want to know more about Catherine Fletcher,' Flo says. 'What was she doing in the days before her murder?'

Liam scratches at his side. He takes a cigarette and a match from his shirt pocket. He lights the tobacco, blows the smoke into the air.

'I don't know her better than anyone else.'

'You must've heard something over the bar. People talk.'

Liam takes a long drag on the cigarette. 'Hard to know what to believe. A lot gets said around here that wouldn't stand up to the slightest breeze. I don't want to be passing on rumours like with poor Missus Watson and her dog.'

Flo turns her head and stares at the ground.

'What seems true to you?' I ask. 'What do you hear that seems like the truth, the ordinary truth, without any extra added to it?'

'Not much seems ordinary about what happened to her, but if something was going to happen to any girl that age, I'm not surprised it was Catherine.'

We share a look, Flo, Sam and me.

'What do you mean?' asks Sam.

'She stayed apart from people, as far as I can tell,' Liam says. 'Didn't have friends. Only person she had was her brother. Doted on him, she did. Someone like that, when someone else pays them attention, they go to it like a moth to a flame. It's like the old boys in the pub, the ones that sit alone at the bar. It's a hunger in them, that need for attention.'

'Why would someone who wants attention get killed?' I ask.

Liam's jaw sets. He stares into the eyes of each of us in turn. 'If I find out any of you said this came from me,' he says, leaving the rest to our imaginations.

'You won't,' I say. 'Tell us, please.'

85

Liam looks left and right but we're the only ones near. 'Some people make the most of that need in others. She was only young, but I heard she had a sweetheart, only it wasn't someone her own age. The man she was going with was older.' His voice trembles at the edge of each word. 'I heard her mother found a bag in the house, after the body turned up. It had clothes and a little money, the kind of bag you pack when you think you might want to get away fast.'

There's a heavy knock at the back door. Liam's face twitches. He opens the door. 'Scared me half to death, Elliot,' he says.

There's a cook standing at the door, wearing a white apron and holding some plates. He doesn't blink. He's a stocky man, around thirty years old. His skin glows with a layer of sweat and oil, even in the shade.

'Got to knock with my boot when my hands are full,' Elliot says. 'You want these or not?'

He nods at Flo and Sam, then his eyes land on me and they go wide, only for a moment, before settling back to the way they were before. Dull and unblinking.

'This here is Morris,' Liam says. 'His dad's the one looking into Catherine.'

Elliot nods at me and I nod back. He hands out plates to Flo and Sam and me. 'Sausages and mash,' he says.

We say our thanks. Elliot turns and leaves.

'Tell us more about Catherine,' Flo says to Liam, her mouth half full of mash. 'Who else knew she had a sweetheart?'

Liam scratches his chin. 'Not sure. What I can be sure of is her father didn't know. If he had, he'd have done something to stop it. No way he'd let his daughter run off with some bloke.'

'Maybe he did stop it,' Sam says.

Liam stares at Sam. 'Be careful what you say about Will Fletcher where his daughter figures in. It's all right around me, but say that to the wrong person and it'll find its way back to him. That's something you don't want to happen.'

'Why's that?' I ask.

'Let's just say Will Fletcher and the men from the mine will swing an axe sooner than they'll ask a question. He was here the night Catherine died. Got in a fight that night of all nights.'

'Wait,' Flo says, sitting up straight, almost knocking over her meal. 'He was here at the pub that night?'

'Sure he was. It was payday out at the mine. They all come back here to skim some off the top and hand it to us. Will Fletcher skimmed off quite a bit, always does.'

'And he got in a fight? Who with?'

'Can't remember,' Liam says. 'Plenty of fights down here. It's not like watching Jack Dempsey in the ring. They're not something you store away to think about later.'

I picture Catherine's body, laid out near the tunnel. What it would take to do that to someone, the rage you would need to take a life from a body. And then to lay her out, to lay her hair over her face like that. This wasn't someone who killed her and left her in a heap. They pulled her into the tunnel, away from the rain that was about to come. Away from the black clouds gathering between the ground and the stars, Capricornus high in the northern sky.

Capricornus. Before the rain.

'What time did Will Fletcher leave the pub?' I ask, my heart beating fast.

Liam looks at the sky for a moment and then shrugs. 'Must've been around eight or nine. Most of the blokes from the mine have run out of steam by then. They work hard underground and they drink pretty hard above ground.'

I share a look with Flo and Sam. We each spoon the last of our meals into our mouths and stand up on the steps.

'Thanks for the food,' Flo says. 'We'll fix you up later.'

Liam snorts. 'I've got a strict account on you, Florence, and you're not the only one. I'll be clearing it whenever it is you get some money of your own.'

He smiles and it's a warm one, full of feeling. He takes our plates and disappears inside. We make our way around the pub, back into the heat of the main street.

'I've got to get back,' Sam says. 'Ma will be wondering where I am.'

Flo points to the river, across from the pub. 'Meet us here tomorrow after midday,' she says.

'Why?'

Flo taps the skin under her eye. 'Because we're going to keep our eye on Will Fletcher, that's why,' she says. 'We're going to follow him and find out what he's like when there's no one watching.'

14

After Flo's done with her morning chores at the farm and we've eaten enough to last until dusk, we walk to town and set off for the riverbank. Sam's already there, crouched in the shade of a gum tree. The sun is between the hills and the air bites with heat. The three of us pant more than breathe, short, sharp gulps of air. Sam picks up sticks and throws them to the water, and we take our eyes off the street now and then to watch the sticks float downstream.

We're waiting for the men from the mine to walk into town.

'What do you think, Flo?' asks Sam, picking up another stick and tossing it onto the flowing water. 'You sure it was Will Fletcher?'

Flo loops her thumbs under the straps of her overalls and leans back against the trunk of the gum tree. 'Here's what we know,' she says. 'He was at the pub the night she was murdered and he got in a fight, so we know he had violence in him.'

'Same could be said about most men in town,' Sam says.

'But not every man was fighting, getting his blood up, right before she died.'

Sam looks down at the stick he's holding. He snaps it in half and nods.

'He left the pub at the right time to run into her,' Flo says. 'What if he saw her walking away from the house that night? Maybe he saw her in the distance and followed her. Maybe he'd already found out about her sweetheart and decided to stop her. Liam was sure he'd stop it happening any way he could.'

I think about the marks on Catherine Fletcher's neck. I think about the cuts in her back. Whoever took her from the world wanted her gone. They wanted to leave their mark on her body, to change her until there was no more to her than a weight to leave behind.

'We know he's been trying to get everyone to look at the people in the camp,' Flo says. 'He's been stirring up anger, looking for someone to blame, and we know he wasn't crying at her funeral. This is someone who fights, who has a daughter who could bring him shame, who left the pub at the right time to run into her and who works at the mine, so he would know his way around there in the dark.'

Flo crosses her arms and her shoulders slump, as if laying out her case has taken all her energy.

'That it?' Sam asks.

'For now,' Flo says.

'Not a lot, is it?'

'It's the most we have on anyone. Morris, what do you think?'

They both turn to me, waiting for me to play judge. I look away, out over the river, watching the water flow in the currents. I think about all I know of Catherine Fletcher, about the telephone call at night, the photographs I saw, the woman at the hotel on the drive out to Gemini. About what Liam said, how lonely she was, how she wanted attention.

'It's not much,' I say. 'What about her missing shoes and undergarments? I don't think a father would take those.'

Flo's eyes narrow. She rubs the bridge of her nose, thinking it over. 'Maybe he wanted to make it look like a lover,' she says. 'Maybe something else.'

My heart beats a little faster in my chest. I take a few long breaths. I don't want to think about that. 'We need evidence,' I say. 'Something that puts Will Fletcher in the right place that night.'

'Here's our chance,' Sam says, pointing at the street. 'They're here now.'

On the main street, men appear from around the bend. They walk in small groups. Their faces are dirty, cleaned in lines where streams of sweat have run. A few of the men walk down to the river and dip their hands in the water to wash their necks and faces.

I see him before Flo and Sam. Off on the edge of the group, hands in his pockets, feet shuffling more than walking.

'There he is,' I say. 'There's Will Fletcher.'

The group comes closer. They start drifting toward the pub. Will Fletcher peels away from the others. A few men call him over. One man tries to drag him by the arm but he pulls from the man's grip. The man holds up his hands and backs away. The miners file into the pub, all of them except Will Fletcher. He passes us and then we see the back of him, turning up a side street that leads to the slope of Castor.

'Come on,' Flo says.

The streets get narrower the closer we move to the hill. The dirt road is coarse under our feet. Trees grow in the gaps between houses, hanging over the buildings, shading or hiding them. The houses themselves are faded, paint peeling in long strips like bark. They look patched together, with wooden boards nailed over older, rotten boards. There are signs outside, hand-painted and driven into the ground on stakes. The signs talk about rooms for rent or flowers for sale. There doesn't seem to be much use for either around here.

Will Fletcher walks alone past the trees and houses, looking at his feet as he goes. We keep our distance.

'Where are we?' I ask.

'On the edge of Gemini,' Flo says. 'Not much more past here but bush and the paths up Castor.'

'What's on the other side of the hill?'

'Nothing,' she says, shrugging. 'Not for a long way.'

There isn't anybody in the street. The houses we pass are either empty or hiding people who stay inside, away from the sun. The air shimmers in the distance, over where Will Fletcher walks. To my left and right I see small plots of vegetable crops in front yards or running along the sides of houses. The leaves wilt in the heat, drooping toward the ground.

'What are all those crops?'

'Those? Potatoes and pumpkins, mostly,' Sam says. 'My dad says a lot of people have been growing vegetables. They save seeds and the ends of potatoes and shove them in the ground and hope, he says.'

'Why do they grow so much?'

Sam searches me with his eyes, as if seeing me for the first time. 'They need to eat. Where do you think food comes from? They eat all they can or they trade them with neighbours when they don't have money.'

I look at the wilted green leaves around us. They look weak and frail, inches from the brown and grey soil. If there's money deep down under these crops, in the coal that lines the tunnels under Gemini, not much is making its way here. These houses look a step away from the shacks we saw in those clearings. They may be made of wood with brick chimneys instead of board and canvas, but they don't look much of a shield against the wind that's blowing through the world.

'There he goes,' Flo says. 'That must be the Fletcher house there.'

Will Fletcher turns in to a yard near the end of the street. The lower halves of his legs disappear behind weeds. A hundred yards or so beyond the house, the dirt road ends at a line of trees that slope up the hill, climbing to the clouds. Next to the house, there's a wooden fence. It's halfway to fallen down in parts. There's a strip of empty land between the fence and the neighbouring house, a line of sand and ferns that joins this street with the next.

'Come on,' Flo says. 'Let's see what we can see.'

She leads us to the fence. We walk beside it, moving past shrubs and stones until we find a small gap where the wood has fallen away. We huddle around the gap, looking through to the backyard, to the windows that line the side of the house and the kitchen out back.

'There he is,' Sam says.

Will Fletcher comes into view in an open side window. He takes off his cap and wipes it across his brow. He stands at the window, looking out at the backyard. I keep my breath steady and quiet and I watch the side of his face, the heavy bones pushing at the skin of his jaw and cheeks. Then his face moves. He shakes his head slowly, back and forth. He raises a fist and brings it down.

'Mary! Mary!'

Mary Fletcher comes into view in the window, dressed in black. Even from this far away, I can see the dark rings around her eyes.

'What's he doing out there? He can't be out in the heat!'

Mary Fletcher nods. She lowers her eyes, away from her husband's gaze. He leans over her.

'You want another dead child?'

Mary Fletcher lifts her hands and covers her face, weeping. She doesn't see Will Fletcher's arm rise, his open hand hit her ear. She falls to the ground, out of view of the window.

My head feels light. My hands tingle. I can see light shimmering at the edges of my vision. Flo and Sam are on their heels. Their eyes are wide, their breathing shallow.

'We have to do something,' I say.

I can hear Mary Fletcher moan softly, the sound leaking out the kitchen window.

'We can't let him do that.'

Sam looks at the house. He blinks like the cattle on the farm, standing in a paddock, staring at the horizon. 'What can we do?' he asks.

'We should go over there.'

Flo shakes her head. 'You want him to beat us too?'

I look at the window. Mary Fletcher is still on the ground, out of view. Will Fletcher is standing over her.

'We can tell someone,' I say. 'Get someone to come and stop him.'

'How you going to tell them why you're here, staring at the Fletcher house?' Flo asks. She puts a hand on my shoulder and I feel its warmth seeping into my skin. 'We can't do anything.'

Will Fletcher turns and looks out the window toward us. We move our heads away from the gap in the fence. My heart beats like an engine. My legs are shaking.

'Did he see us?' Sam asks, in a whisper.

Flo peeks past the edge of the gap. 'I don't think so,' she says. 'No.'

I look through the gap and see Will Fletcher pouring liquor from a bottle into a cup. He raises the cup to his lips and rocks his head back, letting the liquor fall inside him.

'Get up,' he says to his wife. 'Go and fetch him out of the yard.'

There's a noise on the street, tyres moving over stones. We rise to our toes and peer over the fence. Father's car stops outside the Fletcher house. He climbs out of the car, puts his hat on and walks to the front door. When he knocks, I drop down and stare through the gap. Will Fletcher turns from the window and then Mary Fletcher comes into view. She moves hair away from her face, rubs the skin beneath her eyes. She touches the bottom of her nose and looks at her fingers. She turns and I see Father walk over to her. He bows his head and shakes her hand.

Flo tugs on my collar. 'Come on,' she says. 'We've got to go. Now, before they see us.'

Flo and Sam back away, looking down at their feet, careful not to make a sound. I turn to join them, but something in the backyard catches my eye. At the far end of the yard, in the shade of a wattle tree, Ollie Fletcher sits in his wheelchair, facing me, an open book in his lap. As I back away, as Flo and Sam call out to me in whispers, Ollie lifts one hand slowly, palm facing me. He holds it in the air and his fingers curl over. Behind him, near a wooden shed at the back of the yard, a patch of lilies stand tall in the sun.

15

We move in silence, walking downhill past the houses with signs and vegetables. We're lost in our thoughts, going over what we saw. Thinking about Will Fletcher and what he did to his wife, what he could have done to his daughter. I'm thinking about something else too, something the others didn't see. About Ollie Fletcher, sitting in the shade of the wattle tree, and the lilies growing around him.

As we walk, I imagine stepping into the past and finding Catherine at the mine. She rises from the dirt. The bruises on her neck sink into her body, the cuts on her back heal over. The scratches on her legs blend and disappear. She steps out of the tunnel, into the night. There's someone with her, someone covered in darkness. The person who was with her on the day she left this world, the day she went through the gate of the gods and to what comes after.

Flo leads us to the shade outside the dispensary. She leans against the window. On the other side of the glass, there are vials and bandages and tonics lined up along the shelves.

'That wasn't good,' Sam says, shaking his shirt to fan his body. 'Why did you drag us out there?'

'We had to see it with our own eyes,' Flo says. 'That's all part of being a detective. You've got to uncover the facts.'

I can feel my heart pumping blood through my arms and neck. I don't want to uncover facts, not if it means watching what we saw and walking away. The witnesses in Father's cases, you won't find anyone jealous of them. You don't get any prizes for seeing what you see, only memories to keep you up at night. I stand there in the shade, letting the breeze push air over my face, hoping it will cool my blood.

Flo looks at me and frowns. 'What is it, Morris?'

I imagine Ollie Fletcher sitting under the tree, waiting for the sun to go down, for his father's own blood to cool. I picture him waiting until it's safe to go inside and I think about the way he waved at me, fingers curling down at the sight of me hiding behind that fence. I'm a coward.

'I saw lilies at the Fletcher house,' I say.

Sam stops shaking his shirt. 'Lilies? You sure you saw lilies?'

I nod. The heat begins to leave my face.

'Where did you see them?' Flo asks.

'They were out back,' I say. 'Over near a shed.'

Flo moves away from the window. She starts pacing in short lines outside the door to the dispensary. 'Why didn't you tell us?' she asks. 'You could've told us when we were there.'

'We were trying to get away. I thought that was more important.'

'More important than evidence? There's nothing more important,' she says, pacing faster now. She stops and stares at me. 'Were they the same as the ones in the photograph, the ones near her body?'

I shrug. I don't want to think about that photograph.

'Maybe.'

'Maybe?'

'Yes, I think so.'

Sean Wilson

'This is it,' Flo says, her voice getting higher. 'This is the sign we needed.'

'I don't know about that,' I say. 'Lilies can grow anywhere.'

'Not around here. Look, it's all wattle and waxflowers. You see lilies growing wild?'

Flo goes back to pacing in front of the door. She shakes her head as she walks and then it changes, slowly, from shaking to nodding. 'What about you, Sam?' she asks. 'What do you think?'

'I don't know. It's something, I guess,' he says. 'Anyone could've gotten lilies though. She could've brought them herself.'

Flo snorts, not breaking stride. 'What girl brings lilies to meet her sweetheart? It's a sign. It's another arrow pointing at Will Fletcher, that's what it is.'

Flo keeps pacing. She starts humming to herself. Me and Sam share a look.

'Are you all right, Flo?' Sam asks. 'You're not having a fit, are you? Our dog made a sound like that last summer before he lay down and started twitching.'

Flo stops, holds up a finger. 'Here's what happened,' she says. 'On the night Catherine died, Will Fletcher gets worked up at the pub, fighting and drinking. He gets kicked out and spots his daughter walking off into the night. He asks himself, where's she going? He's heard rumours that night at the pub. Maybe that's why he was fighting. It couldn't be true, could it? He follows her, down empty streets, past shops and houses and out where there's only bush. He catches up with her and makes her confess. He can't have this. His life is bad enough. He can't have his daughter running around town like this. So he loses his temper, what's left of it. He wants to show her how much she's hurt him. Wants to hurt her back. She gets away and he pulls a knife from his pocket. He chases her down

98

and he puts all his anger into that knife. It runs out of him, through his hands and down that blade. It all comes out of him and she dies. She dies right there in front of him. Now, maybe he regrets it, but there's a body and he has to do something with it. He drags her to the only place he can think of, a place he knows well. He takes her to the mine, to the tunnel where he works, and he lays her down and covers her face with her hair. He doesn't want to see her face again. But how does he make sure no one comes after him? How does he make it look like a sweetheart did this? He's going over it on the walk home and then he sees them, the lilies. He picks a few, walks back to the tunnel and lays the flowers by her side, but it's not enough. He takes off her shoes and he reaches around her and pulls off her underthings, then throws them away, letting the bush swallow them. Then he walks home, back to his wife and his other child, thinking all the time of who he can blame.'

Flo takes a deep breath, sucking in all the air she let out in her story. She leans against the window again. 'That's what I think happened on the night Catherine Fletcher died.'

'Why would he kill her with a knife?' I ask. 'Who carries around a knife?'

'This isn't the city, Morris,' Flo says. 'People aren't carrying around tram fares and theatre tickets.'

'We've got to tell someone,' I say. 'You saw the way he was with his wife. We've got to tell my father.'

Sam and Flo look at me and then at each other. A wind blows through the street, turning up the dirt. A horse tied to a wooden post near the dispensary sweeps its tail.

'People don't talk here,' Flo says, her voice softer now.

'What do you mean? Missus Fletcher's in danger. You saw it. We have to do something.'

Flo lays a hand on my shoulder and I find that I'm shaking. My body is shaking all over, light and fast.

'If that's true,' she says, 'then we're all in danger. He's a killer and we won't be safe until he's locked away. That's what we need to be set on.'

She steps to the edge of the shade and looks out over the street.

'Think about it,' she says. 'If we tell people what we know now, Will Fletcher will realise we're onto him. He'll cover up his crime, even more than he has. You won't see those lilies in his backyard. He'll tear them up. You probably won't even see him. He'll pack up his family and leave. The best thing we can do is find enough evidence to put him away for the murder. That's what we need to do. We need to find the evidence.'

'What evidence?'

The question comes from behind us. There are two young men and a woman standing by the door to the butcher's. Older than school age but not by far. The woman is holding on to one of the men, the shorter one. The other man is taller with dark, slicked-back hair. I've seen him before. The scattering of freckles on his nose, spreading out like a galaxy on his cheeks. He's the man from the falls, Eamon. The one who was sitting on the boulder. He leads the others closer to us.

'What's this evidence you're talking about?' Eamon asks.

Flo shakes her head. 'Nothing,' she says.

'No, go on. Tell us about this evidence. Is it anything like the evidence of Missus Watson killing her dog and feeding it to the town?'

The couple behind him laugh. The short man sticks out his tongue and pants like a dog.

Flo watches him. 'I didn't think it was possible to look uglier than Missus Watson's dog but there you go.'

The short man makes a face like he's sucking a lemon. He seems to be thinking of something to say, but the moment passes.

'Who's your friend?' asks the woman.

'That's my cousin,' Flo says. 'His name is Morris. His dad is the detective.'

Something passes over Eamon's face. It's a flash, lightning showing the clouds in the night sky, and then it's over, everything going back to darkness. He moves his tongue along his bottom lip. 'You're the city detective's boy?' He looks me up and down, and then holds out his hand. 'I'm Eamon,' he says.

I reach out and shake his hand. He nudges the man next to him with his elbow.

'This is Keith and that's Rebecca. You need anything for your dad, any help on the case, you're better off asking us,' he says. He points at Flo. 'That one there couldn't find a gold ring in a jewellery store.'

Flo lifts her chin, juts it out. 'What would you know?'

'I know you think you're one of those lady detectives. I've seen you reading those books. What's the name of that lady detective people are talking about?' He looks at Keith and Rebecca, searching for an answer. Rebecca shrugs. Keith scratches his chin.

'Missus Maple,' Keith says, his voice tripping over the sounds.

Flo laughs through her nose. 'You mean Miss Marple?'

'That's what I said,' Keith says, looking between Flo and Eamon.

'I heard you say Missus Maple,' Sam says. 'Maple like maple syrup.'

Keith's face blooms red as a spring rose.

Rebecca grips his arm, holding on tight. 'He said Marple,' she says.

'Did he?' Sam asks, playing the fool. He tilts his head and taps a finger on his lips.

Keith leans in closer to Sam. 'That's what I said. Marple.'

'Why do I feel hungry all of a sudden, then?' Sam asks.

Keith looks ready to swing at Sam. Eamon waves an arm between the two of them.

'Enough of that,' he says. 'The point is, Flo here thinks talking about evidence is enough. She thinks talking is going to make her a detective.'

He walks over to Flo and steps around her, the way people walk in a museum. A visitor staring at an exhibit. 'Look at you. What are you supposed to be? You'll never make it as a lady detective dressing like that. You look like a fat little boy.'

Keith and Rebecca laugh. Eamon drinks in the laughter. His body seems to swell with it.

'Leave her alone,' Sam says.

Eamon turns and moves over to Sam. 'And what about you? Prancing about all the time like a ballerina. I've seen you. You ought to swap bodies, you two. You should be the girl and her the boy.'

He lifts a finger and holds it up, pointing at Sam's eyes. 'You were born all wrong, like her. Nothing is going to make you right.' Eamon lifts Sam's cap off his head. He holds it in the air and dashes away from Sam, who follows after him, arms waving, clutching for the cap.

'Give it back.'

'I would,' Eamon says. 'I'd love to give it back but this is a cap for boys, not girls.'

Keith slips out of Rebecca's arms and runs over. Eamon throws the cap to Keith. They pass it back and forth to each other. Sam stands in the middle, moving to catch the cap now and then. Rebecca leans on a post, laughing like she's watching a film at the pictures.

'Give it back to him,' Flo says.

'Don't you want it for yourself?' Eamon asks, holding the cap in Flo's direction. 'That's what you want, to be a boy?'

Flo looks at the ground. I see a single tear run a path down Sam's face. I step forward out of the shade, into the sun. The tips of my fingers are tingling.

'Give him back his cap,' I say.

Eamon and Keith stop moving.

'The city boy speaks,' Eamon says. 'I thought he might be mute, didn't you?'

'You want to come get it?' Keith asks. He holds the cap out to me. I'm a few steps away. If I rush, I can make it. I could pull the cap from his hands, give it to Sam. I could stand in front of them, these two men, holding my ground. I could stare them down, Sam on one side, Flo on the other. I picture what it would be like. The looks on their faces, the anger in their eyes.

The feeling inside starts up again. I can feel the churning in my guts. My heart starts to pound. I take one step forward and then rock back on my heels.

'Come on, then,' Keith says, looking down at the cap in his hand and back at me.

There's a sound of soft bells ringing. The door to the dispensary is open, the bell above it swinging back and forth. A man stands in the doorway.

'Eamon Slater and Keith Hanlon. I might've known.'

The man is heavy, white shirt rolled to his elbows. His arms are thick and hairy. There are two pencils poking up from the breast pocket of his shirt. He's the chemist.

'You got something there doesn't belong to you?' The chemist nods at Keith, his jaw set tight. His hands are on his hips.

'We got something ought to belong to a real boy,' Eamon says.

Keith laughs once, quickly, then goes back to staring at the chemist. I watch his knuckles, grip starting to loosen on the cap.

'Why don't you go swing an axe or push a broom instead of running off that mouth? When's the last time you did a day's work?'

Eamon looks down at the dirt road and pushes a stone with his boot. His shadow seems to dance behind him. 'It's not like that,' he says. 'Not that easy.'

'My backside it's not,' the chemist says. 'You knock on a few doors and ask if they'll have you. Then you show up on time and put your back into it. Couldn't be anything simpler in the world.'

Eamon spits on the ground. He looks at the chemist and there's a burning in his eyes, something that's drawing from deep inside him.

'There's nothing more pathetic than a country boy who's work shy,' the chemist says. 'Your ma's more man than you are. You don't see her missing a chance to work.'

Flo snorts and starts laughing. I laugh too. It's hard to keep it in, the laughter. My body seems to want to let something out, a valve letting off pressure.

Eamon is staring at me. 'What you laughing at, city boy? I've been working since I was younger than you. What would you know about it?'

The chemist takes a step out of the shade and into the street. 'You give Sam there his cap and clear off from my shop,' he says. 'Now, Hanlon, unless I need to have a word with your old man again?'

Keith tosses the cap at Sam's legs. It falls in the dirt. Sam picks it up and runs a hand over it.

'Now, clear off,' the chemist says.

Rebecca walks into the street and puts an arm around Keith. They walk off together up the road. Eamon stands for a moment, staring at the chemist. The chemist raises his eyebrows and Eamon turns and walks after Keith and Rebecca.

'Thank you, Mister Townsend,' Flo says.

Mr Townsend nods and moves away inside his shop, bell above the door chiming softly after him.

We walk in silence. Sam holds his cap in his hands, his hair shining in the sun. When we get to Sam's street, he turns and walks toward his house.

'See you tomorrow, Sam,' Flo says.

Sam doesn't speak. He keeps walking. We watch until he reaches the bend in the street, moving out of sight.

'Come on, then,' Flo says.

We walk along the main street. We pass some women shopping and a man fitting a saddle to a horse. Outside the pub, three men smoke cigars, their eyes following as we pass. The river comes into view between the shops, cool water running past the trees and ferns. In the distance, I see the cleared-out land of the farms on the edge of town and the puffing smokestacks of the mine.

'What Eamon said doesn't change anything,' Flo says. 'We know what we're doing. We're going to do some more digging.'

Flo walks with pace, as if trying to outrun something the world is trying to press on her. A kookaburra calls from the riverbank, its laugh, piercing and shrill, echoing between the buildings in the street.

'We have to go to the scene of the crime,' she says. 'That's what we'll do. We'll go to the mine.'

16

We go past Sam's house early in the morning. He takes some time coming out, and when he does, he's not wearing his cap. We set off for the mine and the heat builds on the walk. When we get close, we see crows nosing the ground in the shadows of the smokestacks. They're almost invisible, matched as they are to the coal-smeared dirt.

The mine is different to how I pictured it. This place has been filling up space in my head since the night of the telephone call, pushing into the corners and running along the edges like a slick of oil. The mine is bright and dry. I've only ever pictured it wet with rainwater, a floor of mud and the dark opening of a tunnel. A place black as night, where there are no constellations, only the carved-out insides of the ground.

Flo leads me and Sam through the grounds of the mine. We pass the brick smokestacks that reach to the sky like stalks without leaves. We pass buildings dusted black with coal, and iron tripods wrapped in cogs and pulleys and wire. We pass men with darkened faces and hands, their eyes and fingernails shining like jewels against the darkness. They watch us, muttering quietly to each other.

'Here it is,' Flo says.

We round a corner and I see it. A slope lined with a rail leading to an opening that's small and flat and dark, a wound in the earth. Tall yellow weeds ring the opening, swaying in the breeze. From the other side, you wouldn't see the cut that leads to the tunnel. The weeds are a curtain, hiding what's below. In the distance, I can see the main part of Gemini. The steeple of the church, the white walls of the town hall, the shops bending around the river. The tunnels beyond this opening stretch under the town. I picture the veins of them, twisting deep below Gemini in search of coal, in search of money, the way a tree's roots hunt for water.

We crouch behind some shrubs and stare at the opening. There's a sign beside it, hammered onto two wooden stakes. *Long Tunnel East.*

'That's where he dragged her,' Flo says. 'Down these tracks and up to that place.'

There are flowers by the opening. Bunches of yellow and red and white and green against the black ground. We watch men come up from below leading a pony, its white coat powdered grey. The pony drags a cart filled with jagged black rocks. This is coal, fresh from down below. The men glance at the flowers. They lead the pony and cart along the tracks. Another group of men pass them and these men also glance at the flowers before pushing on into the tunnel.

'We shouldn't be this far in,' Sam says. 'I'll get in trouble if my dad finds out.'

'He's not going to find out,' Flo says. 'Look at them. They don't care about us.'

'What are we doing here?' Sam asks.

'We're looking to see if anyone is acting suspicious. It's basic detective work, Sammy boy.'

'Suspicious? They're only working.'

'Sam's right,' I say. 'Maybe we should go back to the entrance and talk to someone there.'

Flo picks up a stick from the ground. She points it at the tunnel, a knot at the end of the stick shaking in the air. 'We need to look under the surface,' she says.

'Under the surface is the tunnel,' I say. 'We can't go in there.'

Flo makes the sound through pursed lips. 'I mean under the surface of these people,' she says. 'You two don't get it, do you?'

'There's nothing going on here,' I say. 'It's only people working.'

Flo shakes her head. I look at the mine, at the dirt, at the men. I start to stand.

'Come on, Sam,' I say. 'Let's go.'

Flo pulls on the sleeve of my shirt. I come back hard to the ground, one leg twisted under my body.

'There he is,' Flo says. 'I can't believe he's there. He's right there, where she died.'

She points with her stick. Out near the entrance to the tunnel, Will Fletcher is standing, ringed by a few men. Other men walk toward the group. Will Fletcher is waving his arms. He kicks at the dirt beneath him.

'We've got to get closer,' Flo says. 'This could be important.'

We follow her, crouching as we walk. We move near the group of men and hide behind a cart. It smells of iron. I can almost taste it, a sharp, metal taste of blood. Will Fletcher is shouting to the men around him. We're so close I can see the spit coming from his mouth, arcs of it that fall like rain.

'These useless coppers aren't gonna do a thing about it,' Will Fletcher says. 'They need to be out rounding up the outsiders, that's what.'

A few of the men shout agreement at Will Fletcher. He points at a man. 'What about you, Tom? What if it was your little girl next? What would you do?'

The men mumble. They curse quietly. They look at each other, moving in close to Will Fletcher until their shoulders are touching.

'What about you, Ed? Would you sit on your hands if it was your kin they came for? We've got to do something. We don't know where they came from, how long they'll be here. We don't know anything about them.'

A man near the edge of the pack digs a heel into a patch of grass. More men walk over from the tunnel entrance.

'They're trying to steal our jobs,' says another man. 'I saw them up near the mine office the other day, cap in hand.'

'There aren't enough jobs around here as it is,' Will Fletcher says. He seems to rise above the group. 'We can't have them coming in and taking what's ours.'

The pack of men has grown to thirty or forty. There's a pressure in the air like a storm building, a wind raising up dirt and leaves. This is a storm in people. There are other men, ones that don't walk over to Will Fletcher. These men stay back, shake their heads and look down at their hands.

Will Fletcher raises a pickaxe over his head.

'Let's show them,' he says. 'Take back our town.'

Men take up shovels and lengths of iron. They hold them in front of their chests like trophies. Will Fletcher turns and moves away from the tunnel and the other men follow, each one driving his boots into the ground as he walks, kicking up coal dust until it's a dark fog that spreads around the group. Flo stands and starts after them, moving around the rusted cart. Me and Sam pass a look between us. Neither of us wants to be the one left behind at the tunnel. We follow behind Flo, crouching low to the ground.

The camp is close to the mine. It's out in the bush, a little further from town, out in the direction of the dark, distant mountains that colour the horizon. There's a path from the road that slices between the trees like a scar cutting through scalp. The men stamp along the path. There are tyres and cracked plates and broken chair legs beside us. I see a picture frame leaning against a tree. Mud is smeared across the photograph but I make out a family posing in front of the sea.

'There it is,' Sam says, in a whisper.

My heart begins to pound. The trees thin out and the camp appears. Shacks made of board and tarred hessian, fifty or sixty of them. Low to the ground, slanting at odd angles. Roofs of rusted corrugated metal or flattened kerosene tins nailed together. The smell of kero and rotting food. There's a car pitched to one side, missing two wheels. Another car with the hood up, high like a sail, a sheet made of patched hessian bags running from the back of the car to fallen tree limbs propped up in the dirt. A few skinny chickens pace inside a run made of twisted branches. There's a dog sitting in a rocking chair. It barks when it sees us. At first, I can't see any people, only the shapes of the shacks and tight lanes of mud and flattened grass. Then a woman with sunken cheeks and thin hair walks out of one of the shacks. She wraps a shawl around her shoulders and moves toward the men.

'What do you want?' the woman asks.

The men don't seem to see her. They look past her. Will Fletcher drives his pickaxe into the side of one of the shacks, punching a hole in the board. Another man kicks over a box, sending cutlery to the mud.

The woman stands in their path. 'What do you want here?'

Will Fletcher pushes her and she stumbles back, shoulders rocking like the hull of a ship in high seas. She falls to the mud and the men walk past her. The woman lifts a hand and pulls the hair from her eyes, leaving a streak of mud on her face. There's a tightness in my throat. It's

110

hard to breathe. It's a hand pushing on my windpipe, fingers squeezing the air out of me. Flo and Sam walk into the camp, staying out of sight. I follow. I pass the woman as she lifts herself out of the mud.

Sounds of snapping and cracking. The men swing axes and shovels and bars. Splinters of boards rise and fall. Cups and plates and copper pots spin in the air like planets. I see some children run from the camp. They pass into the bush, rushing through the curtain of leaves. Everything moves slow, as if the world is pushing through treacle. I hear shouts and calls and I know that the men from the mine have found the men of the camp. I turn and see Sam's face beside me as we move. We're running.

Flo holds out an arm, stopping us. We move over near some other children, out on the tree line, away from the men. We look toward a broad fire, drawn down to its embers.

Will Fletcher is holding a man by the collar. His other hand holds the pickaxe, pulled back, ready to strike. Will Fletcher is shouting and the words are bombs falling around us.

'Who killed her?'

The children next to us are shaking. I look down at my hands and find that I'm also shaking.

'Where's the bastard that did this?'

The man tries to pull away but he can't get loose. He turns one cheek to Will Fletcher and then the other. People are gathering around. Some men from the camp start to appear. The men from the mine, the ones behind Will Fletcher, move closer.

'What happened? What did you people do?'

Will Fletcher pushes the man toward the fire. He kicks at the man's legs until they buckle and he holds the man's body over the fire. Men from the camp come forward but they're met by the men from the mine. I hear the sounds of fists against flesh. A baby screams in the distance. The man's body hangs limp above the fire. He doesn't move, doesn't try to get free. He's the still point at the centre of the universe, chaos swirling around him.

Something moves into view, shapes passing the shacks. There's a wave rushing to the shore. I catch sight of Father's beard as he runs toward the men.

'Let him go!'

The police weave through the crowd, taking hold of men from the mine. The men drop their axes and shovels and pipes. They fall to their knees in the soft mud. Father walks over to Will Fletcher and pulls on his shirt. Fletcher and the man fall back, away from the embers. The man crawls, low to the ground, over to the line of men from the camp.

'You got no right doing that,' Will Fletcher says.

'I've got every right,' Father says. 'I'm police. It's me who questions people.'

Will Fletcher stands and pats the mud that's clinging to his clothes. The men from the camp are backing away, the police officers moving them on. Will Fletcher stays standing in front of Father. 'You ought to be out here rounding them up. Don't need to be a fancy city copper to know this is where to look.'

'Leave that to me,' Father says.

'I don't leave it to anybody. It's my daughter who's gone. Mine.'

Will Fletcher looks past Father, over to the line of men from the camp. There are women holding babies on one hip. There are other women herding children away, back to the shacks near the edge of the bush. Father stands between Will Fletcher and the people of the camp, feet set apart. Will Fletcher watches Father for a moment and then spits on the fire. I hear it sizzle, a quick burn, over in an instant. Will Fletcher walks to the other men from the mine.

Father turns to the man Will Fletcher held over the fire. He places a hand on the man's shoulder and whispers something in his ear. Smoke rises from the fire, gathering in a low cloud above the shacks. It lingers around Father and the man, coating them in a thin grey.

'Did you hear Fletcher?' asks Flo. 'What did I tell you? He's laying it on thick. Wants everyone to blame the outsiders. It's a fake, all a big fake.'

We're crouching. My knees are burning and there's an ache that's flashing between my shoulders.

'I don't know,' I say. 'Seemed real to me. I don't know if anyone fakes holding a man over a fire like that.'

Flo's face tightens, skin wrinkling above her nose. 'City boy like you surely been to the pictures. You never seen anyone act angry? I can spot a fake a mile away.'

'I don't know,' I say. 'His daughter died. How much faking could there be?'

Sam's blinking next to us, the whites of his eyes getting smaller with each blink.

Flo jabs his ribs with a finger. 'What do you think, Napier? You think it was one of the men from the camp killed Catherine or you think it was the man just now trying to kill someone over a fire?'

Sam looks away from us. 'I think we're in trouble,' he says.

A shadow falls across Sam's face. I look up and see Father standing over us, blocking the sun. The outline of his face and the hairs of his beard are all in shadow.

'You children take a wrong turn into town?'

Father has a way of talking when he doesn't approve. He doesn't yell, doesn't threaten. He offers you an out, a means to talk your way out of what you did. I know better than to take it. He's testing to see if you'll take the easy way or the hard way. The easy way doesn't get you anywhere. The hard way is about building character, owning up to what you did. Flo and Sam don't know it yet.

'Yes, sir,' Flo says. 'We got lost and then we heard some shouting.'

Father steps out of the light and I can see his face. He looks down at Sam. 'That the way it was, Sam?'

Sam doesn't speak. He only nods, slowly, like his head is swaying in the wind. Father looks down at me. The light is shining in his eyes now. A blue like the surface of the ocean. Calm before a storm. 'What do you say, Morris?'

A police officer walks by, taking Will Fletcher by the arm. Fletcher looks over at us and his eyes land on me. His face sets like it's been fired in a kiln, and the hairs on my arm stand tall. The officer pulls on Will Fletcher and they're gone, lost between the shacks and trees.

'We followed the miners here,' I say, looking up at Father. 'We were at the mine when we heard them shouting and taking up axes. We followed them here.'

Father nods. Every drop of his chin is a hammer driving a nail into my coffin. It's hard but it's better this way. It's better to watch him listen to the truth than to lie and have him know the lie. A quick punishment, better than a lasting stain on you.

'Right, then,' he says. 'Follow me. I'm driving you back to town.'

Father sets off the way we came in. Sam rises to his feet and falls in line behind Father. I get up and reach out a hand to help Flo. She slaps it away and gets to her feet under her own power. She dusts off her overalls and we start off after Father and Sam.

'Why did you do that? We had him thinking it was all an accident, us ending up here.'

'You don't know,' I say. 'This is what he's like. He wants to know if you'll lie or own up to it. He knew enough of the truth already.'

Flo is quiet for a while. We push on through the lanes between the shacks, twigs cracking beneath our feet. After a while, Flo starts nodding. 'That's the way I'll be when I'm detective,' she says. 'I'll keep people guessing.'

We pass a rusted dray. There's a lean-to set against one of its flanks, a shelter patched together from potato sacks. In the shade under the shelter, a woman sits on a wooden crate nursing a baby. She doesn't seem to notice us. She looks into the distance, arms cradling the baby, gently rocking back and forth. We pass without saying a word.

'It's good we came out here,' Flo says.

I look ahead to Father's back. I see a line of sweat running from the back of his hair down under his collar.

'I'm not so sure about that,' I say. 'We're in for it later.'

'Maybe, but at least we got to see the show Will Fletcher put on.'

'Some show. It was awful.'

'You're right about that. It was awfully bad acting.'

'I don't know about that.'

Flo sighs. She aims a fist at my arm and jabs. Pain shoots up to my shoulder.

'You still don't get it, do you? He's shifting the target away from himself. That's what this was for. You don't get people pointing fingers at you if you're the one doing the pointing.'

We pass more shacks made of hessian and board. Some have fern leaves laced together on the roof. They look damp even with the heat of the day on them. There are cracks in some of the walls that are so wide you can see clear through to daylight. I picture more camps springing up with shacks like these, all over the country. I think about the problems that lead to shacks like this, if they'll ever get fixed or if they'll only be patched up, the way these shacks are. Held together with wire and twine, clinging on until the next storm.

The path continues on past the shacks and then we're clear of them, back on the track we took off the road, the one that brought us here.

Flo points at a man. I hadn't seen him there, standing in the shadow of a gum tree. 'What about him? You think he could kill Catherine Fletcher? You never know.'

The man watches us as we pass. His face is like the boards of the shacks, weathered and plain, but his eyes are something else. Small, sharp eyes that shine at us, even in the shade.

We leave him behind as we follow the path through the bush, aiming our bodies at Father's back.

17

'We're taking out the telescope,' Father says.

I'm sitting with Father and Lottie at the kitchen table in the cottage. The lamp shines on one half of Father's face, setting the other side in shadow. Lottie rolls her eyes. She takes up the plates and cutlery and walks over to the sink.

'Go on,' Father says. 'Get your coat.'

There are no clouds in the sky, the first truly clear night since we came to Gemini. When we walk out the front door of the cottage, when I look up at the sky, I could fall to my knees. There are more stars than I've ever seen. I stand in front of the cottage, head back, neck straining. I can see Taurus the bull and Canis Major the great dog. I can see the winding tail of the Milky Way.

'Come on,' Father says. 'Plenty of time to look once we're out there.'

We walk in silence along the path between the cottage and the big house, Father carrying the telescope. The path is dark, the stones lit only by a faint glow from the distant stars and the sliver of moon. When we get to the big house, Flo is standing outside the back door. Uncle Jimmy is on the back steps, a lantern in hand. He sways, the lantern swinging in front of him. I can smell the gin five yards away.

'Beth told me you need Flo,' he says. 'That right, is it?'

Father stops a few yards away. 'Only want to show her something,' Father says. 'Teach her a couple of things.'

Uncle Jimmy snorts. His nostrils flare above the lantern. 'Got a lot of life lessons now, do you?'

'Come on, James,' Father says.

'"Come on, James," he says. Got to make way for what Jude wants. Jude's got to do what he wants to do.' Uncle Jimmy spits over his shoulder. It passes through the light and falls in the shadows. 'You got a nerve telling anyone in this town what to do.'

Aunt Beth appears in the doorway. She taps Uncle Jimmy on the shoulder. 'Get out of it,' she says. 'It's too late in the day for that.'

Uncle Jimmy stares at Father and then shakes his head. He gives the lantern to Aunt Beth and walks into the house. I can hear his boots falling on the boards, moving away, a storm carrying off distant thunder.

'Go on with your uncle, Florence,' Aunt Beth says. She looks up at Father. 'Don't be too hard on her.'

Father nods at Aunt Beth and sets off in the direction of the paddock. Me and Flo look at each other.

'You better keep up with him,' Aunt Beth says.

'What for?' Flo asks. 'What's going on? Is this what city folks do when they come out here?'

I shrug. A breeze passes, carrying a chill through the air and I dig my hands into the pockets of my trousers. 'Don't ask me,' I say. 'We were eating tea and then he took off over here.'

Aunt Beth blows out the lantern and steps back into the house. 'You'll lose him in the dark and then you'll be in for it,' she says.

We rush off after Father. Flo is ahead of me, moving through the dark like she's tracking a scent. I can't see where we're going. I look down as we walk and I can barely make out my boots as they move over the ground.

'Where'd he go?' I ask.

Father must have this paddock in his memory. The way dogs always know their way back, even if you drop them miles away. He's out there, somewhere in the black, pushed on by the memories from his childhood.

'This better be good,' Flo says. 'It's colder than death out here.'

We keep moving. I think I see Father ahead. We get closer and I see that it's only the outline of a tree stump, cut down at the height of a man. Stripped of bark, grey wood showing. I'm about to tell Flo we should head back to the big house when Father appears. He's facing us, the telescope set up and pointing at the sky.

'Who wants a turn?'

We don't answer. Neither of us wants to be the one to take the medicine. There's a reason Father has us out here in the dark. We followed the miners to the camp. We went where we shouldn't have. This is the time when Father tells us how we ought to behave, how we need to be better.

'Flo,' Father says, 'you can go.'

In the dark, I hear Flo drag her feet through the rough dirt and patches of grass. I watch the outlines of Flo and Father as he moves her to the telescope.

'What do you see?'

Flo bends over the telescope. I listen to the sounds of the three of us breathing and the crickets and the wind pushing through the grass.

'It's incredible,' Flo says. There's a brightness to her voice, something I've never heard from her. A power coming from far below, let free the way spring water pushes to the surface through layers of rock. 'They're so close.'

'See that bright pair of stars. Those are Castor and Pollux, the twins of Gemini. They're the stars that gave this town its name.'

'I see them,' Flo says.

'There's another story about these stars,' Father says. 'It comes from this land. There were different names for this part of the sky. Yurree and Wanjel, the fan-tailed bird and long-necked tortoise. See the shape of the bird's wings, that bend in the sky.'

'Yes,' Flo says. 'I can see it.'

'There's more than one story in the stars,' Father says. 'More than one way to look at them.'

He takes hold of the telescope. Flo steps away and Father leans over the eyepiece, swings the telescope. 'All right, look again,' he says.

Flo leans over the telescope. She clasps her hands behind her back.

'Keep it steady,' Father says. 'That's good. Do you see the stars off to the side?'

'Yes, I see them,' she says.

'Join them together until you see a line carving through the sky. Does it look like a river from above, moving over the land?'

There's another silence, shorter than the last. I picture a river rushing across the sky, water floating above us, moving with the currents of the wind. It makes my skin cold, colder than it was before, as if I've been plunged in water.

'I see it,' she says. 'I've got it.'

'Good. That's what the Greeks called "Eridanus",' Father says. 'They had a story that went with this one about Phaethon, the child of the sun god, Helios.'

Father clears his throat. I can't see him clearly in the dark but I know the way he's standing. I know the way his head is tilted, the way he'll reach up and stroke his beard. I've heard him tell these stories so many times. I know everything about the way he does it.

'As the god of the sun, Helios would drive his chariot across the sky, taking the sun from sunrise to sunset. In the story, the young Phaethon wanted to drive his father's chariot. He begged and begged until one day his father agreed. Helios gave Phaethon instructions to follow the track of wheel marks Helios had left in the sky. Phaethon took the reins of the chariot, but the horses sensed that the rider was different. They leapt into the sky, leaving the track behind. Poor Phaethon wasn't ready for this. He couldn't keep hold of the horses and the reins slipped from his hands. The horses took the chariot down close to the land and it caught fire, making deserts that stretched over the earth. The great god Zeus was angry and he struck Phaethon with a thunderbolt. Phaethon's hair caught fire, and he jumped from the chariot and fell in the river Eridanus, never to be seen again.'

I hear Father's voice catch at those last words. *Fell in the river. Never to be seen again.* Something inside me starts to boil. I hate the river in the story. I hate the way it swallows him. I've never hated anything more in my life. I don't know what this feeling means. My breathing start to race and I try something Mrs Clayton taught me. I breathe in quick and deep then let the breath out slowly. I take hold of the chain around my neck. I rub the heather between my fingers. I keep doing that, holding the heather and breathing in quick and deep then out slow, until the feeling starts to fall away.

'Do you know why I told you that story?' Father asks.

Flo thinks for a while. I can hear her scratching at the ground with her heel. 'You think we're going to set fire to something?'

'Not quite,' Father says. 'Morris?'

I don't need any time. I know what Father's stories mean.

'You think we're not ready to take the reins,' I say.

I know, out there in the dark, that Father is smiling. I can feel his smile as sure as the ground beneath our feet, the dark belt of grass around us.

'Good lad,' he says. 'I know you both want to find out what happened to Catherine Fletcher but this isn't the time for you. Everything comes at the right time. Leave it to me to drive this one.'

I hear the clicks of metal on metal. Father is packing up the telescope, pulling the legs of the tripod together. I can just see the shape of him hitching the telescope over one shoulder.

'I know what's happening isn't good, but trust me that everything will come around,' Father says. 'There's a lot of bad in the world, but we have to believe that the good will win out. We have to believe it because that's how we keep going on, despite the bad.' Father begins to walk away. We fall in behind him and he talks to us over his shoulder. 'I'll find who did it. Working a case is like looking at the stars. There's not much to go on at first. It can look like a mess. But in time, when you look closely, you start to see the connections.'

We walk back to the big house in silence, me and Flo following Father through the cold and empty paddock. We walk slowly, each of us creeping up on our thoughts as they race ahead of us, out into the darkness.

18

We're not allowed out. Father makes us work on the farm with Uncle Jimmy and Aunt Beth. He takes off each morning, a plume of dust rising behind the car. We stay behind, putting our noses to the grindstone so we keep them out of other people's business.

Uncle Jimmy has us rising at dawn to milk the dairy cows. We mend fences in the heat of the day, sweat dripping from our brows onto the wire and wood. We pump water from the well, arms aching with the effort. We herd in the sheep at twilight. Aunt Beth lets us feed the chickens scraps from the kitchen. I like this part best, watching the chickens strut around the run, each one dipping its head to lift the scraps and shake a piece loose.

Lottie also leaves each day after breakfast. She rides with Father to town or else walks off down the drive, not coming back until sundown. I don't know what she does all day but she comes back beat, as if she's been running for miles. There's a glow to her skin in the evenings, a sheen that lasts all the way through tea.

Me and Flo are taking a break from mending fences, sitting in the shade of one of the sheds and pulling prickles from our socks, when Uncle Jimmy tells us he's in need of a coil of wire.

'Get onto the tray of the truck,' he says. 'We're heading to town.'

'But we're supposed to stay out of town,' I say. 'We're supposed to stay here.'

Uncle Jimmy snorts. He rubs the skin above his eyes. 'I may be the baby brother but it's my word around here,' he says.

Flo leans in close to me and whispers, 'You want to stay out here with the stinking sheep? Fine by me. I'm going to town.'

I watch Uncle Jimmy and Flo as they walk to the truck. Flo pulls off the cap she's wearing, the one made for a boy her age, and climbs onto the tray. I'm still for a moment and then I run to catch up.

It's loud in the back of the truck. We crouch, holding tight to the wooden slats that run along the sides, above the tray. The wind pulls my hair and flies sting my forehead and cheeks. Uncle Jimmy is in the front, in the cabin, his elbow out the window. Flo hits me on the arm.

'I've been thinking,' she says. 'Maybe Mister Fletcher killed Catherine out of jealousy.'

'What does that mean?'

Flo runs some hair past her ear and tucks it into her bun. It comes loose again, trailing behind her in the wind.

'Think about it. Catherine was getting older, sneaking out to start her life. Imagine it from his point of view. Here he is in Gemini, back in the town he tried to leave, and now he's stuck with a job scraping coal underground. Stuck with a wife at home and a son crippled from polio. Maybe he was jealous that Catherine was about to start her life and leave him alone with that.'

'Why would he be jealous?'

Flo hits me on the side, knocking me in the ribs. 'You've got no idea what it's like to be stuck in a small town, do you? You see the same people every day, hear the same problems, go to the same store, eat the same food. I know I'll get out of here one day but it must be hell to know you're stuck here. He's got a family to look after and he needs the job. They're not giving out jobs all around the country, are they? He's like a tree in the ground, roots holding him down. He can't move. What must that be like? You see your daughter getting ready to leave the place you're stuck in, leave you behind with all your problems. Think how that must feel, what it might make him do.'

We get to the main street and Uncle Jimmy parks the truck near the river. Me and Flo get down off the tray and Uncle Jimmy comes around the back to meet us, cracking his knuckles. He lays a palm on Flo's back and another on mine and pushes us toward the shops.

'Go on. Clear off,' he says. 'I've got things to take care of. Make your way back home for tea.'

Uncle Jimmy walks off in the direction of the Union Hotel. We watch him disappear through the pub doors and then we move on, further into town. Opposite the bandstand, we see a dozen or so people standing in a tight group. They're watching a man scrub the outside of a shop. He's on his knees, dipping a rag in a tin bucket and running the rag over the wall. Black paint, as dark as the man's hair, has been smeared on the shop. The windows have been smashed, a few shards of glass left clinging to the frame. The people shake their heads and murmur as they watch him scrub. Nobody helps.

'That's the Chinese shop,' Flo says.

We get closer and I make out one of the people watching. It's the man from the meeting, the one who wants to be mayor. Cornwell. He stands with his hands on his hips, looking at the people around him.

'Nobody likes to see this, least of all me,' I hear him say, 'but these people were giving supplies to the camp. We've all seen them giving wood and boards and nails to those people, not charging them a penny for it. Can't have a camp if there's nothing to build with.'

The man stops scrubbing. He turns and stares at the group, a blank expression on his face, and then goes back to his task.

'Serves them right,' a man next to Mr Cornwell says.

'These people don't think the same way as us,' Mr Cornwell says. 'I don't like saying it but that's the way it is.'

I think back to one morning, back in Melbourne, when there was news in the papers about fights between Chinese people and some labourers, out near the market gardens. We were sitting at the kitchen table, Father with his legs crossed, resting one knee against the tablecloth. He placed his tea on the saucer and pointed at the paper.

'It's not about how long you've lived in a place, not with people who think a certain way,' he said. 'It's about who you are, what you look like. It's about what tongue you speak in your family. About where you pray and what you believe. Some people are just afraid to let anyone in.'

I watched as he shook his head and turned the page, and I thought about what it might have taken for Father and Mother to leave the place they're from. What made them leave Gemini.

I catch sight of Lottie. She's over in a lane between two shops, standing with some other people. One of them has his arm around her. It's a man, younger than Father but older than Lottie. He's whispering in her ear. It's Eamon.

'Isn't that Charlotte?' Flo asks.

'That's her,' I say.

'She's picked out wonderful new friends.'

We watch as Eamon's face dips, as his lips fall on Lottie's neck.

'Disgusting,' Flo says. 'Come on, let's get going. We'll get some sodas.'

I keep my head down as we pass the laneway and continue on down the main street. We reach the general store, a wide building facing the river, covered in posters advertising newspapers, milk and sweets. Under the awning, at the far side of the building, Ollie Fletcher is sitting in his wheelchair. He's facing the river, watching magpies fly between the trees on its banks.

'You go in,' I say to Flo as we reach the door. 'I'll stay out here.'

Flo looks past me. She taps the side of her head. 'Good thinking,' she says. 'See what clues you can get from him.' Flo reaches for the door and she pauses. She turns back to me. 'Don't give anything away. He doesn't need to know who our suspect is. Better that way.'

She opens the door and walks inside the store. A bell rings and Ollie looks away from the river, looks at me standing by the door. I feel a heat rising in my face, a burning in my cheeks and on my forehead as if I've turned my face to the midday sun. Ollie is thin and slight. He looks like a paper doll, no thickness to his body. I think about the photograph of the boys in the hospital beds. Legs bandaged, eyes pointed away from the camera.

'I get left outside a lot,' he says.

'Oh,' I say. 'You do?'

He points past me to the entrance of the store.

'Stairs,' he says.

He looks down at his wheelchair and back at me. The blanket that usually covers his lower half is pulled up around his waist. I can see his legs, two shapes, thin as arms, strapped to the chair below the knee.

'Oh,' I say. 'Stairs. Of course.'

Ollie smiles and then looks out at the river. It's quiet under the awning. There's only the sound of water running over stones and of wind passing through leaves.

I take a deep breath. 'I'm sorry about your sister,' I say.

Ollie turns to me and his face softens, his shoulders slump, as if the memory of Catherine numbs all feeling in his body, smooths out all muscle.

'Thank you,' he says. He looks me over, from my boots to my eyes. 'Your dad's the detective, isn't he?'

'That's right.'

'I'm Ollie.'

'I know,' I say, taking a small step forward. 'I'm Morris.'

'I know,' he says. He sits up straight in his chair. 'Pleased to meet you.'

'Pleased to meet you too.'

A horse and buggy rush by. The driver raises a whip and brings it down on the flank of the horse. The sound of the whip striking the horse hangs in the air, echoing around us after the buggy has passed.

'Do you always look in at people's houses?' Ollie is staring at me. His eyes hold me in place. I remember the way he looked at me that day, from the shade of the wattle tree. The way he waved to me as I moved from the fence. The way the lilies behind him shone in the sun.

'No. I promise, no.'

'Our house isn't an easy one to stumble on.'

'I was following my cousin, Florence. Do you know her?'

Ollie laughs, as if I've asked him if he knows what bread is or what direction the sun sets in the evening.

'Of course. Everyone knows everyone in Gemini. I guess it must be different in the city.'

'You've never been there?'

'It's hard to go places,' he says, looking down at his wheelchair. The steel frame and leather seat look cold in the shade. Ollie picks at a corner of an armrest. 'Tell me something about the city.'

'What do you want to know?'

'Anything.'

128

'All right,' I say. I clear my throat and scratch the hair under my cap. 'Well, there are a lot of high streets, I suppose, with all sorts of shops. Trams run up and down the high streets, carrying people back and forth. There are tall buildings in the centre, in town, taller than a church steeple, some of them. Ships come into the bay from all over the world, carrying food and spices and everything else. Tea from China and wine from France and cotton from America. There's always something arriving from somewhere else. And there are sporting matches every weekend, gardens to walk in. Houses as far as you can see, full of so many people you could never hope to meet them all. In the evenings, when the sun is going down and everything starts to go still, you can see bats flying through the sky and hear the howls of dogs from all over the city.'

I look out over the main street of Gemini, wide and dusty and almost empty of people.

'There's something about that time,' I say. 'The time between day and night. It makes you feel like you're part of something.'

Ollie turns and looks out over the river. The trees on the banks and up the side of Pollux shiver in the wind. 'Thank you,' he says.

Two men walk in the street, past the shop. They take off their hats and bow their heads when they see Ollie. He nods at them and they walk on along the street.

'Your dad has been around to see us a lot,' Ollie says. 'I don't know how many times. He's almost a part of the house, like the curtains or the bath. He comes around to talk to my dad.' His face changes. Lines fan out from his eyes. I get the feeling he's holding something in, pushing something down. 'Is that normal?'

I nod, slowly at first and then quicker. 'Sure,' I say. 'That's normal. It's part of his job. He's only getting information. He'll be over at a lot of houses, doing the same.'

'All right, then.' There's nothing in his voice, no change, no relief. He doesn't believe me. He looks past me, up the street in the direction I came. 'Awful what happened to the shop today,' he says.

'You were there?'

'Earlier. We couldn't help but look.'

'Don't blame you,' I say. 'You can't help running over when something like that is going on.'

I look down at Ollie in his wheelchair. My breath catches in my throat. 'Sorry,' I say. 'Sorry.'

'You don't have to worry,' Ollie says. 'I know about running. It's not a secret.'

'Of course. Sorry.'

Ollie folds his arms in front of his chest. 'Say sorry one more time and I'll call out for my ma. You don't want that, do you? The new boy making the poor boy in a wheelchair call for his ma?'

I hold up my hands.

'No. I don't want that. Please. I promise I won't.'

Ollie unfolds his arms. He goes back to picking the leather on the armrest. 'All right, then,' he says. 'As long as you promise.'

'I do,' I say, smiling quickly. 'Apologies.'

Ollie's lips draw tight, his eyes narrow.

'I suppose I have to let that one go.'

I watch butterflies float above the river and birds rise into the low clouds that ring Pollux. It calms me, watching the hill, something so old and set. It makes me feel steady, knowing there are hills like these where not everything shifts as time goes on. Some things stay the same, no matter how much changes around them.

I look back at Ollie and I see he's also watching the hill. His eyes look like the windows on a house in the early morning, shining with dew.

'It's strange,' he says to me, to the hill. 'It feels as though she's only gone on a trip somewhere, that she'll be coming back home soon.'

An elderly woman passes in the street. She smiles at Ollie and me. Most of her teeth are missing. Ollie doesn't seem to notice her.

'I know she's gone, I saw them bury her in the ground, but I can't stop feeling that she'll be back. I've been feeling it ever since they found her.'

I hear the sound of the shop bell.

'Has that ever happened to you?'

In my mind, I see the muddy brown water of the Yarra. The current swirls near the banks, pulling dirt and stones from the edge and dragging them into the river. I'm standing near a boathouse. It's beautiful, this building. There are lights on strings and white cotton bunting hanging from the eaves. People sit at tables near the bank, sipping tea and cutting scones in half. Out on the water, I see wooden rowboats painted green and white, red oars hanging over the sides like wings. Couples float in the current. They hold hands and whisper to each other. Families float by, the father rowing, the children looking over the edge at their reflections. Further away, out near a bend in the river, I see a woman sitting alone in a boat. Her back is to me, hair hanging over her shoulders and down her white dress. I watch her float alone, getting further and further away until the rowboat she's sitting in melts into the water.

Ollie is looking at me. I blink the pictures away.

'She won't be gone as long as you remember her,' I say. 'Not all the way gone.'

'I suppose so,' he says. He takes in a deep breath. 'Dad only talks about catching who took her. He doesn't talk about her. Ma isn't much better. Any mention of Catherine's name is like pulling a plug. Ma goes down the drain and then she leaves the room and she's gone for hours. Nobody talks about anything before that night. They don't talk about how she could beat anyone at checkers, how she could listen to the radio for hours. They don't talk about how she would stare up at the sky whenever an aeroplane went by. We used to talk about going away together, flying away on one of those aeroplanes, somewhere far from here. That's how I know she wasn't leaving when it happened. She wouldn't go without me.'

The bell rings behind us and Ollie's eyes go wide. He shuffles back in his chair, straightens his back.

'Don't tell anyone about that,' he says, in a whisper.

I hear footsteps. A short woman in a black dress walks past me and behind Ollie. Mary Fletcher. There are dark rings around her eyes. She reaches around Ollie and pushes the blanket over his legs.

'Ma, this is Morris,' Ollie says.

Mary Fletcher's mouth drops open a little. She takes hold of the handles on the wheelchair.

'Hello, Morris,' she says.

'Hello, Missus Fletcher,' I say. My feet shift around below me. 'I'm sorry about your daughter, about Catherine.'

Mary Fletcher nods at me. She turns the wheelchair. 'Come, Oliver,' she says. 'We must be getting back now.'

She wheels Ollie away. They move into the light. Ollie turns and waves at me. I stand there, in the shade of the general store, waving back. Mary Fletcher takes hold of Ollie's arm and pulls it down, and they move around a corner, out of sight.

'What did you find out?'

Flo is next to me. I didn't hear the bell ring in the store this time. She hands me a soda bottle and my hand cramps at the touch, so cold after so much heat. I bring it to my lips and let the cold fall inside me.

'Nothing,' I say.

'Nothing? I've been wandering around in that store for ages,' Flo says. 'How long do you think it takes to buy some sodas? I almost turned to stone waiting for Mary Fletcher to do her shop. You must have found out something.'

I imagine Ollie Fletcher sitting in his wheelchair, going up that hill, watching the trees get thicker, the houses get smaller. I imagine what it would feel like to be pushed back to that house. To be stuck there, unable to leave.

'Father's been going over to their house a lot. More than just the time we saw. He's been going to talk to Will Fletcher. Ollie said he's like the curtains.'

'Like the curtains? What does that mean?'

'He's been there a lot. He's always there, like the curtains.'

Flo lifts her soda bottle to her mouth and sips. She frowns, as if studying the flavour. She lowers the bottle and licks her lips. 'Interesting. That's interesting,' she says. 'Seems we're not the only ones trying to find out more about Will Fletcher.'

A woman and three small children arrive at the store. The woman smiles at Flo and nods at me. The children elbow each other, aiming to be the first to get through the door. Flo waves for me to follow her. We cross the street and sit on a wooden bench near an empty building. I can see the Chinese shopkeeper in the distance, stooped over, picking up glass. There are more people walking over to the shop to watch.

'Whoever did that,' Flo says, 'they're doing their part to take the attention away.'

'What do you mean?'

'Think about it,' Flo says, hooking one thumb under the strap of her overalls. 'You put the eyes of the town on people who are already on the outs. It's like Will Fletcher getting the other miners up about the people from the camp. Nobody looks at you if you turn their heads and get them looking at someone else.'

I remember Will Fletcher holding the man over the fire, the veins on his arms like the roots of trees. It made me think of how roots can push out of the soil after a storm. That's the way he seems, Will Fletcher, soil washed away, everything on the surface. I can't imagine him hiding something like this.

'Sure is a shame to have your shop attacked like that though,' Flo says. She drinks the last of her soda and takes the empty bottle out of my hand.

Flo looks off into the distance. I think about Father and Mother, moving away from Gemini and staying away. What was it that made them move? Did something happen that made the people of Gemini turn on them?

We set off up the street, past the shops and the hotel and out in the direction of the farm. I imagine Catherine Fletcher leaving this town, before the night of the storm. I imagine her pushing her brother up the hill, along the river and away from Gemini, never to return.

19

Lottie glides around the cottage. The hem of her skirt rises over the rough boards, her feet seem to float through the air. She whistles as she moves through the kitchen. Father sits at the table, watching her between bites of toasted bread. This mood has made her a different creature. She's a butterfly, free from the cocoon, stretching her wings.

'You seem happy,' Father says.

Lottie turns her head as she moves. 'And what's wrong with that?'

'Nothing. Nothing wrong with it. It's good to see you enjoying yourself.'

'I wouldn't go that far,' Lottie says, turning a shoulder and floating over to the icebox.

Father nudges me with his elbow. 'I don't know, Morris,' he says, winking. 'She seems transformed to me. Must be something she likes about being out of the city, don't you think?'

I think of Lottie standing near the Chinese shop, Eamon close to her, his arm around her waist.

'Must be,' I say.

'There you have it,' Father says, leaning back in his chair. 'The jury finds you guilty of enjoying your summer. I'm afraid I have to sentence you to two months of joy and cheer, and ask that you wear a smile while carrying out your sentence.'

Lottie rolls her eyes at Father. As she moves away to open a cupboard, I see her smiling despite herself. It's faint, the two corners of her mouth lifting gently like flowers in the morning rays of the sun.

'There's a food drive in town today,' Father says. 'The women's association is putting it on for the people in the camp.' Father sends a look in my direction. I sink into my chair, letting my backside slide down. 'This is the way we help. We'll gather up some tins and some flour, and we'll take them to town.'

'We don't have much,' Lottie says. 'We only have enough for us.'

'We can get some more. It's not so easy for others to do the same.'

Lottie opens cupboards and shifts items around, pulling out the odd tin. Father gets up and takes them from her, stacks them on the table.

'Give her a hand, Morris.'

I go to one of the cupboards. I take out a tin of brisket beef and another of tomatoes. I turn them over in my hands, watching the pictures on the labels come and go, and I think about who might hold these cans next. Lottie hands me a package of flour. Some of the flour spills and coats my fingers. White powder, the opposite of coal dust.

'Come on, Morris,' Father says, clicking a finger near my face. 'We're not cutting diamonds here. No need to inspect each and every one.'

I drop the flour on the table. Father gathers it with the other items and lays it all inside a cardboard box. The tin cans shine in the light coming through the kitchen window.

'Come on, now. Get your hats and meet me out by the car.'

We walk down the path to the big house. Father lays the box on the front seat of the car. Lottie gets in the back with me. Uncle Jimmy's truck pulls out ahead, carrying him and Aunt Beth and Flo. Father starts the engine and drives onto the tracks left by the truck. Up ahead, the truck has churned so much dust it feels as though we're driving in a cloud. I can just make out the steel wire of the tray catching the light.

I nudge Lottie with my elbow. She looks at me sideways, frowning.

'I saw who you were with the other day,' I say, in a whisper. 'When that building was attacked.'

She turns her head to face me, pulls some hair away from her eyes. 'And?'

'Eamon Slater,' I say. 'He's no good.'

'Says who?'

'Says me and Flo and Sam.'

She looks down at her fingernails. 'The team of investigators,' she says. 'Why don't you worry about who left their purse behind at the town hall or whatever case you're trying to solve? Leave me out of it.'

'Is he your new beau?'

'Listen,' she says, dark eyes staring at me now. 'This is as far outside of your business as anything could be. You understand?'

Father shifts the gears. He glances back at us. 'What are you two talking about?'

'Nothing much. Only something about the stars,' Lottie says in a bright tone. She elbows me in the ribs. 'Isn't that so, Morris?'

I look at the back of Father's head, bobbing up and down as we pass over the rough drive. Gum trees rush past the window, leaves still and silent.

'Yes,' I say, 'we were talking about stars.'

The main street is a flood of life. There are horses of all colours outside the pub and the town hall, dipping their heads to drink from troughs. A few dusty cars stand together near the bank of the river,

wheels almost touching. Tables line both sides of the street, covered
with boxes, bags and loose items of food. Women from the association
sit behind the tables, backs straight and tall, hair tied up or hidden
beneath hats. They tally the goods on wide sheets of paper. There's a
small band playing in the bandstand near the fire station.

I'm walking with Father and Lottie, carrying a box heavy with
food wrapped in paper or tin. A man walks out from the shade near
the post office. It's Art Napier. He's decorated like a Christmas tree,
medals and buttons polished and gleaming. I have to squint when I
look at him. There are ribbons around the medals, stripes of different
colours. I've seen the same medals back in the city, pinned to men
down by the river or sitting near tram stops. Mr Napier's clothes and
these medals seem to be saying something about him that he wouldn't
say with words. It's a way to talk about the past, about something
painful but honourable, without having to open your mouth.

'Good to see you,' Mr Napier says. 'How do you do today?'

'Fine, thank you,' Father says. 'Good to see you too.'

'And here's the rest of the Turner gang,' Mr Napier says.

I look over my shoulder and see Uncle Jimmy, Aunt Beth and
Flo walking behind us. Each of them has a few tins and parcels in
their hands. They've brought less than half of what we have.

'Art,' Uncle Jimmy says. 'Where do we drop this?'

'Anywhere you please. Right over there would do fine.' He
points at a table and then doffs his hat at Aunt Beth and the girls. 'If
you'll excuse me, I have to do the rounds.'

Mr Napier walks off, whistling a tune. We make our way
through the crowd. There are people dropping off armfuls of food on
tables. Tins of beets and peas and beans. Boxes of oats and corn flour
and wheat biscuits. I see tins of condensed milk and bottles of sauces.
At other tables, far from the crowds, women from the association

hand out sealed boxes. The people taking the boxes keep their eyes low, staring down at their shoes or their hands as they reach out to take the charity. They're wearing their best clothes, I can tell. The clothes hint at better times, of strolling down a high street, spare coins calling out a tune from their pockets. Now the men's hats are dotted with holes and the dye in the women's dresses is washed out. Some of the children hobble around in shoes too small for their feet, tripping forward as they walk.

'Let's drop off here and be done with it,' Uncle Jimmy says.

Father nods and leads us to a table outside the bakery, one that has less than the others. The woman behind the table greets us. She takes down our names and records our donations on the paper in front of her. She chats with Aunt Beth and Lottie, talking about the weather and how the sheep are doing.

Father and Uncle Jimmy take a few steps into the street, looking over the crowd. Me and Flo follow them. The Chinese shopkeepers are nowhere to be seen. The windows on their store are boarded up, the front door shut.

Flo taps me on the shoulder. I look at her and then follow her eyes to a man. He's standing in the middle of the street, people moving around him in all directions. He's wearing a dusty jacket and cap. His shoes are worn down, scuffed on all sides like they've been roughed with sandpaper. He has a scar on his face, reaching from eye to chin. It looks like a track in his skin, a path in the wilderness. He's staring at us, across the mass of people.

'Who's that?' I ask.

Father holds a hand over his eyes. 'Never seen him before,' he says. 'Might be from the camp.'

The man with the scar keeps staring. He must know we're watching him, talking about him. He doesn't seem to care.

'What do you think he wants?' asks Flo.

'No idea,' Father says. 'Might have us confused with someone.'

Father waves at the man. A moment passes as the man stays there, watching us, before he lifts a hand and pulls on the rim of his cap. He turns and walks away, blending in with the crowd.

'Strange,' Father says. He stands beside us for a moment, calculating something in his mind before he rubs his belly. 'Shall we see what we can get to eat?'

Uncle Jimmy nods and turns to get Aunt Beth and Lottie. Father looks over the crowd, scanning the faces, watching the movements. I look at Flo and she raises her eyebrows. She's thinking the same as me. The man with the scar must've been looking at Father for a reason.

We pass through the mass of people. Lottie sticks close to Aunt Beth, the two of them talking and pointing at people in the street. There are so many people, it's hard to see where the crowd starts and finishes. All of Gemini and most of the camp must be here.

'That man with the scar,' Flo says, walking close and whispering. 'He had a look about him. That wasn't an ordinary kind of look.'

'I know,' I say. 'I think he's from the camp.'

Flo scratches her chin, her eyes dart around.

'We need to get another look at that camp,' she says.

My heart kicks in my chest like a racehorse at the starting gates. I think about the tight lanes between the shacks at the camp, about the boughs of trees leaning over, about the shadows settling around the board and hessian and tar.

'That's a bad idea,' I say.

'This time will be different,' Flo says, winking at me. 'We won't get caught.'

'How are we going to get in there?'

'Leave that to me. I know a way.'

The smell of grilled meat pulls my mind from the camp. Outside the general store, grills and smokers are stacked with meat and corn. I see piles of boiled potatoes and turnips. It's past noon and my belly shudders, letting off a growl that rises to my throat.

'Who's hungry?' Aunt Beth asks. She turns around and smiles. 'Seems as good a place as any.'

We move toward the grills. On our way, we see a bake sale. There are cakes, scones and biscuits spread out over two tables. I see lamingtons stacked high, columns of chocolate and coconut and jam. I watch women dig into their purses for coins that they place on the table like they're planting precious seeds. The way they put down the coins, I can tell they don't want to part with them. They watch as their money is taken up, passed back to a jar behind the table and gathered for people more unfortunate than them.

Flo nudges me and points across the table. At the edge, two children, a boy and a girl, are standing near the sweets. Their faces are clean, skin pink and mottled from scrubbing, but their necks are filthy. They keep their hands by their sides. The boy's trousers are two inches higher than his boots. His wrists show past the ends of his shirtsleeves. The girl's dress has patches like leaves on a tree.

'They can't buy any,' Flo says. 'There's no way they can buy those cakes.'

An old man with white hair and a cream suit walks over to the children. He whispers something to them and points to the table. They look at the sweets and back at the man. He nods his head. The children watch the sweets for a moment, as if they might disappear, then they each point to something on the table. The old man reaches into the pocket of his waistcoat and takes out two coins. He hands them to the children and they place them on the table. It's all careful, the way it happens, as if they're practising a play. The children take the sweets in their hands. The boy bows to the man and the girl curtsies. They walk away, curling around the tables, and into the crowd.

As we pass the bake sale, I watch the old man in the cream suit. His eyes are dark and shiny like boots buffed with spit and polish.

Father and Uncle Jimmy buy us sausages and bread and corn and potatoes. We lean against the posts outside the general store, eating the meal in silence. I can feel sweat pouring out under my clothes as I put the hot food in my mouth. I have a feeling that someone is watching us, but each time I look up from my plate there isn't a soul looking our way.

A man's shout rises above the other noises. People turn their heads, others start moving toward the sound. Flo taps my shoulder. We drop our plates and rush off, Aunt Beth's words of protest stretching behind us like a tail.

It's hard to pass through the mass of people. I remember the time Father took us to Flemington to watch a horse race. I remember how hard it was to pass through the crush of people on our way to the edge of the track. Everyone pressing forward, aiming for the thundering sound of hooves on turf. I get the feeling I'm there again, carving a path through the grass by the track, trying to get near the action.

We get closer and the words become clear. I can see who's shouting. It's Will Fletcher. He's over near the pub, near one of the donation tables. Mary Fletcher is at the edge of the table and he's leaning over her. Ollie is off to the side, looking on like the rest of us.

'Pack up everything you put down,' he says, voice thick and slow. 'You ask for it back.'

Mary Fletcher turns and looks at the lady from the association, the one behind the table. The lady picks up a few parcels and cans and starts placing them in a paper bag.

'You think I spend my days scraping away underground so you can give our food away? Think I want my food going to these filthy beggars?'

Mary Fletcher glances at us. Ollie looks at his lap. This feels like watching a car accident, seeing the tyres spinning, the smoke rising above twisted metal. Will Fletcher takes a few steps into the street. His legs bend and buckle beneath him.

'You disgust me,' he says, pointing at a young man in the crowd. The young man wears a suit flaked with dried mud and a hat that's too small for his head. 'You're pathetic. We don't want you here. Time you went back to whatever hole you crawled out of.'

A few other men from the camp walk over near the young man. Their faces are set. They stare at Will Fletcher, arms straight as poles by their sides.

'It's pathetic. You're all pathetic,' Will Fletcher says. 'Don't you know we haven't got enough for ourselves? They're cutting our wages at the mine. You know that?'

Will Fletcher's body sways as if pushed by winds. He waves an arm. 'Look at this town. Look around. You're bleeding us dry.'

Mr Cornwell walks out of the crowd, smoothing his moustache with thumb and forefinger. He's wearing a fine wool suit. He puts a hand on Will Fletcher's shoulder.

'Mister Fletcher's right about that. He's right about a lot, you know. People in this town are selling off furniture. They got barely enough for themselves. Some are eating horse meat if they're lucky.'

'How can you sleep?' Will Fletcher says. 'We're hurting here and you're asking for charity.'

People around us whisper. I look over at Flo, her eyes set on Will Fletcher. A voice rises above the noise.

'Got enough for a pint though, don't you?'

Will Fletcher's head whips around. 'What did you say? Who said that?'

He searches the crowd. When his eyes pass over me, my chest

starts to thump. I remember his hand rising and falling on Mary Fletcher, striking her down to the ground. I remember the way he stood over her, as if looking down on an animal.

Mr Cornwell steps away from Will Fletcher and leans toward the crowd. There's a look on his face, in the way his brow reaches for his cheeks, that says he hadn't counted on that turn. A few men come out of the Union Hotel doors, Liam, the publican, at the head. He walks behind Will Fletcher and puts a hand on his shoulder.

'Come on, Will,' Liam says. 'Let's go back and have another drink. On the house.'

Will Fletcher rocks on his heels, falling back on Liam's hand. The men from the camp lead the young man away, draining into the mass of people.

Will Fletcher looks left and right and settles his eyes on his wife. 'Take those home.'

Mary Fletcher picks up the paper bag and holds it low to her body. Will Fletcher lets himself be led to the pub. Whispers wrap around us the way air moves around a mountain. It feels like being back in the city, in close with a pack of people, the sound cloaking my mind, taking away all thoughts.

'Let's have some music,' Art Napier says. He whistles and points to the band, who take up their instruments and start plucking and strumming. The music stops the whispering, the notes flicking a switch in the crowd. People walk away, finding interest and amusement in other parts of the street. Art Napier leans in close to Mary Fletcher and says something to her. She nods slowly and hands the paper bag to Ollie. Mary takes hold of the wheelchair and pushes Ollie along a lane between two buildings, away from the street, away from the people, away from the music and away from the whispers.

20

Days pass before we have another chance to leave the farm. One morning, after Father has left, Lottie goes with Aunt Beth to visit neighbours. They take scones Aunt Beth has baked, a dozen of them wrapped in a tea towel, cradled like a newborn, steam rising around Aunt Beth's arms.

After they've left, me and Flo slink around the farm. We push crickets around with our boots. We lean against the stable in the shade. We throw gumnuts at a post.

Uncle Jimmy watches us as he takes feed to the cows and drags a wheelbarrow filled with manure. He stares as he carries eggs back from the chickens. After a time, he walks past us and points to the truck. We know what this means. He'll drive us to town, if only to get rid of our sour faces.

We get dropped off near the fire station. We're watching Uncle Jimmy drive away when I see someone walking along the railroad tracks that skirt the town, moving on toward the mine.

'Isn't that Sam?' I ask.

Flo squints in the direction of the tracks. 'Could be,' she says. She cups her hands around her mouth. 'Sam! Sam!'

The figure keeps walking. Either he doesn't hear or he doesn't want to hear.

'Sam!'

The figure keeps walking and then he's lost behind the buildings and trees. If that was Sam, it's a curious place to walk. There's nothing along those tracks other than a few empty houses, stretches of cleared land baked hard as stone by the sun and, at the end, the blackened mine.

'Florence. Come on over here.' The voice comes from behind us, from the bandstand. We turn and see a group of three young women standing in the shade of the shelter. One of them waves at us. 'Florence. Over here.'

We walk to the steps of the bandstand. When we get closer, I see the women are girls, only a few years older than us. They're wearing dresses that look fine from far away but as we get closer I see they're faded, the material fraying at the hems, stitching so loose you can see through it in places. As we walk, Flo leans in and whispers in my ear.

'Remember the town meeting? When that woman talked about the men from the camp staring at her daughter?'

'Sure,' I say.

'That's her,' Flo says, nodding at the girl closest to us.

The girl waves as we climb the steps. She's pale with bright ginger hair. She's wearing white gloves stained yellow in places.

'Come on out of the sun,' she says. 'It's awfully hot already.'

'Hello, Clara,' Flo says. She smiles wide at Clara and then less so at the other girls.

'Florence,' Clara says. 'I knew that was you.'

'How could you mistake her in those overalls?' one of the other girls says.

The girls laugh, heads close together. They stare sideways at Flo.

Clara doesn't laugh. She takes off a glove and snaps her fingers at the others. 'Don't make light of Florence. She's a dear friend.'

Flo's shoulders twitch. She cracks her knuckles. After a time, she shakes her head and waves a hand in my direction.

'This is my cousin, Morris,' she says. 'He's down from the city.'

Clara looks at me and lines appear on her forehead.

'You're the detective's son.'

The other girls take a step back, all at once. They might be worried they'll catch something from me. I can't tell if they're thinking about polio or the murder that brought Father here. Either way, it's clear they don't want me around.

Clara doesn't back away. She takes a step forward. 'Do you think they're any closer to catching the killer?'

'I don't know,' I say, shrugging. 'Father doesn't talk about the case.'

Clara pulls at her hair. She twists a few ginger strands around one finger, glancing between me and Flo. 'They ought to be looking at the camp,' she says.

Flo's back straightens. She seems to grow a foot taller. 'Why do you say that?' she asks.

'Whoever she was meeting that night, she was meeting them out near the camp. I saw her walk that way not three nights before she died.'

'You shouldn't be talking about that,' one of the other girls says. 'It's not polite.'

'It's the truth. There's nothing to fear about the truth, that's what they say at church after all.'

The girl behind Clara closes her mouth. It snaps shut like a gate at the mention of church. She leans against her friends, lips pursed, arms crossed.

There's a sound in the street behind us. I turn and see two boys, not much younger than me, swinging sticks as if they're swords. One of them pulls a billy cart by the string with his other hand, the cart made of a packing box and old pram wheels. A girl walks beside them a little ways off, careful to stay away from the sticks. They have the look of children from the camp. Skin grubby, clothes tight, hair a mess of knots.

Flo passes me one of her looks and then we're saying our goodbyes to Clara and chasing after the boys and the girl.

'Where you headed?'

The boys stop fighting. They let the sticks drag along the road, carving a jagged path in the dirt. The girl moves a little closer to the boys. I see cardboard nailed to the bottom of her shoes where the soles used to be.

'We have to get back,' she says.

'Back where?' Flo asks.

The girl moves closer again to the boys. 'Just back.'

There's a breeze behind us. I get the feeling we shouldn't be walking with these children.

One of the boys starts to stab the dirt with his stick as we walk. 'We got to help set traps for rabbits,' he says. 'Got to dig them into the burrows.'

'I'd like to know how to trap rabbits,' Flo says. 'Wasn't I just saying that?'

Flo looks at me and the others follow her eyes. I nod my head slowly.

'He's as keen as me,' she says. 'He's too excited for words. That's Morris and I'm Flo.'

The children introduce themselves. Polly, Harvey and Bobby. They tell us we can tag along. We can follow them out of town, along the bend in the river and out to the camp. I take hold of Flo's arm as we walk behind the others.

'You live on a farm,' I say, in a whisper. 'Don't you already know how to catch rabbits?'

'Quiet,' Flo says. 'They don't need to know.'

We smell the camp before we see it. All the way along the dirt track, the smell thickens. The air is wet with it, covering our skin and clothes. This time, walking to the camp is like going into a butcher's shop. Smoke and steam rise from the middle of the camp. We pass the shacks, trying not to stare at the people huddled inside. The smell is coming from the main campfire, two vats, wide as wheels on a car, each with something bubbling away inside. People gather around the fire. Their faces are waxy and tight. Behind them, strung up on wire stretched between two gum trees, are the skins of a dozen rabbits. They look like soft toys in a shop window, save for the blood dripping from their paws.

Harvey leads us to a man who's stirring a vat with a long stick.

'These are friends from town,' Harvey says, pointing a thumb at me and Flo. 'They've come to help with the traps.'

The man stares at us for a moment. He's tall and thin, with cheekbones like tent poles stretching out a tanned canvas of skin. His old suit hangs loose on his body. 'Better have a feed before we go out there,' he says.

The man waves at a woman and she hands us plates and forks. He dips a wooden spoon into the vat and loads the plates with something soft and brown. This must be rabbit meat. The woman breaks off pieces of a flat loaf. She adds the bread to the plates and we follow the man out to a lean-to near the edge of camp. He squats in the dirt. One of his toes is showing through the old leather of his boots. He lifts the soft meat to his mouth and we do the same.

'What's this?' I ask, holding up the flat bread.

Polly looks at me as if I've asked what a shoe is. She giggles, dips her bread in the stew.

'That's damper,' the thin man says. 'Bread you bake in the coals.' He looks back at the campfire, watching as the other men break sticks over their knees and throw them on the flames. The rabbit isn't bad eating and the damper is only halfway stale. The thin man gulps his food like water, and so do we, trying to keep up.

'Do you know a man with a scar on his face?' Flo asks the thin man, holding a finger up to her face and dragging it down her cheek. 'We saw him in town, at the food drive.'

The man watches Flo while he chews, breathing hard through his nose. He swallows and licks his lips slowly.

'Haven't seen anybody like that,' he says.

'He must be from the camp. Never seen him before in Gemini. Are you sure?'

The man pulls some meat off a bone. 'Sure as the day's long,' he says. 'People come in and out of camp all the time. Some folks only stay a day or two before moving on. Others been here a long time. I keep to my business. Don't need any more trouble than I got.'

We finish eating in silence and we follow the thin man through the camp. He taps men on the shoulder and knocks on the makeshift doors of shacks. Our group grows larger, swelling with men and children who look down at their feet as we walk. The thin man tells us to get the traps and we follow Harvey, Bobby and Polly down a narrow path. We pass some men digging a well for groundwater and walk past another hole further along the path where the water has dried out. We reach a clearing on the far side of the camp. Harvey, Bobby and Polly stop a few feet into the clearing and I trip over something, almost falling. I look down and see a steel trap, teeth closed, jaws locked together. It's made of rusted iron, the colour of soil. I look up. It's hard to make them out at first, but after a few moments I see a couple-dozen steel traps scattered all around, a constellation at my feet.

We're crouching and picking up the traps when I notice

something in the distance, at the end of the clearing. Gleaming white in the sunlight. Bones. I see a pile of bones.

'Where did those come from?' I ask.

'Rabbits maybe,' Bobby says, shrugging. 'Maybe something else. All the bones get thrown over there. Keeps the foxes out of camp. They go to the bones first and lick them clean.'

I stare at the bones while we sling traps over our shoulders. The bones look far too big to be rabbits.

We follow the thin man through the bush, crouching to set traps near burrows and trails. I try to pull the teeth apart but the traps are too tight. The man pulls the teeth for us, sweat beading on his forehead, and we take the traps further into the bush, past the gum trees, bottlebrush and ferns, our small bodies better for ducking under the low branches. When we've set all the traps, the thin man nods at us and we follow him along the trail back to camp.

'You did good,' the thin man says, when we get back to the shelter. 'Stay for some lemonade. My wife found lemons growing wild near the river.'

'Thank you,' I say. 'We ought to be going.'

'Another time,' Flo says. 'We'll come back.'

The thin man looks at Flo like she's speaking another language. It's clear we're the first outsiders to talk about coming back to camp. This is a place you go when you can't go anywhere else, a place you drop into, falling and reaching out to save yourself. This is not a place you choose to come.

We say our goodbyes and make our way through the twisted lanes between shacks. We pass a woman washing her feet in a shallow enamel bowl. We pass another woman pulling clothes off a wire strung between two trees. A boy dips a cloth in a bucket and wipes at the grime on his face. The sun is under the hill and a cool wind is blowing through the camp, picking up leaves and pressing them against the boards and hessian of the shacks.

'You think he really doesn't know the man with the scar?' Flo asks.

I look at the faces of the people around us. I can't imagine ever forgetting these faces. Each is like a star in the night sky, fixed and shining.

'I think he knows him but he doesn't want to know him.'

'That's what I think too,' Flo says.

We pass a low shack made of jagged boards and pallets. The roof is rusted corrugated metal, weighed down by wires that look like the strings on a bow, each end coiled around a brick. There's a front fence made with offcuts of steel pipes. It reminds me of the hideouts me and George used to make, leaning fallen branches against the thick trunks of gum trees. Covering them with leaves and bark until we blocked out the sun. We used to spend whole summer afternoons in those cool and dark hideouts, telling stories, sweeping the floor, patching the roof. Playing at real life.

These places are different. These are homes where people eat and sleep.

In front of the shack, there's a small hearth, wrapped on three sides by bricks and iron, a short chimney above. A man, hatless and balding, not many years older than Father, squats on the ground in front of the hearth. There's a little girl on his lap. She's wrapped in a blanket so that only her long brown hair and ruddy cheeks are open to the breeze. The man holds his hands out to the fire. As we pass the shack, as we make our way out of camp, I see him pull back his hands and hold them to the girl's cheeks.

21

The days are hot in the paddocks, and the nights press the cold in from every direction. Clouds flow in a current above our heads, sometimes puffy and soft as wool, sometimes thin and long, scars on the blue. I never knew life could slow like this. In the city, it's never this way. There's always something happening, people moving around, buildings going up, trams rolling by, games being played. Now, time seems to be measured out by the shadows passing over the tall grass, the ticking of the axe when we chop wood, the animals going in and out like the tide. I wonder if this is what it's like for George, his mother keeping him inside, away from the polio, time slowing down within those walls. There's space out here in the paddocks but there are walls all the same.

Father leaves every morning, comes back every evening. I watch his face when he returns, looking for any change, any clue that he's closer to catching the killer. He doesn't give anything away, doesn't talk about the case. His work is outside the farm and he sheds it like a heavy cloak when he comes back. But I can see some of it on him. I can see the heaviness, the heat it traps. It's what I see when I try to talk of Mother, when I bring up her name or try to talk about their past in Gemini. Father likes to tell stories, tales about the stars and the constellations that wander across the sky, but there are no stories about what happened before he left Gemini.

'Do you know why they left here?' I ask.

Me and Flo are feeding the chickens, throwing kitchen scraps on the turned soil. The hens peck at the scraps, jerk their heads to the side. The sun is low and the hens cast shadows that stretch across the run.

'Who left where?'

'My parents,' I say. 'When they left Gemini.'

Flo turns over her hand, looks down at the scraps coloured brown and grey and green. 'How would I know?'

'Don't your folks ever talk about it?'

Flo throws the scraps and they hit the wire at the end of the run, some of the food clinging to the wire and bending in the wind. 'They don't talk much about those days,' she says. 'I know Grandpa wasn't a nice man and he died of drink.'

Aunt Beth walks by carrying a bucket, heading out toward the well. She smiles as she passes and we wait until she's out of sight, holding our tongues and scattering the scraps.

'Come on, I'll show you something,' Flo says.

We leave the run and I follow Flo to one of the tin sheds out near the edge of the paddocks, where the grass gives way to bush. There's a rusted latch on the door and it creaks when Flo pulls it free. Inside, the light catches piles of metal and wood, fence posts and car bonnets and gallon drums. A layer of dust on everything, no footprints on the dirt floor.

'Up there,' Flo says. She points to a wooden box. It's on a shelf on the far wall, covered in a lattice of cobwebs. 'There he is. Those are his ashes.'

The varnish on the box is faded. I can see cracks at the joins in the wood. Inside that box is the man who raised my father.

'I think he ran him off,' Flo says. 'Grandpa ran off Uncle Jude, or he was part of it. Something to do with the way they got together, your folks. I've heard about that much. There's a story about a man dying at the falls, and your folks left not long after that.'

'Who died?'

'Don't know. You never can tell. Nobody talks much about those things here, and stories get all mixed up. People around here like to carry on and put things behind them. That's the way they are.'

Flo peers up at the box. 'I guess my dad didn't like Grandpa much. That's why he's up there and not in the cemetery.'

We wash up for tea and take our seats at the table in the big house. The same as every night, a sliver of meat with root vegetables and beans. My tongue is numb to it. I eat because I know it's food, but there's no joy in it. I spoon some potato into my mouth and I think about the people in the camp, the vats bubbling with rabbit day after day.

Aunt Beth is scraping off the plates when there's a knock at the door.

'Who could that be, at this time?'

It's after dark and the house is far from the main road. Uncle Jimmy pulls the cloth from his collar and drops it on the table. He rises with a sigh and walks to the front door. There's a silence, then Uncle Jimmy's voice carries down the hall. He's shouting.

Flo stands and starts toward the door. 'I'll see if I can help,' she says.

I watch her move into the hall and I start to follow her. As I pass Father, I see his mouth drop open, as if to speak, then close again. He won't stop me, but he'll make sure I know what he thinks later. He'll catch me if I fall but only after I've felt the fear of the drop. I go down the hall, all the same.

Uncle Jimmy is in the doorway, the faint light of the house showing grey leaves and dirt in the space around his body. His voice is quieter now. I can barely make it out. I'm walking slowly, trying to make out the words, when a hand reaches into the hall and takes hold of my arm. It pulls me into the front bedroom. Flo holds a finger to her lips and waves me over to the window.

There's a small group of people out in the drive, near the front door. They look sickly and thin in the grey light. One of the women has her hands out in front of her, holding some small items. There are deep shadows under her cheeks. I know this woman. She's the one Will Fletcher pushed over when we followed the miners to the camp.

'We've got pincushions and some pokerwork,' she says. 'They're lovely. Made by hand.'

'I don't need it,' Uncle Jimmy says.

'Please, take a look.'

'I'm not giving you any money.'

'Whatever you can spare,' she says. 'There are children who haven't eaten for days.'

The people look at the door. I think about them walking over here, stopping at the farms on the road, watching all the other doors close in front of them.

'We're desperate,' the woman says. 'The rabbits and the food from town only go so far.'

I hear Uncle Jimmy clear his throat. When he speaks, his voice is strong but there's something beside that strength. There's a faint high pitch in his voice. 'This farm is losing money,' he says. 'Has been since prices fell.'

'Whatever you can spare,' the woman says. 'Please.'

Uncle Jimmy clears his throat again. 'I got children here too. I give to you and the wolf will be at my door next. Can't do it.'

'Please,' the woman says, holding her hands higher. 'Anything.'

'You ought to try another town. Might be work somewhere else. Gemini's not the place. There's nothing for you here.'

The woman lowers her hands. She turns to face the other people and they shuffle away, out into the darkness, toward the trees that line the drive. One man stays staring at Uncle Jimmy. He stays there while the others move away.

When he finally turns, when the moonlight passes over his face, I see a scar running down one cheek. And then he's gone, melting into the darkness with the others. We listen as their footsteps mix with the sounds of crickets and cicadas, until we hear the door close and Uncle Jimmy's boots trail back through the hall.

22

Aunt Beth says there's less money for help these days, even with the price of help so low. She does other people's laundry for a few coins or trade, has her hands in suds most days, her fingers dry and cracked. It's less than amusing the way Lottie goes missing when there's talk of help on the farm. I wonder why Father lets her out alone in a town where a young woman was murdered. But he's working the case, his mind locked on Catherine Fletcher. Lottie has nothing holding her back. No commitments. Nothing except five feet and ten inches topped by slicked-back hair.

Me and Flo run wheelbarrows up and down the paddocks, shovel stones into ditches. We pull bugs from plants in the vegetable garden. Endless hours under the sun, the skin on my face and neck turning pink then settling to an almond brown. Flo's voice is always next to my ear, running over what we know and what's still a mystery. Her mind wraps around the same subjects, smothering them in words. Out here, baking in the full sun, she finds a new thought to fix on.

'Where's Sam been hiding? We haven't seen him for ages,' she says. 'Why's he keeping clear of us?'

'We've been here on the farm most days,' I say. 'We've not been around.'

Flo spits on a fence post, darkening the wood. 'That boy used to come knocking every other day. I couldn't get rid of him. Now he's nowhere to be found. Strange, isn't it?'

'I guess. I don't know him well.'

'I'm telling you it's strange,' Flo says. 'We've got to find out where he's been.'

When Uncle Jimmy heads out of town to talk to an animal doctor, me and Flo slip away from the farm. We cut through the bottom paddock. Jagged, dry grass pushes through our socks. We hop a fence on the other side and Flo leads me to a track that cuts through the bush. When we come out of the bush, out into the bright world, we're not far from the main street. We follow the river along the far bank until we get to a little footbridge and cross to the street. Flo marches toward Sam's house.

'Hello, Missus Napier. Is Sam about?'

From my place at the front gate, I see confusion written on Mrs Napier's face. Lines appear between her eyes, her lips are thin slits. 'He said he was meeting up with you,' she says.

Flo slaps her thigh. 'You're right,' she says. 'I just couldn't remember if we said we'd meet here or not. My mistake.'

Mrs Napier's head tilts to one side. 'He is meeting with you?'

'Of course,' Flo says. She waves a thumb over her shoulder. 'Me and Morris been out in the sun too long. My head's a fried egg. Sam's probably wondering where we are. We best get going.'

She turns and marches down the path, pulling on my shirt as she passes, making me stumble after her. I look back at Mrs Napier, standing there on the doorstep, one hand on her hip, watching us go.

Flo waits until we're well away before she lets it out. 'That Sam Napier,' she says. 'What's he up to? That's what I'd like to know.'

We walk on into town, past the general store and the butcher's and the dispensary. There's a smell of gum trees burning. There must be a fire out beyond the hills, the smoke creeping through town, hitched to the wind. It's a message of danger, a telegram from a place where fire is crawling over hills and valleys.

There's shouting ahead and we break into a run. It's coming from the police station. There's a group of people out front, mostly women. They hold handkerchiefs to their faces. They seem to be moving in close to one woman. We walk near and I see it's the woman from the town meeting. Mrs Wade, the one who talked about her daughter. Mr Cornwell is next to her. Sweat darkens his thin hair, pulling it flat on his scalp. He has a hand on Mrs Wade's back. He seems to be pushing her forward.

'There's no telling what he would've done if I didn't stop him,' Mrs Wade says, her voice high and loud.

There's movement near the front of the station and I make out two people. The one in front is hunched. It's a young man dressed in dirty clothes, the white cotton stained dark as tobacco. His feet are bare and filthy. It looks like he's been running through the bush. The man behind him comes into view. It's Father. He has a hand on the young man's shoulder, leading him forward. Father's jaw is set, his eyes moving between the young man and the group.

'I caught him with her,' Mrs Wade says. 'With my Clara. He had her down by the river, had her lying down on the bank. My Clara. He's stained her name.'

The young man keeps his eyes down, watches the stones beneath him.

Mr Cornwell steps out in front of the townspeople, thumbs looped around the suspenders under his coat. 'What you going to do to him, detective?'

Father stops. He keeps his hand on the shoulder of the young man who also stops, eyes fixed on the stones.

Father runs his tongue along the back of his teeth, clears his throat. 'That's my concern, Mister Cornwell,' he says. 'Move these people on.'

Mr Cornwell points a thumb over his shoulder.

'Do you see these people? See how they suffer? I think it's all our concern.'

Father looks out over the crowd. He seems to be counting the people, maybe counting how many men there are among the women. Me and Flo huddle close behind a woman on the edge of the group, out near a paperbark tree. I can feel the bark from the tree, strips that have split from the trunk, reaching out into the air.

'I'm going to talk to him, Mister Cornwell,' Father says.

'You ought to do more than talk. You ought to teach this boy a lesson. He's laid his filthy hands on a young girl, forced himself on a young member of our community. You ought to do a lot more than talk.'

Father shakes his head. 'There's nothing to say he made her go down to the river, not yet.'

Mrs Wade steps forward, stamping her feet in the dirt. 'How dare you,' she says. 'How dare you say that.'

Father turns and pushes the young man forward. They move on along the path, toward the barred windows and the station door.

'Move on, now,' Father says, as he goes. 'Let us do our work.' He nods to a constable as he leads the young man through the door.

The constable steps toward the people, arms outstretched. 'Move along,' he says. 'Move along.'

Mr Cornwell offers his arm to Mrs Wade. She takes it and is led away from the station, crying and mopping up her tears with a handkerchief. As the group drifts away, me and Flo walk over to the pub and find the shade out front. We watch as the constable walks slowly inside and closes the door.

'What do you make of that?' Flo asks. She wants answers from me, the son of a detective.

'Father questions a lot of people in his cases,' I say. 'Not all of them are guilty.'

'Mister Cornwell seemed pretty sure of it.'

'He sure did,' I say.

We stay there in the shade, sweat cooling on our faces, and we watch the dark length of the station, the bars on the windows glinting in the sun.

23

Father gets back to the cottage just before sunset. He doesn't speak of the young man or the police station or Clara down by the river. He washes in the bath. The sound of water moving fills the cottage. When he comes out, the skin on his neck is as pink as the clouds outside. He makes me and Lottie wash our faces and forearms in the basin, and we dress for tea.

The light is fading as we walk over to the big house. We pass Red and Blue near the back steps. They lift their muzzles and sniff the air when we open the door.

'How was your day, Jude?' Aunt Beth asks. She's serving mashed potatoes beside fried liver and onions. Lottie is helping. There are a few shards of liver on my plate, darker than meat but dull and dry. I move the liver around with my fork and I look up to see Uncle Jimmy staring at me. He doesn't blink. He lifts his glass of beer and draws in a mouthful, watching me shift around the liver.

'It was fine,' Father says. 'Just another day.'

Father cuts into his liver, knife and fork squealing on the plate. The high sound reminds me of Mrs Wade, of the way she spoke to Father. He doesn't talk about what happened, just goes on cutting his liver and raising pieces to his mouth. I look over at Flo and see that her eyebrows are halfway to her hair.

The telephone rings and Uncle Jimmy walks over to the wall, feet dragging on the boards. He sniffs as he listens to the caller. 'It's for you,' he says, holding the receiver out toward Father.

Father takes the telephone and listens. 'How many of them? All right. I'll leave now. Don't let them in, whatever you do. Shoot in the air if you have to.'

Father lays the receiver down. He sighs and smooths the sides of his beard with his hands. His eyes are dull and weary looking, like the eyes of sheep out in the weather through all seasons. 'There's trouble at the station,' he says. 'I won't be long.'

'What kind of trouble?' Flo asks.

'None for you to be worried about, young lady,' Aunt Beth says. 'You finish your liver.'

Father takes his coat and hat from the rack in the hall. His movements are hurried but his face is blank.

'Can me and Flo come?' I ask.

Father looks back at me, down the hall. I'm halfway out of my chair.

'Yes, can we go with you?' Flo asks.

Father puts on his hat. He straightens it and shakes his head. 'No, stay here,' he says. 'Finish your tea. I won't be long.'

He fades into the dark hall. I see the back of him when he opens the door and the moonlight catches him, then he's out the door and gone. I hear the car pull out onto the drive and the engine firing as it passes the house and reaches out into the night. A hush falls over the table. There's only the sounds of cutlery scraping on plates and the curtains flapping in the breeze. When we've finished eating, we take up our plates and help Aunt Beth wash up. I watch a layer of grease form on top of the water, ringing the basin, showing the high-water mark.

Uncle Jimmy drains his beer glass, tipping his head back, letting the ale tumble into him. He belches and rubs his belly. 'Well, come on, then,' he says. 'I'll take you to look.'

Aunt Beth drops a rag in the water. She turns and watches Uncle Jimmy.

'Don't stare at me,' he says. 'This is my house. I'll take them if I see fit to do it.'

'You can barely walk,' she says.

Uncle Jimmy rises from his chair. He leans over, arms outstretched toward his toes. He can't quite reach, comes up short. 'I could run a mile,' he says, straightening. 'Come on, Morris, Flo. Let's get down there.'

I walk over to Uncle Jimmy. He's breathing heavily. The skin on his nose is a dull red like the embers in a burned-down fire. I look back over my shoulder as I take my coat from the rack. Lottie is standing next to Aunt Beth. I watch her shake her head and then I follow Uncle Jimmy and Flo out to the truck.

People are walking through the main street. Men, all walking in one direction, moving like a herd, their hats pulled low over their brows. Uncle Jimmy parks the truck near the pub and we follow the crowd, listening to the low voices, faint as the distant rumble of thunder. When we get closer to the station, we hear other voices, loud and forceful. The lamps at the front of the station cast a dull glow over the men so only the edges of their faces can be seen, pale as ghosts. A few men at the front carry what look like long sticks. One man turns his wrist and I see the clear shape of a cricket bat.

Father is at the door of the station, flanked by two constables. One is old, his eyes halfway closed, as if set for bed. The other is young. His eyes couldn't be more open.

'Go on home,' Father says. 'Go back to your families. There's nothing for you here tonight.'

The crowd parts, the men lowering their sticks and bats, making an aisle like at a strange and dark wedding. A man makes his way to the front. He steps up to the fence that wraps the station like the cliffs on a coast. I see the side of his face in the lamplight. Will Fletcher.

'Let us have him, Turner,' he says. 'Give him over to us.'

Father runs a hand down the lapel of his coat. His fingers curl around the lapel and it moves away from his body. Something dark and metallic catches the light. A pistol. 'Go on home, Will,' he says.

Will Fletcher looks behind him, moves his sight over the men, and turns back to Father. 'We're not leaving,' he says. 'Not without what we came for.'

The young constable holds a baton tight and close to his chest, his knuckles white against the wood. The older policeman swings his baton low beside his knee.

'He didn't do it,' Father says, speaking over the heads of the crowd, his voice carrying over the street. 'I want you all to know he didn't do it, wasn't anywhere near Gemini the night of the murder. He was shearing out in Wonnangatta.'

Will Fletcher snorts. He nudges a man beside him with his elbow. 'You'll have us believe that?'

'You can call them up yourselves,' Father says.

Whispers in the crowd. A few men at the edge turn away and walk toward the pub.

'And what about the other girl,' a man says. 'He's messed with her. That's why you have him.'

'I don't know what you've heard,' Father says. 'He hasn't done anything to that girl worth you coming out here.'

'How do you know?'

Father clears his throat. 'I don't mean to say it,' he says. 'Not out here.'

Will Fletcher puts a hand on the gate. The old constable stops swinging his baton. He grips it tight by his side.

'You're going to have to say it,' Will Fletcher says.

Father looks at the sky, out to where the stars blink on and off between the clouds. He looks back down at the men. 'The girl's intact, Will. Doctor confirmed it.'

Fletcher looks at the men beside him. More whispers in the crowd. 'What's that mean, intact?'

'It means he didn't touch her, only talked to her.'

A man beside Fletcher leans in and talks to his ear. Will Fletcher starts to nod.

'Go on home, all of you,' Father says. 'Unless you want to sleep in a cell yourself tonight.'

Men turn from the station and walk away into the dark until it's only Will Fletcher at the gate and us, a few yards away in the shadows.

Will Fletcher leans forward over the gate. 'You can't protect them all,' he says.

Father lets go of the lapel on his coat. He rolls his shoulders forward. 'That's exactly what I aim to do.'

'You should be protecting this town,' Fletcher says. 'But I suppose they mean more to you than this town.'

'Go on home, Will.'

Will Fletcher stares at Father, at the constables, at the station lit by the soft yellow lamplight. He takes a few steps back and then turns and walks into the night. Uncle Jimmy walks forward, and me and Flo follow. I keep my head low, glancing up at Father. He's showing the constables back through the door when he sees us. He looks fit to skin us. His face is wild, nostrils flared, teeth showing, but I see his eyes are on Uncle Jimmy.

'You damn fool,' he says, voice thick and deep. 'What are you doing bringing them out here?'

Uncle Jimmy laughs. I stand a step behind him, looking out around his side.

'I don't see what the fuss is about,' Uncle Jimmy says. 'This is part of life out here, or have you forgotten that?'

The constables make their way into the station and Father pulls the door shut. He takes a step toward us and raises a hand, finger pointed out at the darkness beyond. 'Take them back. I don't want to see you here again. You're as dull in the head as the rest of them.'

Uncle Jimmy sways in the half-light. Faint sounds of shouting and laughter carry to us from the pub.

'You should've let them have him,' Uncle Jimmy says. 'We could've run them all out of town. They're good for nothing, that lot at the camp. They don't belong here.'

He turns and walks from the station. Me and Flo follow behind him. I look over my shoulder as we move into the dark and see Father smoothing the sides of his beard, his breath coiling in front of him, then vanishing into the cool night air.

24

Wind covers the town. Grass is whipped low. Gum trees bend and sway. Stones tumble on the driveway and paths, collecting in ditches. Birds rise and dip in the sky, each one showing the shape of the wind, painting the gusts with their wings.

We eat tea in the big house while it's still light out. Aunt Beth's eyes dart to the walls and the roof each time a window rattles or the chimney creaks. Lottie pushes at some beans on her plate. Father and Uncle Jimmy aren't speaking. They keep their eyes away from each other, twisting their bodies in different directions, staying apart like oil and water. Me and Flo keep our heads down for the most part, spooning food into our mouths. Nobody speaks.

A light rain starts to fall, tapping at the kitchen windows.

Uncle Jimmy finishes the last of his meal and leans back in his chair. He turns toward Father, lifts his chin at him. 'Now's the time to show them, what I was saying the other day. We'll do it now,' he says.

Father looks at Lottie and me. 'Now isn't the time, James,' he says, talking through his teeth.

'They got to find out sometime. Can't be swaddled in the city their whole lives, wrapped up like babies. That the way you want to raise them? We weren't raised like that. We found out pretty early. They got to find out the truth of the world.'

Father scratches the side of his beard. I can see him running his tongue along the back of his teeth, can see it in the way his jaw pitches left and right. This is what he does when he's thinking on something important.

'Find out what?' I ask.

Lottie drops her fork on the plate and it chimes like a bell, a warning. 'What are you talking about?' she asks.

'Come on,' Uncle Jimmy says, slapping a hand on the table. He rises from his chair. 'Follow me.'

Father is still for a moment and then he nods. Me and Flo and Lottie push our plates to the centre of the table and walk to the hall. Father takes our coats from the hooks on the wall and hands them out. Aunt Beth stays behind. As we pass through the hall and out the front door, I hear her saying something about Uncle Jimmy enjoying this too much.

The rain peppers our faces, drops stinging our cheeks. The light is almost gone from the sky. There's a crack in the clouds where the last of the sunlight streams through. A knife slicing clean through the sky. We follow Uncle Jimmy along the path that leads to the work sheds. He doesn't look back. He presses on, back arched to the oncoming wind. I look up and see the crack in the clouds close over, the wound healed.

I hear the bleating before we get to the shed. It's a high-pitched cry. It carries on the wind, rising and falling in volume, the air bending around the sound. Uncle Jimmy opens the shed door and waves us in. I follow behind Father, Lottie and Flo. When we're all inside, Uncle Jimmy shuts the door, drops the latch. The wind eases to a hum. It's dark in the shed and it takes a few seconds for my eyes to get used to it. I look around, searching for the sound. And then I see it, at the far end of the shed, tied with rope to a beam. A little white lamb.

'Be gentle about it,' Father says, looking square at Uncle Jimmy as he rounds us and walks toward the lamb.

'No use making a ceremony of it. This happens every day on a farm. It's as natural as the rain falling outside.'

'It's their first time, James.'

'Makes no difference. Remember Dad ever giving us an easy run? He'd have had us hold the knife.'

I watch Father bite the skin around his thumb. He looks down at the dirt ground and shakes his head, breathing hard through his nose. Every mention of his father is a charge passing through the air, a sheet of lightning.

'This is how the meat on your plate starts out,' Uncle Jimmy says. 'This is what it takes to turn an animal into a meal.'

He picks up a long knife, long as his forearm bone. The metal shines in the light coming through the shed window. He walks over to the lamb.

'No,' Lottie says. 'No. No.'

Uncle Jimmy crouches next to the lamb and grips its two front legs with one hand. Time slows. I watch the knife move past Uncle Jimmy's leg. It's a leaf in a stream, floating in a gentle current. A question comes to me, rising from my toes all the way through my body, pushing past my blood and my bones until it reaches my head. I feel it tingle as it passes through me. Is this what death is like? Is death so powerful that it can slow the world, make the planet stop spinning?

Flo takes hold of my hand. She squeezes.

'This is what it means to be alive,' Uncle Jimmy says. 'Taking life is a part of life.'

He slides the knife into the belly of the lamb and pulls. I see the blue and red parts fall to the floor, slick as oil, and I look down at my boots and watch them spin below me.

The storm pushes against the cottage. I'm in bed, the blanket pulled to my chin. I can hear Lottie breathing slow in the bed next to me. It took her a long time to get to sleep. I listened to her cry for what felt like hours. I don't know what time it is now, can't see any stars through the window, only the faintest moonlight peeking through the dark clouds and wash of rain.

There's a sound outside the window like the grinding of stone. I turn over and kneel on my bed to get a better look. Nothing, only the ghostly outlines of trees, grey limbs swaying in the wind. I hear the sound again, closer now. Another sound, of metal chiming in the darkness. I lean in close to the window, blinking, trying to see through the black. And then I see it, moving along the stone path between the cottage and the main house. A man leading a horse through the rain. From the shape of him, I can tell it's Uncle Jimmy.

I pull on my boots and tiptoe out of the bedroom and down the hall. I open the front door of the cottage and the wind rushes at me, driving me back. I bend my body into the wind, and then I'm outside in the black night, pulling the door closed behind me.

I listen for the chime of the bridle. It's a beacon, a north star that leads me through the dark. I stay far enough behind to be sure Uncle Jimmy won't hear me following. The rain soaks my hair and runs down my back. Branches scratch my arms and face. I think of Catherine Fletcher, lying in the tunnel entrance, rain falling all around. That familiar feeling rises in me. My nerves take over, speeding my heart and slowing my legs. I keep going. I keep following the sound.

The trees part, the sheds come into view and I remember the sound of the lamb. Up ahead, I see the shape of Uncle Jimmy mounting the horse, feet slipping in the wet stirrups and then taking hold. He holds the reins and urges the horse into the dark.

I'll never be able to keep up with him on foot. I look around and I see it, leaning against the wall of a shed not more than ten yards away, metal wheels shining in the faint light. Flo's bicycle.

The wind pulls my hair and dashes it over my eyes. I pedal fast, enough to keep pace with Uncle Jimmy but slow enough to stay out of earshot. He keeps the horse at a slow trot as we pass the empty black paddocks. When we make it to the main road, I have to race to keep up. My legs are pistons, firing in the dark. The muscles burn. My knees and ankles start to seize. It's flat here in the valley. I'm grateful we're not climbing the hills. I keep pedalling, moving as fast as I can. Even so, Uncle Jimmy and the horse begin to disappear. I can only make out their outline and then they're gone, and I'm alone.

I follow the tracks of the horse, deep prints filling with rainwater in an endless line. I keep following and the line turns. I know where they're going. I know where this is. The tracks turn into the path that leads to the camp.

I let the bicycle glide, hoping the tyres don't give me away. It's not long until I see him. Uncle Jimmy sitting on the horse near the entrance to the camp. He's still. I lean the bicycle against a tree and creep forward. I'm close enough to hear the grunts of the horse. I wait, the rain washing me, and I watch as Uncle Jimmy slides off the horse and wraps the reins around a tree branch. There's a break in the clouds, long enough for some moonlight to fall on us. I move behind a tree. I can see Uncle Jimmy clearly now. He walks to the side of the horse, unclips the saddlebag. He reaches in and takes something out. It's newspaper, long sheets wrapped into a parcel. He unfolds it, resting it on one arm, and there it is. Thick, long cuts of meat, deep red and wet.

It's the lamb. This is the lamb he slaughtered tonight.

I'm following Uncle Jimmy through the camp. There's nobody around. The clouds leak over and the moonlight fades. It's hard to see the way. I step around shacks, creep past corrugated iron flapping in the wind. I think about the people on the other side of these walls. About the hungry people sleeping there, huddled in close to each other for warmth. It makes me think about when I used to go to Lottie, back when we were little. The times of nightmares and her holding me until my breath slowed.

Uncle Jimmy stops in a clearing. I know this place. I've been here before. This is the centre of the camp. He's standing near the fire, the last of the coals glowing below rough black logs. I stay back, hiding behind an old copper washtub. Uncle Jimmy stands near the fire, hair whipping in the wind. He stays there a long time, then someone walks toward him from out of the shadows. It's a man, judging by the shape. I can't see his face, only his outline. The man walks to Uncle Jimmy and shakes his hand. Uncle Jimmy offers the man the meat.

I can scarcely believe what I'm seeing. Uncle Jimmy hands over the meat and the man walks away, into the shadows. This is the man who turned hungry people from his door. The man who gave as little as he could at the food drive. Uncle Jimmy rode through a storm to give meat to the people of the camp.

I stay hidden behind the washtub. Uncle Jimmy passes me and makes his way to the horse. I listen for the sound of him riding off before I make my way past the shacks and back to the bicycle.

Something has changed in me tonight, I can feel it. I could've turned back. Nobody would have seen me go. I could've gone back to bed, left the questions there without an answer. This time, I didn't let the nerves hold me back. I pushed against them, and I saw something good in this world. Uncle Jimmy, riding through a storm to feed the starving people of the camp. A man taking the lamb he'd raised and slaughtered, and giving it to the people who need it most.

25

I keep that night to myself. In the days that follow, as Flo talks about Will Fletcher and the camp and the lilies and the man Catherine Fletcher was seeing, I don't breathe a word about the night I followed Uncle Jimmy. It's for me alone. Something good and secret to keep inside.

It's Sunday morning. Father is in the hall, stringing a tie around his neck, tilting his head left and right as he loops and measures. I'm in the bedroom, trying hard to do the same. Lottie is sitting on the front step of the cottage, the door open to the breeze, picking lint from her good socks. We're getting ready for church. It's something we've been doing every Sunday since we got to Gemini.

I'm trying to get my tie straight but I can't keep my mind on it. I keep looking down at the table beside Lottie's bed. There's something that I can't take my eyes off. I look away and my eyes wander back, fish following the bait. On the table, standing in a jug of water, are ten stems of lilies. There are lilies in the bedroom.

'You right to go?' Father is standing in the doorway. He looks at my tie and raises his eyebrows.

'It looks awful,' I say. 'I can't get it straight.'

Father roughs my hair and then straightens it again, smoothing it down with his palms. 'It's close enough,' he says. 'Come on. Let's find your sister. She'll curse us if we take any longer.'

Lottie is standing out on the path to the big house now. Her body is turned, as if ready to sprint. Father stops and puts the door and the windows on their latches. I run ahead and catch up with Lottie.

'What took you so long?' she asks. 'You have to spin the cotton for that shirt or just put it on?'

'Pardon?'

'Never mind.'

She starts walking along the path. I rush to match my steps with hers, marching on the stones beside her.

'Where did you get those lilies?'

Lottie glances at me. Colour floods her cheeks, a river inside bursting its banks. 'Why? You want some for yourself?'

'I'm just wondering who gave them to you,' I say, trying to keep my voice light.

'It's none of your business.'

She hurries into the clearing in front of the big house. I stand there, where the bush meets the drive, and watch Lottie fall into Aunt Beth's embrace, almost knocking her over. Uncle Jimmy and Flo are by the truck. I can hear the engine ticking over, warming up. They don't see the way Lottie moves toward Aunt Beth, the way she seems to need her like the trees need the sun.

Father reaches me and rests his elbow on my shoulder, not laying any weight on it. He watches the way Aunt Beth tucks Lottie's hair behind her ear, the way Lottie rests her head on Aunt Beth's hand. I see his chin fall to his chest, only for a moment, before he raises it again. A force inside him, more powerful than gravity, more powerful than sorrow, keeps his head from falling for long. We stand in the early morning sunlight, already sweating under layers of cotton and wool. We watch the women, and I wonder if Father has seen the lilies standing in the cool water inside the cottage.

The sermon is about want and poverty and greed and disease. There's something about Jesus calming the storm and having faith in the will of the Lord to see you through danger. There's the story of Jesus feeding five thousand people with five loaves of bread and two fish. How even in hard times we have to share not only our faith but also what few worldly goods we have.

There's the story of the Good Samaritan, about a Jew who was robbed on the road from Jerusalem to Jericho. He was beaten and stripped of his possessions and clothes, and the only man to stop and help was a Samaritan. An enemy of the Jews. The Samaritan poured oil and wine on the man's wounds. He took the man to an inn and cared for him. He gave silver to the innkeeper and asked that he spend it on the beaten man. All this for an enemy of his people, for someone who may have walked by if it were him lying in the road. Go and do likewise, we are told. Go and do likewise.

I look around the church. Flo is looking down at her lap, minutes from sleep. Uncle Jimmy is staring at the altar. Aunt Beth is nodding along to the words. I keep looking around the church, at the faces lined up in rows, skin scrubbed clean of coal and dirt. I keep looking until I find Will Fletcher. His face is a beacon, deep red and shining. He looks to be boiling over, listening to this sermon. There's a fire inside him, cooking his insides, melting it all down to one colour.

Lottie is sitting next to me on the pew. There's something on her neck. I didn't notice until now. It's something I've seen before, but not on Lottie's skin. It's the same mark I saw in the photographs of

Catherine Fletcher. A dark stain under the skin. A map to a secret. I wonder if Father has seen this mark. He's been giving Lottie a lot of room lately, keeping his distance like he's tracking a wild animal. Maybe he hasn't noticed.

Outside the church, after the sermon, the women's association hands out food. Steam rises from the soup and potatoes. The people from the camp don't come to church. Even without them, there are plenty of takers for the food. Locals are thinning under their clothes. Since we first came to Gemini, they've been drawing into their bodies, the skin on their faces wrinkling like prunes. These people dip chunks of bread in the soup. They let the bread wait in their mouths, stewing it inside themselves, each one holding on to the taste before they swallow.

Flo takes my arm and leads me to the side of the church. She walks quickly, shoes kicking the stones that line the church grounds. Up ahead, standing alone, watching the people lining for food, is Sam.

'Where you been hiding, Samuel Napier?'

Sam turns, startled. He takes a deep breath and his face sets. He's playing a part. He looks the picture of confidence, not giving anything away.

'I haven't been doing any hiding,' he says.

Flo's eyebrows rise. She's playing a part too, one she's taken from those detective stories. 'That's not true. You've been hiding from us. We haven't seen you for days.'

'I've been busy is all.'

'Busy telling your ma lies. We came to your house and she said you were meeting us.'

'Come on, Flo,' I say. 'Let's leave it.'

'No, I want to hear him talk his way out of this. I want to know what he's been up to.'

Sam kicks at the stones and sends a handful sailing toward the white boards of the church wall. 'You're going round the bend,' he says.

'Me? You're the one who's changed. Maybe you killed Catherine Fletcher.'

They go quiet. Sam and Flo watch each other, staring each other down. There are only the sounds of people talking, of plates being stacked, of the wind rushing around the steeple. Sam turns and starts walking away.

'If you have to know,' he says, over his shoulder. 'If you really have to know where I've been, I'll show you.'

We follow Sam through the empty streets in our Sunday best. Everyone else is either at church or hiding from the knowledge they're not at church. We walk past houses with peeling paint, cracked walls. We pass houses leaning to one side, falling slowly to the ground as if they're in need of rest. Sam leads us to the railway tracks and we walk between the rails, stepping on the faded wooden sleepers. We keep walking as the tracks take us out near the start of Castor, where the trees thicken and colour the land like a bruise.

Near the edge of town, the tracks pass an old building. It's made of brick, sturdy and squat, with a tin roof that's rusted and pocked with holes. There are deep cracks running in a pattern down the walls, marking out a puzzle.

'It's an old supply shed,' Sam says.

He walks to the door and kicks until it creaks open. He pushes and makes a space just big enough to squeeze through. Once he's inside, he reaches a hand back through the opening and waves us in.

It's dusty inside. The only light falls through gaps in the mortar high on the walls and through the holes in the roof, thin beams running down to the floor, each one a tiny spotlight. The shed is empty, save for some clothes hanging from hooks on the walls. Hats, scarves, coats and ties.

Sam stands in the middle of the shed. He holds his arms out wide, an actor on a stage the moment before a bow. 'This is where I come to rehearse,' he says.

Flo walks over to the clothes. She pinches the material, pulls the clothes and lets them fall to the wall. I hold the sleeve of one of the shirts. It's soft to the touch, smooth and cold.

'They're my parents' old clothes,' Sam says. 'They have so many they won't miss them.'

'What are you rehearsing?' I ask.

'It's a secret,' Sam says. 'I'm going to debut before Christmas. Somewhere they can all see.'

He stares at the gap in the door, the crack of light that leads to the rest of Gemini.

'If I can't get on a stage then I've got to bring the stage to me.'

We walk around the shed, under the holes in the roof, a hundred little stars in the tin. We take the clothes from the hooks, wrapping them around our bodies even though they make us sweat like racehorses. We chase each other across the dusty floor, laughing and joking. Here in the shed, it's as if the rest of the world doesn't exist. All the trouble, all the hard times, they melt away as we move between the beams of light. Time passes in the shed and the heaviness lifts from us, rising from our shoulders and necks, moving into the air and vanishing like steam. I can almost forget about Catherine Fletcher and the person who killed her, the one who's walking around out there, somewhere past that crack of light in the door.

26

There's a festival in town. Mayor Napier's idea, a way to get people together, to keep the spirit strong in the community. That's what Father told us. I think it sounds like a prayer, a voice sent up to the heavens. I remember hearing about a Mexican custom at school. An object is hollowed out and filled with sweets. It's strung up on a beam or branch, a weight dangling on string. People take turns hitting it with sticks. The hitters are blindfolded while they swing. It's an act of faith. You swing the stick, again and again, swinging in the dark, hoping you'll hit on something and your faith will be rewarded.

We're driving to town, gum trees and wattle a blur in the window. Lottie says the festival is only folly.

'What does he think, you put on a festival and that's enough? It might work for one day but it won't last.'

She looks out at the tall yellow grass near the edge of the road. 'Does he think it's so easy for people to forget how miserable they are?'

I wonder where she's getting these ideas. Father whispers something from the driver's seat but it's lost under the groan of the engine. The car rounds a bend and the town fills the windshield.

When we get to the festival, Lottie takes off. She's going to find Eamon, no doubt. Father lets her go. I can see how he wishes to reach out for her, but his arms stay limp by his sides. He turns his head away and moves on past the shops of the main street.

'Where's Lottie?'

It's Uncle Jimmy. He's outside the butcher's, swaying in the afternoon light, one arm hooked around a pole. His clothes are tight, as if shrunk in hot water. His hair is slicked back and wet. Aunt Beth is standing near him, arms crossed over her chest. There's dancing near us, people joined together in the street. Over on the bandstand, musicians with fiddles and horns and drumsticks are playing a jolly tune.

'I thought Lottie would be with you,' Uncle Jimmy says, his words loose, his tongue swollen in his mouth.

'She's here somewhere,' Father says.

Uncle Jimmy stumbles, falls heavy on one knee. Father loops an arm around him, pulls him upright.

'Your brother put in some time at the pub today,' Aunt Beth says. 'His body is thirty per cent ale right now.'

I catch sight of Flo and Sam in the crowd. They're standing near the dancers. Flo is wearing a dress. She's pulling at the fabric on her shoulders, looking at the people, whispering now and then to Sam. Father lays a hand on my shoulder.

'Go on, then,' he says. 'We'll be here.'

When Flo sees me she waves me over, pulls me in and whispers in my ear. Her breath is hot against my skin. 'Look over there.'

She moves her eyes to the left, pointing with them, showing me where to look. Over near the bandstand, some young men stand in a tight group. They have the hungry look of people from the camp, their eyes distant moons in the black of their sockets. They're passing comments back and forth as they watch a group of girls, the girls we met the day at the bandstand. Clara and her friends. The men from the camp watch them the way a hunter watches an animal. The girls don't seem to notice.

'You can picture someone looking at Catherine Fletcher like that,' she says. 'Just the same way those men are looking.'

'I can't keep up,' Sam says, scratching under the cap on his head. 'You think it's people from the camp again? I thought you said she was meeting someone at the mine.'

'That's one idea. We heard she was meeting someone there, but we can't rule out the camp. The mine isn't so far from the camp after all.'

'We don't know anything,' Sam says. 'First it's Will Fletcher, then it's someone from the camp. Then it's anyone from the mine. Then it's Will Fletcher again. Today it's the camp. You've got us chasing our tails.'

Flo pulls on the fabric of her dress, pulling it lower over her legs. 'It's all part of the investigation,' she says. 'We follow the leads until one of them takes us to the end of the road. There's no way around it. We have to keep looking into all of it.'

I watch the dancers and onlookers. There's a thin layer of dust in the air, rising around the ankles of the dancers. People are smiling and waving and blowing kisses. The air is warm and close. I notice Lottie at the edge of the crowd with Eamon and his friends. She's in close to him, one of his arms holding tight to her waist.

'What about Eamon?' I ask.

Sam's head jerks around. 'Eamon?'

'Sure, have you ever thought it might be him?'

'I try not to think about him if I can help it,' Sam says.

'Lottie's been gone a lot,' I say. 'She's hardly ever at the cottage. I think she's been seeing him. She's over there with him now.'

Flo and Sam follow my gaze to where Lottie and Eamon and the others are standing.

'Makes you shudder to think of his greasy arm around you,' Flo says. 'It's like a snake wrapping you up.'

Eamon leans down and whispers something in Lottie's ear. She smiles and worries at the hair near her temples.

'Lottie seems to like him,' I say. 'He gave her lilies.'

Flo swings a fist at me, landing just above my elbow. I stay still, fighting the urge to rub my arm.

'He gave her lilies? Eamon did?'

'They were on her nightstand,' I say, my voice straining. 'She wouldn't tell me where she got them but she blushed when I brought it up.'

Flo's eyes are two suns, burning bright and round. Sam is watching Eamon.

'That's not everything,' I say. 'She has a mark on her neck. It's a lot like some of the marks on Catherine Fletcher, the ones I saw in the photograph.'

'Might be a love bite,' Sam says.

I nod, acting like I know what Sam means. He draws a small circle on his neck with his finger, a little ring under his chin.

'Comes out small and round like this. It's what happens when someone kisses the skin on your neck and sucks at it. That'll be Eamon's doing.'

I try not to imagine Eamon's lips on Lottie's neck. I try not to imagine the sound, a sound like someone sucking marrow from a bone. A sound like feeding.

'This changes everything,' Flo says. 'This puts Eamon at the top of our list.'

I watch Eamon. The way his eyes narrow when he laughs, the

way he runs his tongue along his lips. The way he pulls Lottie tight to him. I wonder what Father would do if he saw.

'What do we do next?' I ask.

'Come on,' Flo says. 'We're going to get a closer look at Eamon.'

Me and Sam follow Flo away from the crowd, breaking into a run to keep pace with her long strides. We move down the street in the direction of the pub. A man catches my eye, his silver coat buttons casting off the sun. It's Mayor Napier. His face is close to the ear of a woman, speaking where only she can hear. He moves his hands as he talks, palms down, as if patting down a bed. The woman listens for a time and then she steps away from Mr Napier, from his words, and walks to another man's side. The man reaches around her and holds her shoulder. She leans on him. I've seen this man once before, at the pub. This is Elliot, the cook. Mr Napier watches the backs of the cook and his wife. The woman looks over her shoulder and shakes her head at Mr Napier.

We move away from the street, up a lane between two shops, weeds reaching out from cracks in the foundation, purple flowers closed to the shade. The sound of the music and the dancers thins behind us.

'Where are we going?' I ask. 'Eamon's back that way.'

'We're not getting a look at him,' Flo says.

We turn out of the lane and onto a street with low houses, a rusted coach at one end, no people in sight. She points ahead, to the end of the street, where it joins with another road.

'We're going to look at his house.'

27

We walk along a winding road, no people, only a handful of dogs that sniff at the gutter or else lie on their sides in the shade. The road narrows and the trees get thicker and taller. Flo leads us to a squat cottage, shaded on one side by an overhanging gum tree. The front yard is empty, patches of grass rising here and there, mud that's baked in the sun. It looks like muddy river water frozen in place. The cottage leans a little to one side. There's a sleepout on the lower end with a slanted roof made of sheets of tin. A rusted car blocks most of the passage down the other side.

'Let's go around the back,' Flo says. 'See if anyone's home. Then we'll go in.'

'Who else lives here?' I ask.

'Only Eamon and his ma,' Sam says. 'His dad died in the war, I think. Mother never remarried, went to work instead. She's a nurse.'

'She might be home,' I say. 'Maybe we should come back another time?'

'This is the best time to get into a house,' Flo says. 'Everyone's out in town. It's bound to be empty.'

Flo leads us along a track of weeds between the houses. There are small flowers on the weeds. Flo doesn't see them. She lays some of them flat with her boots as she moves. I step around the few flowers that still stand. I see Sam doing the same.

The backyard is littered with tools, a few tyres and an enamel basin. There's a small brick shed to one side, double doors leaning open, firewood logs stacked waist-high inside. Flo leads us to the shed and we crouch beside the wood. We're quiet, watching the windows at the back of the house. There's no sound, save for the cockatoos calling from the trees and cracking nuts with their beaks.

Flo picks up a few small stones and throws them onto the roof of the house. Nothing. She picks up a few more stones and throws them at the back door. We wait. The house is quiet, still.

'Come on,' she says. 'Let's see what we can see.'

The back door is open, no lock in sight. It looks as though it can't close, an inch of space between the door and frame. Flo pulls it open and walks inside. I hold the door for Sam. The wood is chipped and rough to the touch. When we're in, I pull the door to the frame and look out the back window to see if we've been spotted. There's no life out there, the yard baking in the sun.

The cottage is dark and cool. We make our way through the small kitchen and into the hall, laying our boots down gently as if we're walking past a sleeping baby. Flo leads us to a sitting room, smaller even than the kitchen. There are two faded armchairs beside a fireplace. Above the fireplace, on the mantle, is a small frame with a photograph of a man in uniform. Above that, tacked onto the wall, is a crucifix.

'This place gives me the chills,' Sam says.

On one of the armchairs, on the seat cushion, there's a half-finished scarf trailing wool and two knitting needles. A cup and saucer rest on the floor next to the chair. The cup is filled with a dark liquid. I crouch next to the cup and touch the side. It's not hot but it's not all the way cool.

'Someone was here not long ago,' I say.

Sam's eyes spread wide. 'Let's get what we need and go,' he says.

The next room over has a large bed with a floral-print spread on top. The furniture around the bed is plain, the wood worn smooth by years of touch. There's a closet against one wall. Flo opens it and takes out a long, dark-green gown.

'Something for your costume collection, Sam?'

Sam rolls his eyes at Flo. He takes the gown and hangs it back up in the closet. 'Not my size,' he says.

'Let's keep looking,' I say. 'There's not going to be anything in here.'

The other room is Eamon's. A single bed with plain white sheets and a grey woven blanket. A few hats and caps hang from nails on the walls. There's a closet and a small cabinet next to the bed. I walk over to a framed painting hanging on one wall. It's small and it shows a man in old-fashioned clothes. He's in a clearing in the bush, crouching over a fire, a billy above the flames.

'This more your style?' Flo is at the closet, holding some trousers by the suspenders. She dangles the trousers in her hands, pretending to walk the legs along the floor.

'I wouldn't wear that if you paid me,' Sam says.

'I think you'd look rather good,' Flo says. 'You could go down the mines if the stage doesn't work out.'

'Let's be quick,' I say. 'I don't want to be here any longer than we need to.'

I open the drawers on the side table and move the contents around, searching through the mess of playing cards, razors, chewing gum and pennies. It's hard to make it out in the faint light. I keep searching until my hand touches something cold and hard. My fingers wrap around it. It's heavy and polished. I pull it out and hold it near the light coming through a gap between the curtains.

'What's that?'

Flo and Sam walk over. I'm gripping it now, holding tight. It's a handle, short and thick. There's a lever to one side and I pull it down with my thumb. My body kicks at the sound, a single shake that runs from my shoulders to my legs. Sharp steel fires out of the handle, faster than my eyes can follow. A knife.

'A switchblade,' Sam says. 'Here, let me have a look.'

I give the knife to Sam. He turns it over in his hands.

'It's a beauty,' he says. 'Must be an heirloom. From his dad, maybe.'

I watch the steel moving around in Sam's hands. The blade catches the light, reflecting it at my eyes. Sam pushes the blade back down into the handle.

'Catherine Fletcher had two wounds,' I say. 'They looked about as wide as that blade.'

Flo narrows her eyes and stares at the knife. 'Why would he hold on to the knife he used to kill her? Every book I've ever read, they throw the murder weapon in a lake or a river or a well. They don't clean it up and put it away in their house.'

'Would you throw out something like this?'

'Where'd you find it?' Flo asks.

I point at the drawers on the side table. Flo walks over and starts going through the rest of the drawers. She pulls out the deep drawer, the lowest of four, empties the contents on the bed and spreads them out flat, sweeping them with her hand as if she's washing them.

'Nothing.' She slaps the bottom of the drawer, a look of frustration covering her face. A thin sound, not at all like solid wood.

'Give me that,' I say.

Flo hands me the drawer and I reach inside and tap on the bottom with my knuckles. I feel around until I find it. A small opening in one corner. I reach into it with my little finger and hook the other side. The bottom of the drawer comes away.

'A false bottom,' I say. 'Look.'

Underneath the wood panel are a dozen or so photographs. I pick up the photographs and drop the drawer on the bed.

'Let's see those,' Sam says.

Flo and Sam hold out their hands and I pass them each a few of the photographs. I already know what I'm going to see, who will be on every print. I know what someone would want to hide in this town.

'Catherine Fletcher,' Flo says. 'With Eamon.' She raises a photograph, holds it like an exhibit. It shows Eamon wearing a suit and tie, Catherine in a fine dress. Eamon's arm is around her waist and she has one hand flat to his chest. Their faces are close together, almost touching, their lips a couple of inches apart.

'This is it,' Sam says. 'This is proof.'

'It's proof they were close,' I say. 'I'm not sure it's proof of anything else.'

'If they were so close, why didn't we all know about it? Why keep it a secret and hide it in a drawer?' Sam asks.

'I don't know. I don't know what goes on here.'

'It's not that different from anywhere else,' Sam says. 'When two people are sweet on each other, you can see it a mile away. It's like a neon sign, but I never saw that with them. Did you, Flo?'

Flo shakes her head, still looking down at the photograph.

'Do you think he did it?' I ask her. 'Could he have killed her?'

'If he did, we have to warn Lottie.'

Sam takes off his cap and sits on the edge of the bed, placing the cap down next to him. He runs his fingers through his hair. 'Eamon,' he says. 'Eamon all this time.'

I hear a sound outside, in the street. It's a woman laughing and then the low rumble of a man talking. I peel back enough of the curtain to see out. In the street, turning toward the house, are Eamon and Lottie. He has his arm around her waist as they walk, same as in the photograph.

'It's them,' I say, turning away from the window. 'It's Eamon and Lottie.'

Sam leaps from the bed. Flo picks up the drawer and starts tossing in the contents.

'Help me,' she says.

I help Flo fill the drawer. We move fast, our hands colliding, skin slapping together. Sam looks out between the curtains.

'They're almost here,' he says. His voice is high, urgent, panicked. 'They're in the yard.'

Flo slides the drawer back into the side table. I'm still holding two of the photographs. I put them in my pockets.

'In there,' Flo says. 'In the closet.'

I follow Sam and Flo across the room. We each climb into the closet, pulling aside shirts and trousers and coats to make room. I reach out and pull the doors closed behind us, wings folding in, gates swinging closed. Then it's dark and quiet. The only light comes from gaps between the wooden boards of the doors. I can feel blood pulsing in my ears. We stay there, among the clothes and dust, waiting.

We hear the front door open. Muffled voices that grow clearer. There are footsteps that get closer, each one a sound of danger, a mortar shell falling. Eamon and Lottie come into the bedroom. I can see them through a gap in the boards. Eamon has his arms around her. Lottie has her hands on his face. They're kissing. She's walking backwards, him forwards, his feet falling toward her. It's a dance moving in one direction, moving toward the bed.

Sam takes hold of my arm. He lifts his other hand and points to the top of his head. All I see is his hair. He points at the closet doors, toward the room, toward the bed. His cap. He left his cap on the bed.

'We shouldn't be away long,' Lottie says. 'Someone might look for us.'

Eamon's hands are moving around Lottie's back.

'There's enough going on back there. We won't be missed.'

Eamon's head dips and he kisses Lottie's neck. Her head falls back.

'Careful,' she says. 'Don't leave those marks again.'

Eamon lifts his lips from her neck, enough to speak. 'I want people to know you're mine.'

Lottie pulls away from Eamon. She laughs, dropping to the bed. A foot away from her, laying flat on the grey blanket, is Sam's cap.

'You know I'll have to leave soon,' Lottie says. 'When Father solves the case. We might not be here the whole summer.'

Eamon walks over to Lottie. He stands at the edge of the bed, leaning over her. 'You won't leave me,' he says.

Lottie laughs again, head rolling to the side, hair like a pool of water around her. Eamon moves closer. He presses his hands on the bed, either side of her face, leaning in close. He stops. He looks to his right.

'Whose cap is that?'

'What?'

Eamon stands and points at the bed. 'Right there,' he says. 'There's a cap.'

Lottie rises and moves the hair away from her face. Eamon picks up the cap, holds it up in front of his eyes.

'It's not yours?' Lottie asks.

'No. It's not mine.'

'Are you sure?'

'Yes, I'm bloody sure. I think I'd know my own cap when I see it. This is a child's.' Eamon throws the cap on the bed. 'Someone's been in here.'

28

I can feel the blood pulsing in my neck. I try to keep my breathing shallow, keep it steady to save from giving us away. On the other side of the wardrobe, in the crack between the boards, I watch Eamon as he crouches and peers under the bed. Lottie stands and pulls down her dress, hips moving left and right.

'Do you think your mother came home?' she asks.

'It's not her,' Eamon says, standing and looking around the room. 'It's a child's cap. It's someone else.'

He turns and looks at the wardrobe, looks at the boards of the door. My heart kicks in my chest, the speed of it rising. Eamon takes a step toward the wardrobe and stops. We can't escape.

'There's someone in there,' Eamon says. 'In the wardrobe.'

Through the gap in the boards, I see Lottie's face. Her mouth drops open. I want to be home. I want to go back in time, to be small again. I want to walk through the dark hall to Lottie's room. I want her to tell me it's going to be all right, to pull back the covers and drape them over me. Hide me from all the bad in the world.

'No,' she says.

'Yes.'

Eamon pulls on the doors. They open like a pit in the ground. We tumble out, me and Flo and Sam. I feel a tightness around my neck. The ground is falling back. I'm a constellation rising to my place in the night sky. The gods are lifting me up beside Capricornus and Orion and Scorpius. Is this how it feels to die? Is this how Catherine Fletcher felt? My neck is caught. I can't breathe. There's no air here. I'm being pulled away from the world by my neck, my mind pulled from my body, split in two.

'Let go of him! You're choking him!'

It's Lottie's voice. She's calling from across the room. There's a darkness between us. She's a thousand miles away, drifting into the fog. Black floods across the room, from the walls to the centre.

'You little bastard!'

The voice is at my ear. So close I feel the breath on my skin. It's Eamon. He's behind me, holding me. I feel the tightness in my neck and I know he has his arm around me. The arm that was around Lottie, the arm that was around Catherine Fletcher. Holding back the air. My arms and legs fall limp. I'm sailing into the fog. It's all around me, closing in. And then I see him. In the centre of the room, the only light left in the darkness. Sam is there, standing in the spotlight, the stage empty around him. He lifts his hand and pulls down with his thumb. A flash of silver rising to the light.

'Let go of him!'

I'm falling. The fog lifts, light floods in. The world rises up to meet me. I'm on my side on the ground. It hurts to fall from the heavens, to fall back to Gemini. There's a gentle hand on my face. It's Lottie. She's leaning over me, stroking my forehead, my cheek.

'You hurt him,' she says.

Sam is standing in front of Eamon. He's holding a knife. It's the switchblade we found in the drawer. His hand is trembling. Flo is at the other end of the room, body flat to the wall.

'Use it if you're going to,' Eamon says.

A single tear runs from the corner of Sam's eye to his jaw.

'Go on!'

Eamon rushes in. He takes hold of Sam's arm and the knife falls to the floor, slicing the air. Sam stumbles back and Eamon picks up the knife.

'You think you can steal from me? I'll show you what happens to little thieves.'

Eamon points the knife between Sam's eyes. They roll back into his head. I open my mouth and try to call out but the words don't come. There's only a faint sound coming from my throat, dim and distant like speaking underwater.

'I'll teach you to take from me.'

Flo steps away from the wall, holding a photograph of Catherine Fletcher. Eamon and Catherine, stuck in time. It shakes in the air.

'You going to do what you did to Catherine?'

Eamon lowers the knife to his side. Sam falls to his knees.

'Where'd you get that?'

'In your hidden drawer,' Flo says. 'Where else?' She's standing straight, chin held high. She's a cat arching her back, trying to make herself strong in the face of danger, but I can see through it. We can all see through it.

'You've got no right.' Eamon snatches the photograph from Flo's hand. He holds it in front of his eyes and stares for a moment. A look of pain flashes over his face before it sets again. 'Right,' he says, looking around the room at Flo and Sam and me. Eamon places the photograph in the pocket of his trousers. He walks over to Lottie and offers his hand. She slaps it away.

'You could've killed him,' she says.

Eamon's face sears a dark red. He takes a step back. He seems to shrink, body falling, head pulling into his shoulders.

'Why did you take her to the mine?' Flo asks. 'You were sour on them for laying you off, weren't you?'

Eamon looks down at the knife in his hand. His nostrils flare.

'People like Will Fletcher getting the shifts and you going without,' Flo says. 'That why you did it there?'

'That's not what happened,' Eamon says.

'You couldn't make it with them so you thought you'd take something from them,' Flo says. 'That's it, isn't it? You can't use your hands for work so you use them for something else.'

Eamon raises the knife. He waves it around the room, pointing at each of us. 'You know nothing, the lot of you,' he says. 'You don't know what it's like, what a working life is. What it's like to go down in that tunnel day after day and to need it because there's nothing else. You lot have it easy. You don't know what a hard life is like.'

Sam shuffles over to Flo. I see Flo reach out and pull him close.

'Come on,' Eamon says. 'We're going for a ride.'

We're in the car, the rusted one that was parked beside the house. Eamon is driving, Lottie in the seat beside him. Flo, Sam and me in the back. Flo is holding my hand. Her skin is cold and slick. Eamon has the knife pressed flat against the steering wheel, his other hand working the gears.

'Let us go,' Lottie says. 'We won't tell.'

Eamon snorts and turns the steering wheel. We're moving through the backstreets of Gemini, past empty houses and the odd horse eating feed in the shade. We haven't passed another person. He's steering us clear of the main street.

'I'll let you go,' Eamon says, 'but it won't be where you want to be.'

More turns. More empty houses. The car struggles along the edge of Castor. We rise above the town and then the road takes us down. We pick up speed and Lottie screams. Eamon laughs as he shifts into a higher gear.

We drop down to the road heading out of town. Up ahead, an old man leads a horse by the reins along the edge of the road. A grey dog trots beside them, fur matted and patchy, sniffing the dirt. Flo squeezes my hand. Eamon waves the knife in the space between us, the steel blade shining in the light.

'Don't even think about it,' he says.

We pass the old man, Eamon slowing the car, the knife low in his lap. He clears his throat and nods. 'Henry.'

The old man waves, the horse grunts. And then they're gone, falling away behind us, joining all the others who can't help. Eamon is in control. This is what it's like to be under the will of a man, to have him take away all the decisions you could make. You become no more than a body locked to theirs, a planet orbiting a sun.

The smokestacks of the mine are still. No puffs of black smoke rising into the air. Eamon turns the car into the parking lot, soil singed black with coal. There's no life beyond a half-dozen crows stalking the dirt and shifting it with their beaks.

Eamon stops the car. 'Out you get,' he says. 'Come on.'

We walk in single file through the mine, Eamon taking up the rear. He calls out the lefts and rights when he wants us to turn. I don't need directions. I know where we're headed.

'She was my sweetheart for a while,' Eamon says. 'I don't pretend it didn't happen. She's the one wanted to keep it quiet. I wanted it to last but she broke it off. Told me someone like me couldn't get her away from this town. Came a time all she wanted to talk about was getting away.'

Rails appear in the dirt, two lines, side by side. These are the tracks for the coal carts, the ones that lead to the tunnels. We follow them, stepping inside them, locking onto the rails as if we have wheels. The ground starts to slope down. The dirt darkens beneath us, the sickly paint spread thicker here.

'Why should I want to get away? My friends are here. My ma's here. I had some work at the mines, every other day. I told her we could have a life. We could find a place of our own. Have children, raise them up right. She said it wasn't far enough away. It had to be the city. What would I want with the city? I told her I wouldn't live like a rat in the shadows. I live my life in the open. She said I didn't understand her.'

Long Tunnel East appears in front of us. The wound in the ground, carved out of the dirt and scrub as if with a knife.

Flo turns her head and looks back at Eamon. 'Why'd you hide the photographs in your room?' she asks. 'If you've nothing to hide, why hide them?'

We're moving down now, getting closer to the tunnel. The memorial flowers we saw last time are still here, leaning against the rain-smoothed rock either side of the tracks. The flowers are wilted, stems drooping to the ground. A picture flashes in my mind of Mrs Clayton's roses. For a second, I'm back in the city, standing in a gentle breeze, looking over the fence at Mrs Clayton tending her roses, each upright and strong, petals full of life. And then I'm back here at the mine, looking at the memorial flowers reaching for the ground, for a place to rest.

'I knew how it would look,' Eamon says. 'You think I don't know? Nobody knew how close we were. She wouldn't have it. I was working shifts at the mine, alongside her father. You think I don't know what he'd do if he found those photographs? I'd be gone. They'd never find me.'

I remember the last time we were here, the pack of miners walking to the camp. Shacks splintering like firewood, screams echoing around the trees. A man held over the fire. I know the power of a word of blame. I've seen with my own eyes, how it can twist men into a single beast, each man a limb reaching out in anger. I know the hunger men feel to fill something with their pain, the way you fill a coffin and bury it deep in the ground. Put it down and try to go on living.

'If you ask me,' Eamon says, 'I'd say the killer's long gone. If they have any sense, they'd have left Gemini by now.'

Sam trips on a sleeper beneath the rails. I catch him as he falls and pull on his arm to get him back on his feet. I can feel his body shaking beneath the cotton.

'Just let us go,' Lottie says. 'Please.'

Eamon's face shifts. He seems to remember why he brought us here. He holds the blade high, pointing it at Lottie.

'You're going in,' he says. 'You got to know how it feels.'

The air is cooler the closer we get to the tunnel. We walk through the tunnel entrance into a small chamber, dark rock on all sides. There's a steel gate at the far end, the two halves locked tight with chain and padlock. I try not to look at the dirt near the gate. I try not to picture Catherine Fletcher's pale skin, the shroud of her hair, the bruises on her neck.

Eamon digs a hand into a pile of tools and rocks. 'Perk of the job,' he says. 'I know where the foreman hides the key.' He hands me a damp and rusted key. 'Go on. Open it.'

I walk to the gate and open the padlock. I drag the chain through the steel mesh, the links rattling like a hacking cough. The tracks slope down past the gate, fading into the black. Eamon clicks his fingers and I hand him the key.

'Come on,' Eamon says, shaking the knife. 'In you go.'

We link hands. Flo to Sam to me to Lottie. Flo takes the first step. The sound of her boots on the rough soil echoes down the tunnel. Sam follows and I start walking. I can see Sam's arm leading me into the tunnel, and then it fades. Darkness covers us, as black as the night sky, the space between the stars. I can't see my own hand. There's the sound of water dripping all around. We stumble forward, the air growing cooler with every step. My skin prickles. There's a strange smell in the tunnel, damp and dust below another scent that reminds me of the smell that sometimes flows in the air from Richmond, when the wind is just right. It's a smell that reminds me of places I shouldn't go.

There's a scratching sound behind us, metallic and sharp. Dim light fills the tunnel. Eamon is holding a lighter above his head, the flame flicking like a flag in the wind. His other hand grips the knife.

Wooden beams stretch above our heads. There are posts beside the walls, black dust everywhere.

'You want answers? You want to know the secrets of Gemini?' Eamon waves the flame above his head. The walls shimmer like tar in sunlight. 'You got to start living like the rest of us.'

This is a place to disappear. This is where Catherine Fletcher disappeared.

'Go left up here,' Eamon says.

The tunnel forks in front of us. A cart filled with coal blocks the right-hand passage. The rocks look fit for another planet. Mercury or Mars or Neptune. Those old words from the leather books in Father's library. I want to be back in the city, back in our house before this happened. I want to be sitting with Father in his study. I want to hear him reading from his books, the light from the lamps filling the room and keeping the darkness outside. I want to go back to before Catherine Fletcher, before Gemini, before all of this.

'Please, Eamon,' Lottie says behind me. 'Let us out. We won't tell anyone.'

'You city folk think you can talk your way out of everything. There are some things words can't fix. You make a choice with your body. That's the way it works out here. You slap my hand away, you make your choice. Catherine made her choice, walking away from me. There's nothing stronger in this world than what you do with your body.'

'What about killing?' I ask.

'I haven't killed anyone. I can say I wish it hadn't happened to her but it's not going to change anything. She's gone, and no words are going to bring her back.' Eamon's voice shakes. The words seem to catch in his throat, the pipes inside him going tight. We keep shuffling forward. The tunnel forks again and again, the air growing cooler and cooler. We're somewhere deep below Gemini.

'Here's where we say goodbye,' Eamon says. The light starts to fade. We turn and see him backing away, moving the way we came. The flame flickers, casting dim patches of light on the walls, the shadows growing longer with every step Eamon takes. He holds the knife beside the flame. The blade shines.

'Don't leave us here,' Lottie says.

'You made your choice,' Eamon says.

He turns a corner and the darkness drops like a curtain. There's no more flickering flame, no shining steel blade. There's only black, covering everything.

'Eamon!'

'Come back!'

Screams in the darkness. I hear shuffling and stomping. There's movement all around. I stay still. I feel as though I'm dropping into this emptiness. In this pure black, I'm not sure where I am, where my body is.

The sounds stop. Nobody moves for a moment. I hold my hand in front of my face but there's nothing there. I stumble forward, arms outstretched. I keep moving until my hands touch something cool. The flat face of rock like wet skin.

'Morris? Flo? Where are you?'

I move my hands over the rock until I feel something else. Not as cool but almost as hard. It's a wooden post, the ones that run from the ground to the beams. I stand with my back to the post and touch the chain that hangs around my neck. I rub my fingers over the heather Mrs Clayton gave me. The one she said will bring me good luck. I hold it in my hand and my breathing slows. My head seems to rise out of an ocean. There are more shouts in the dark, more feet shuffling around in the dirt. The voices echo down the tunnel.

'Walk to me,' I say. 'Walk to my voice.'

'Morris? Is that you?'

'Where are you?'

I take a breath in and let it out slow. I'm in a field of white heather, a gentle wind moving around my ankles.

'Walk slowly,' I say. 'Keep walking until you find me.'

I hear shuffling, the sounds of boots scraping over stones.

'Keep walking. Follow my voice.'

I keep talking and, one by one, they find me. We link hands.

'We're going to walk uphill,' I say. 'Walk slow and keep hold of someone's hand.'

We shuffle forward. Nobody speaks. The only sounds are from our boots on the ground and the water dripping above us. The sound of the water calms me.

We keep shuffling until we see some faint light ahead. When we get to the tunnel entrance, the light is almost blinding. I have to squint to stop so much getting in my eyes. The gate is open. Eamon is gone.

We follow the tracks up the slope. We look like miners, faces charred black. I look at Lottie and we laugh, our eyes and teeth shining among the soot. We keep walking past the smokestacks and the work sheds. The mine office looms in the distance, over near the road. Eamon's car is gone.

'I suppose we're walking back,' I say.

'Would you have got back in the car with him anyway?' Flo asks.

We walk past the office, empty and quiet. The sun reflects off the windows, each pane of glass sparkling like a star fallen to Earth.

We start down the road toward town. The river comes into view and we leave the road without a word, all of us moving down the bank to the water. I dip my hands in the cool water and wash the coal dust off my face. Flo, Sam and Lottie do the same, all of us crouched by the river, letting the current take the coal away downstream. Lottie turns her face to me, touching the skin below her eyes.

'Is it all gone?' she asks.

'Yes, it's gone,' I say. 'Just you now. Welcome back.'

We leave the river and join the road again, walking in the gutter to one side. Flo and Sam walk ahead. Lottie falls back and walks beside me. She takes hold of my hand. We let our hands swing between us as we follow the others to town.

29

Eamon left town. On the day of the festival, while we were finding our way out of the tunnel, Eamon packed his clothes and set off in his mother's car. Lottie found out from Eamon's friends, the sour-faced couple Keith and Rebecca. I saw her talking to them in town. They must've known something happened between Eamon and Lottie. They turned their bodies from Lottie as they spoke to her, casting her off.

If Eamon's mother has questions, if she guesses he's running from something, she's not letting on. Sam says he's seen her in town talking to friends and neighbours as if nothing has changed. I suppose if you've already lost so much, losing the rest may not be a surprise. Maybe she saw it coming, with a son like him.

The loss of Eamon has barely left a mark on the town. There's plenty else to talk about. Last night, I heard Father say the mine has been cutting pay and hours, and a lot of people have been leaving Gemini. I've seen it with my own eyes. Families have been shutting their doors, boarding up their windows. They've been packing everything they own and heading north or south to the cities, joining the stream of others in search of work. On the way out, they pass other families moving into the camp. Sam says he heard his father say the families are camping there for days or weeks before moving to somewhere else.

With so much coming and going, Eamon hasn't made a dent.

Christmas is getting closer. Heat shimmers on the paddocks, the grass dancing in the distance. The morning dew on the leaves dries as soon as the sun rises over the hills. Flo says to Lottie and me that we ought to go to Gemini Falls. We pick up Sam on the way out there. We have it to ourselves, despite the heat. We shed our shirts and dresses and overalls, taking off everything that's not needed, and rush into the water. Lottie swims to the waterfall and we follow. The sheet of water sparkles in the sunlight. I think of the river in the stars, the one Father told me about. The constellation Eridanus. I think about when I used to stand on the balcony with Father, taking turns looking through the telescope. It seems like so long ago. So much has happened between then and now. Floating here in the middle of the bush, the water falling beside me, it's hard to believe this is the same world.

'When do we tell about Eamon?' Sam asks, calling above the sound of the rushing water. 'We should tell someone what we know about him and Catherine.'

The water seems to darken around us, a drop of ink spreading to the edge. We may be floating at the falls, cooling our skin under the sun, but Catherine Fletcher is still dead, her killer still free.

'Not yet,' Flo says.

'We've got to tell someone. He did it, didn't he?' Sam asks.

'I don't know. We've got to be sure.'

'Morris,' Sam says. 'We've got to tell your dad. Tell him what we know.'

Lottie drifts a little further toward the waterfall. I see her lips turn down.

'We can't tell him until we're sure,' I say. 'You remember what happened when he found us at the mine. Me and Flo were stuck at the farm for days. We have to know before we say anything.'

'It's different this time,' Sam says. 'We've got proof. You've got the photographs of him and Catherine.'

The photographs. I kept them in my pockets when Eamon found us. I kept them hidden when he took us to the mine. They're back at the cottage now, under my bed, a secret waiting to be let out.

'How did we get the photographs?' I ask. 'We broke into his house, remember? That's a crime.'

'We'll make something up,' Sam says.

'He'll know,' I say. 'He can always tell when someone is lying.'

'I'm an actor,' Sam says, lifting his chin high above the pool. 'I can fool him.'

Flo splashes water at Sam. 'He'll know before you open your mouth,' she says.

'How dare you. I'm a professional.'

'If you're a professional actor, I'm a sworn detective.'

'You'd be fired by now if you were a detective.'

Flo points to the top of the waterfall. 'Tell you what,' she says. 'You jump off that rock into the pool and we'll go straight to Uncle Jude.'

Sam tilts his head back, eyes following the silver stream to the top. 'Up there?'

'That's the deal.'

'I can't do that. I'll die.'

Flo raises her eyebrows. Sunlight reflects off the water, dancing across her face.

'Fine,' Sam says. 'If I die, you better mourn me for the rest of your life.'

He swims to the bank. He rises from the water and lifts himself onto a boulder.

'Sam,' I say. 'It's not worth dying over. Come back.'

Lottie stirs from her daydream. Her eyes fix on Sam on the bank. 'Don't do it, Sam,' she says. 'Don't be foolish.'

Sam climbs over more boulders, leaving wet marks on the grey stone. He scrambles up a path beside the waterfall, moving on his hands and knees. He keeps climbing, higher and higher. And then he slips. My breath catches in my throat. Sam takes hold of the trunk of a small tree, stopping his fall. He looks over his shoulder at the way he's come.

'Sam,' Flo says. 'I was only playing. Come down.'

Sam shouts. His voice seems to bounce off the water. 'I'll come down one way or another. In glory or in pieces.'

'That's not funny,' Lottie says. 'Come down, Sam.'

He doesn't reply. He's climbed so high he looks different, no longer one of us. He's a bird winging up to the clouds. He's Pegasus meeting the gods on Mount Olympus. He makes it to the rock at the top of the falls, walks to the edge.

'I hope you know the way to the police, Flo,' he says. 'Is it upriver or down?'

Sam mocks a jump over the waterfall. I hear Lottie gasp. Sam's words bounce off the water. They seem to spread around us, pooling with the river.

'You got your point across,' I say. 'Come back.'

'It's pleasant up here. You ought to join me.' Sam mocks another leap off the rock and then stops. He kneels and rises again, holding something in his hand. It looks like paper. A sheet of paper bending in the wind. He stares down for a moment and then looks at us. 'Get out of the water!' He waves his arms, paper curling in his hand. 'Get out of the water now!'

We splash over to the bank. Sam twists around trees on the ledge and slides down the slope on his backside. We're shaking the water from our bodies when Sam reaches us.

'He's in there,' he says. 'He's in the water.'

'Who's in the water?' I ask.

'The killer.'

Sam hands the note to Flo. She reads it aloud, voice quiet, almost drowned out by the falls. "'I can't go on with the guilt. I was the one who killed the girl from town. I left her by the mine and went back to camp. There's nothing left for me. There's nothing but sorrow.'"

I look over my shoulder at the pool. Ripples stretch out from the falls, spreading in a ring to the bank. The grey stones at the bank darken as the ripples break. The grass at the edge seems to lean in, bending to the water. That's where he is. Out there, down in the deep cool water. Catherine Fletcher's killer.

Sam and Flo run off down the track to fetch help, feet kicking up dust, their steps loud on the stones and dirt, then fading as they go through the bush. The dust settles on the gum leaves and myrtle blooms. Me and Lottie stay behind. We sit by the edge of the pool, each of us on boulders, facing the dark water. Lottie wraps her arms around her knees.

We stay quiet for a long time and then she starts to talk, pitching her words out over the water, as if there's an audience to hear them. 'Being here makes me think of Mother,' she says.

My head gets light, floating above my shoulders. I breathe in and out, shallow breaths that make my body rock back and forth.

'The water,' Lottie says. 'It looks the same.'

I look out at the water, at the ripples running over the clear surface. At the reflections of clouds, the way they seem to twist on the surface.

'Do you ever think of her?' she asks.

'No,' I say.

Lottie turns and looks at me. I don't meet her eyes.

'Not ever?'

'No.'

'It's all right to talk about her,' she says. 'Father doesn't want to, but we can.'

I've been waiting for this for years. I know this is the time to ask questions, to find out the truth. But not with Lottie. I'm not ready.

I hear footsteps and the low sounds of men talking. Flo and Sam come running out through the gap in the bush made by the track, almost tripping to get to us. Behind them are Father and Mr Napier and some other men from town. Father is holding a length of rope, thick as his arms. His eyes lock on me and Lottie. He holds out a hand to call us over. We rise from the boulders and move over to him.

It takes more than a dozen dives into the dark water before one of the men comes to the surface splashing, shouting as soon as his mouth tops the water. Other men swim to him and they dive together. The rest of us watch from the bank. Father, his arm over my shoulder, Mr Napier, Lottie, Flo and Sam. We listen to the falls crashing into the pool. The water where the men dived levels out and goes still. I hold my breath and count in my head. One, two, three, four. I keep counting, each number that passes seeming more impossible. And then the men come up. They shout for the rope. There's something there between them. A colour in the water, pale and creamy like porridge. Father pitches the rope out to the men, Mr Napier holding the loose end on the bank. The men lash the rope around the colour and they swim in, Father and Mr Napier pulling.

'Look away,' Father says, calling out to us over his shoulder. 'Don't look.'

Lottie, Flo, Sam and me draw in close together. Lottie takes hold of my hand.

'Not too hard or you'll break him,' a man in the water says.

Flo and Sam turn away. Only me and Lottie look at the shape the men have brought up from below. It gets close to shore and it's hard to see much, only some rotten strips of clothing, thin as paperbark, and that creamy colour shining in the light. I see some stones fall from the clothing, from pockets in the trousers. They slip into the water and sink from sight. They look smooth and hard, stones that have been a long time underwater. Mr Napier lets go of the rope and vomits in the grass. Father glances over his shoulder at me and Lottie, sees us watching.

'Look away,' he says.

I turn my head, not wanting to upset him. As I turn, my eyes cast over the water one last time. I see a mark on the cream. A scar running from a hole where an eye used to be, down to the jaw.

30

It's overcast on the day of the funeral. The sky is a sheet of grey, tucked low over Gemini. Heat passes through the clouds and stays in. A scattering of people line the main street. Shop owners lean on poles, women wrap their arms around children. Men stand in groups, a few of them with caps in hand but far from all. Father is over near the men. He holds his hat to his chest. I'm standing with Lottie and Flo, beside Sam and Mr Napier. Mrs Napier hovers behind us. She keeps her head low, as if she doesn't want to be seen. Uncle Jimmy and Aunt Beth aren't here. They didn't want to come. Over by Father there are other policemen watching the groups of men. The police mark the first line on the road, staking out a path with their bodies.

This is the funeral for the man with the scar. The one they found at the falls. We overheard his name in town. The confession made its way around Gemini within hours and the name leaked out of the police station within a day. Charlie Coates.

It's quiet for a time and then a song starts to fill the air. It's soft and high, a woman's voice. We hear footsteps and the procession comes around the bend, winding into town from the road out to camp. There are men on either side of a single horse, leading it on. The coffin trails on a low cart behind the horse, open to the weather. It's a simple cart, the kind you use on a paddock. Twenty or thirty people from the camp follow. They are quiet. There's no crying or calling out to the heavens. Only the woman near the front, the one singing, only she makes a sound. The men have their caps and hats in their hands. It's not the whole camp following the coffin. Not everyone will walk to town to bury a confessed killer.

'It isn't right, doing it in the open like this,' Mrs Napier says. She clicks her tongue.

'We've got to see this through,' Art Napier says.

The procession passes shops. The shopkeepers shake their heads. Women look away, turning the faces of their children, hands pressing gently on cheeks. The people from the camp move on, the wheels on the cart squeaking, marking out a beat to walk to. When they pass the pub, a man steps out onto the road. It's Will Fletcher. He staggers into the street. He walks close to the coffin and spits on it.

'Filthy murderer,' he says.

His voice carries over the street, bouncing off the buildings. Art Napier walks out into the street. Father leaves the line and pulls Will Fletcher back. Mr Cornwell is near Fletcher, and he reaches over and pats him on the back as Father leads him on. Mrs Napier takes Sam by the arm, as if to steady herself, and clicks her tongue.

'It isn't right,' Will Fletcher says. 'They shouldn't be burying him up with our people.'

Art Napier crosses the street, walking over to Fletcher. 'We have to see this through, Will,' he says, loud enough for everyone to hear. 'These people got a right to bury their own, no matter what he's done.'

Fletcher pulls away from Father's grip. He takes a few steps back from the coffin. The procession has stopped, the men next to the horse patting its mane and whispering in its ear. The men and women behind the coffin look down at their shoes, glancing now and then at Fletcher.

'He shouldn't be resting anywhere near Catherine. They ought to take him out of town.'

'And put him where? In a ditch in the bush? That's not our way,' Mr Napier says, sending his voice out over Will Fletcher, out over the heads of all who are gathered. 'He needs to be laid to rest, same as anyone, no matter what he did in life.'

Fletcher turns as if to walk away then doubles back. He spits again at the coffin but shoots wide and hits the face of a woman. She turns and shrieks. I see Mr Cornwell smile, all those teeth under his ginger whiskers.

Mary Fletcher comes out of the crowd, into the street. She pulls on Will Fletcher's arm. 'That's enough,' she says, her voice shaking.

Fletcher pulls free of his wife and turns away. He walks from the procession and down a laneway, out of sight. Mary Fletcher stands for a moment, looking out at the street under the sheet-grey sky. She stares at the coffin and then turns and follows her husband.

'Go on, now,' Art Napier says to the men by the horse. 'You go on up to the cemetery. Nobody's going to bother you.'

The men lead the horse along the street. There's no more singing now, only the faint sound of feet shuffling on the dirt and the squeak of the cart. I look at the coffin as it passes. It's bare, no flowers or cloth, only the rough-cut boards showing on all sides. It makes me think of the shacks at the camp, the ones patched together with thin boards and hessian and rusted tin. I look at the people as they walk by. This simple coffin, this box made for a confessed killer, it's no worse than the shacks they've been living in.

'I've seen enough,' Mrs Napier says. 'Come on, Sam. We're leaving.'

Mrs Napier pulls on Sam's arm and leads him away. Sam raises his other arm, waving to us as he stumbles after his mother.

'Seems too easy,' Flo says.

'What does?' I ask.

'This funeral,' she says, pointing at the procession. 'The confession. The body at the falls. It's all too easy.'

'Not much about this seems easy,' Lottie says.

I look at Father. He's standing with his back to the procession, facing the group of men watching on. I wonder if he found this easy, if he found pulling on that rope easy, lifting the body easy. Coming back home to Gemini, the town he left all those years ago, I wonder if he found that easy.

'It was in his note,' Lottie says. 'You ever hear of anyone saying they killed someone when they didn't?'

Flo sniffs, looking out over the crowd. She takes in a deep breath and sighs. 'It's going to be strange going back to the falls after this,' she says.

The final few people pass us and we watch as they make their way along the street. They turn toward the church and the hill to the cemetery. They'll have dug a hole up on the edge of the slope where the cemetery falls away. The cheapest graves are on the edge, Flo told me. They'll have dug the hole straight down, the way you do for a fence post. They'll lay the coffin in upright to stop it sliding down Castor when the rains come. Charlie Coates will be standing for all time, this man who came to Gemini and left behind his body and another body further up the slope.

31

It's almost Christmas. Father drives us from the farm into town. He leans on the horn as we pass people walking beside the road or riding horses. They wave, their faces bright and beaming, merry with the season.

'Good day to you,' Father calls to an old woman walking with two young children, her back a quarter bent to the ground. She raises her head and calls out a greeting as we pass.

There's a lightness around town. The weight of Catherine Fletcher and the hunt for her killer is gone. There's something to celebrate, a holiday to mark and a new year around the corner. The people seem to be rushing to it. They seem to need it.

Out on the main street, there are decorations strung up around the buildings. Ribbons and bunting run from poles and rooftops, colourful fabric hanging over the road. In the middle of the street, floating between the hardware store and the butcher's, is a star made of polished bronze. It catches the light of the early afternoon sun and sends flares around the street. The old white gum by the river, the tallest tree in town, is decorated with baubles and candles. None of the candles are lit, of course. Nobody wants a bushfire, least of all now.

Over on the bandstand, there are musicians playing seasonal tunes.

'Isn't this jolly?' Father says as we make our way past the people in the street. 'It's like being back in the city.'

We pass children sucking on candy canes, pass people shaking hands and walking arm in arm. If you squint, if you don't look at the patched-up clothes and worn-down hats and shoes, the people of Gemini look prosperous.

The music stops and the trumpet player walks out onto the steps. He raises his horn and lets out a shrill call on the instrument. It's an announcement. People rush to the bandstand. We follow, Father helping us ease through the crowd. We find Uncle Jimmy, Aunt Beth and Flo, and we take our places beside them.

'I wonder what this could be,' Lottie says.

The trumpet player steps away. Behind him is Sam. He's dressed in pinstripe trousers, a silk tie and linen shirt covered over with a large velvet cape. I can see sweat beading on his forehead.

''Twas the night before Christmas, when all through the house, not a creature was stirring, not even a mouse.' Sam walks to the edge of the steps and holds up a finger. 'The stockings were hung by the chimney with care, in hopes that Saint Nicholas soon would be there. The children were nestled all snug in their beds, while visions of sugarplums danced in their heads.'

I look around. Art Napier is dressed in his finest suit, dabbing a handkerchief at the sweat on his own forehead. He's over by the dispensary, looking on, Mrs Napier by his side. Sam doesn't look at them. He walks down the stairs and makes his way through the crowd. He hands out the lines to people as if they were gifts.

'As I drew in my head, and was turning around, down the chimney Saint Nicholas came with a bound. He had a broad face and a little round belly, that shook when he laughed, like a bowl full of jelly.'

Sam has the town fixed on his voice. He moves through the audience, almost dancing, circling the patrons. He makes his way back to the bandstand and climbs the stairs. He turns and stretches his cape, spreads it like wings.

'He sprang to his sleigh, to his team gave a whistle, and away they all flew like the down of a thistle. But I heard him exclaim, as he drove out of sight.' Sam drops his cape and crouches. Behind him, as if by magic, is Liam from the pub, dressed as Father Christmas, belly padded with wool.

'Happy Christmas to all, and to all a good night,' Liam says.

Liam, Father Christmas, dips his hand into a bag slung over his shoulder. He pulls out handfuls of candy and throws them to the children. Sam rises and takes his bow to the applause of the audience. He follows Liam down the stairs and walks over to us.

'Good show, Sam,' Father says. 'You've got a great talent there.'

'Thank you, Mister Turner,' Sam says.

'Not bad, Sammy boy,' Flo says. 'Not sure about the cape but the rest was good.'

Sam lets Flo punch him lightly on the shoulder.

Lottie lays an arm around Sam. 'We adored it, didn't we, Morris?'

'It was wonderful,' I say.

Sam looks past us and his smile fades. His lips stiffen. I turn and see Mr and Mrs Napier moving through the crowd. They look upright and proper, two statues drawn through the street. Sam seems to sink under his cape, shoulders hunched, chest hollowed.

'You've done well, Sam,' Art Napier says.

'Yes, that was lovely,' Mrs Napier says. 'Just lovely.'

Sam's face softens. He blinks once, slowly. 'I'm happy you think so,' he says.

Art Napier looks at us and winks. 'Did you see that? See him up there? Not bad at all. Even better to pull off a surprise in this town that his father doesn't hear of. Not many can do that.'

The men and women keep talking. Lottie stays close to Aunt Beth's side, Art Napier holding court. Flo, Sam and me pull away, flowing into the crowd. People shake Sam's hand and pat him on the back as we walk through the street. Over by the bandstand, Liam hands out sweets to the smallest children.

'You're a real star now, Napier,' Flo says. 'You better remember us when you're famous.'

'Don't worry,' Sam says, shaking another man's hand as we get to the edge of the audience. 'There'll always be room at my palace.'

The sun is high and the heat reaches through my cap, flushing my hair damp with sweat. Sam unclips the cape from his collar and pulls it free.

'Let's go down to the river,' he says. 'It's too hot here.'

The air cools a little as we get close to the river. Crows and currawongs perch in the trees, beaks open in a silent scream. Other birds are down near the water, dipping their heads to drink. I see light reflecting off something partly hidden by the trunk of a gum tree. We walk closer and I see it's the steel of Ollie Fletcher's wheelchair. He's sitting alone in the slight shade of the tree, staring out over the water.

'Hello, Ollie,' I say. 'What are you doing out here?'

Ollie turns and smiles at us. He has the blanket pulled up from his legs, letting the sun touch his skin.

'Watching the water run,' he says. 'It's funny how something that's always moving can be so relaxing.'

I look out at the river. In the shallow parts, near the bank, the water is clear. Under the surface, the dark stones make a pattern, an underwater patchwork.

'Where are your parents?' asks Flo. 'Where's your dad?'

'They're at home. Dad has one of the headaches he gets the day after he collects his pay. Ma's nursing him. Our neighbour brought me to town.'

'I know about those headaches,' I say. 'My father gets them when he's near champagne. Must be the sound of the cork popping.'

'Must be that,' Ollie says.

He looks out over the water. The grass is thick and green at the bank. A few feet out, the current moves around a sleek brown rock.

'I only wish I could swim,' Ollie says.

'Why don't we go out on a boat? We could take one from the boat shed,' Sam says.

'Are we allowed?' Ollie asks.

'Who's going to know? They're all here in town,' Sam says.

'Lead the way, then.'

'I'll do one better,' Flo says, walking around to the back of Ollie's chair. 'I'll push.'

We walk along the river, past the backs of the shops on the main street. The back steps and storage sheds are worn, paint chipping off, walls freckled like skin. Pipes run down from the backs of the shops to the bank of the river. On the other side of the shops, there's the sound of talking and laughing and clapping. The musicians are playing and the music floats past us, moving out toward the hill.

We get to the wooden footbridge and we turn to cross the river. Sam, Flo and Ollie go first. I'm about to cross when a sound draws me back. Over by the back of the bandstand, away from the crowd, Father and Uncle Jimmy are standing and talking with another man. I've seen this man before. He's short and stocky, around Father's age. He's not so much talking as telling off Father, leaning into him, pointing at him with one finger. As I turn to cross the bridge, I see Uncle Jimmy throw an arm around the man's waist and drag him back. It happens so fast,

I don't know what to make of it. Father hangs his head like a man condemned as Uncle Jimmy pulls the man away.

The boatshed is narrow and long, the roof slung low. The roof and walls are green, the colour dulled to the same shade as the leaves on the trees. The shed faces onto a gentle slope of clay, dried grey and hard in the sun. There are grooves in the clay running from the shed to the river.

Flo pushes Ollie's chair close to the water. She waves Sam and me over to the shed. There's no lock on the door, only a latch that springs free as soon as Flo touches it. Inside the shed, it's dark and the air is close. We move in and it takes a moment for my eyes to settle. When I can see, I make out a dozen or so rowboats stacked against the walls, oars stretched out above them on hooks nailed to the walls.

'Come on,' Flo says. 'Help me get two of these out.'

I feel a sickness in my guts, looking at the boats. It rises to my throat and I rush over to help Flo and Sam pull two rowboats from the shed. We lay them on the clay slope, each wooden boat painted a white made creamy with time. The bench seats inside are varnished red. They shine almost as bright as the brass oar rings. I swallow hard, over and over, and I try to think about the air going in and out of my lungs. The sickness starts to fade. I help the others thread the oars through the rings and we line the boats on the bank.

'I'll go out with Sam,' Flo says. 'You can row Ollie out. I'll help you get him in.'

I walk over and we lift Ollie, each of us holding under his arms and legs. He's so light, his legs and arms so thin, that it seems impossible he's our age. We move over the clay and lay Ollie gently in the boat.

'This is fun,' Ollie says, dropping a hand over the side of the boat and slapping the boards. 'Let's get out there.'

The river is wide and slow here, downstream of the town. There are ferns and saltmarsh growing near the banks and great river gums leaning over the water. I take hold of the oars and pull us out into the middle of the river, trying not to think about the way my hands tingle and my head aches. Behind Ollie, I can see Flo and Sam launching their boat. They scream as they hit the water.

I row away from Flo and Sam, putting some space between us and their screams. Ducks fly down and land near the banks.

'How long will you stay in Gemini?' he asks.

'What do you mean?'

'With the case,' he says, stumbling on the word. He clears his throat. 'With it all done, your dad must have to get back to the city.'

'I suppose he will,' I say. 'Suppose it won't be long now.'

Ollie closes his eyes. He dangles his hand over the side of the boat, fingers in the water.

'I suppose,' he says.

Flo calls out to us, tries to get us to follow them upstream. I row harder, pulling us away from Flo and Sam. Ollie opens his eyes and looks out across the river. His face changes, darkens. It looks the way the land does when a cloud passes over the sun, casting a shadow.

'Do you think that man had any family?' he asks. 'The one they buried.'

'I don't know,' I say. 'They know his name so they must be able to find out.'

Ollie looks away from the boat, where the light shimmers on the water. 'There's something I haven't told anyone,' he says.

'What's that?'

'That night,' he says. 'The night Catherine went away. He didn't come home for a long time.'

'Who didn't?' I ask. 'Your father?'

Ollie nods.

'I think I saw him coming home at sun-up. It's hard to know now if it's real or if I dreamed it. I can picture him through my bedroom window early in the morning, just coming home, his trousers all filthy. There's dirt all around the knees on his trousers.'

I imagine Will Fletcher walking to his house, the light reaching over the hills. I imagine his hands and what they may have done, what he may be holding as he walks through the weeds to the front door.

'I don't know. It might've been a dream.' Ollie leans his head over the water. 'I love it here. When I die, I want them to push my body into the river and let me float like this forever.'

A picture flashes in my mind. A woman floating in a boat, moving downstream, oars shipped and lying flat to the sides. My throat gets thick and tight. It's hard to breathe. I can only see the back of her. The woman wears a white dress. Her dark hair is pinned up, her shoulders narrow. My fingers go numb on the oars. I start to wheeze.

'Are you all right? What's happening?'

Ollie's voice is faint and far away. Everything around me is bright, blinding. I can't look at Ollie or the water or the boat. I can only think of the woman in white, floating in the current. I picture the colour of the clouds, dark as mud. The way the leaves of the trees weep into the water.

'Get away from the rocks!'

Screams from far away. Ollie takes hold of the oars. I watch them dangle over the side. There are bricks on my chest, pressing down. There's air all around but none getting in.

'Row! Row away!'

It must be Flo calling. Ollie looks at me. There's a warning in the way he looks. I can't do anything. I need to shift the bricks from my chest. All I want to do is breathe. I want air.

'Help me,' he says.

The boat is above me and beside me. The water is cold. I'm inside the river. My leg hurts and I see the wet stones and river weed bending in the current. The water stings my face and hands. Then I see the light. There's daylight above me. I push up to reach it, my leg aching as I kick. And I can breathe again. I gulp at the air.

Flo and Sam are in their boat, rowing toward me. Flo is pointing at the water. 'Ollie,' she says. 'Where's Ollie?'

I look around. All I see are rocks and the boat turned over, pushed against a boulder. I swim over and dive under. There he is, pressed against the rock, the current like a strap holding his body in place. I put my arms around him. I kick and we make it out and into the air.

'Get him to the bank,' Flo says.

Ollie isn't breathing. His body is flat and still on the bank, clothes steaming in the sun. Flo is holding his hand. Sam is lifting his head. They're calling for him to breathe. Breathe, Ollie, breathe. They want him to wake up. They want him to come back. I lay next to Ollie on the bank, watching him, and the picture plays in my head. Over and over it goes, the woman in white floating downriver. I don't want to see the hair pinned up and the oars shipped to the side. I don't want to see the current taking her away around the bend.

Ollie opens his eyes and coughs up brown river water. And he breathes.

32

I wake to the smell of meat. It must be the ham that Aunt Beth set aside at the big house. The smell of it is blowing along the path, past the thick bush to the cottage. Today is Christmas. Lottie's bed is made up and I'm alone in the bedroom. There's a cool breeze leaking through a gap in the half-open window. I pull back the covers and let the air in, a cold that feels like dipping my body in water.

Father is out in the kitchen. He's holding a cup of tea to his lips, staring out the kitchen window. There's a kookaburra perched on a branch outside the cottage. It lets out a call, a laugh that rings in my ears.

'Good morning, Father,' I say. 'Merry Christmas.'

He doesn't reply. He stares out the window, steam rising around his face. The kookaburra calls again and takes wing, dipping low before lifting and disappearing out of sight.

'I'm going to dress and go over to the house,' I say.

Father blows on his tea and sips from the edge of the cup. He turns his head.

When they took Ollie away, when his mother arrived and wheeled him from the festival, he held up a hand to wave. He was looking at me, hair and clothes wet through, sitting there in his wheelchair with the river water dripping down the wheels. His mother reached over and pushed down his hand. I felt a hundred eyes on me, felt the way the people from the camp must feel when they walk into town. They were seeing me for who I am.

We were standing in the main street, me and Flo and Sam, each of us soaked to the bone. The band had stopped playing. People were cupping their hands over their mouths and whispering. Father and Uncle Jimmy and Art Napier were around us, still as statues, each one with hands behind their backs or arms folded. For some reason, they seemed to want to keep their hands hidden, as if there was some guilt written on the palms of our fathers.

On the drive home, Father was quiet. He pulled on the gear shift, pulled hard like a man wrestling an animal. He didn't speak on the way home, didn't utter a word until we were down the long path to the farm and parked outside the big house. He shut off the engine and stared ahead, out through the windshield.

'He's been through enough, that boy,' he said. 'You're to stay away from him.'

That was three days ago. I haven't left the farm since and neither has Flo. Lottie's been here too, even though she wasn't down by the river that day. We've been walking in loops from bed to bath to kitchen, with the odd trip out to the paddocks to do our chores. The world has shrunk again. Father has barely said a word and he hasn't looked my way since the day of the festival.

I leave him in the cottage and follow the smell along the path to the big house. I'm wearing my best clothes, my boots shined with spit and a rag. The sun is over the hill and starting to heat the air. The leaves near the path are curling away from the sun, moving away from danger.

Aunt Beth wraps me in a hug when I get to the kitchen, her hands fanned out behind me to save my clothes from the flour on her fingers. She lets go and steps back, looking me up and down. 'Very smart, young man,' she says. 'I was going to serve you out in the shed with the pigs but I suppose we'll make room for you at the table.' She smiles and pinches my chin, then rubs the flour off my skin with the back of her hand. 'Here, help me with the custard for the pudding.'

Aunt Beth wraps an apron around me and I help her in the kitchen. We glaze the ham and wash potatoes and layer the trifle. We bake the shortbread, trim the ends off brussels sprouts, check the pudding. Flo and Lottie come in from the garden carrying flowers. They set the table with the good silverware and fill a small glass vase with water for the flowers. Uncle Jimmy comes in from the paddocks sniffing the air.

'You better get washed and dressed, James,' Aunt Beth says. 'We're almost ready here. Go over and get your brother after that. Won't have him moping all through Christmas.'

Uncle Jimmy exhales loudly through his nose. 'Anything else, my dear?'

'That ought to be enough, if you can manage it.'

Uncle Jimmy winks at me and Lottie. He walks off toward the washroom. I follow him into the hall.

'Uncle Jimmy,' I say.

He stops and wheels around. His eyes are dark beneath his brow. 'What is it?'

I look down at the rug in the hall and trace the pattern with my eyes, following the loops and curves.

'The other day at the festival,' I say. 'I saw you with someone. You and Father.'

Uncle Jimmy takes a step toward me. I see his boot cover the pattern on the rug. I keep tracing, twisting and crossing with the weaves.

'You saw us with someone?'

'Behind the bandstand,' I say. 'He was angry with Father. Who is he?'

Uncle Jimmy takes another step toward me. When he speaks again, his voice is a low whisper. 'Look at me, boy,' he says.

I raise my eyes and look at Uncle Jimmy. I can see the patches of red on his face, the shades where the sun has burned him. I can see the freckles on his nose and the lines beside his eyes. The cheekbones that match the ones on Father's face, the eyes a pale mirror of the ones I've seen all my life. It feels like the first time I've truly seen my uncle and the first time he's seen me.

'There are some things you don't know about your father,' he says. 'It's not up to me to tell you. You'll have to ask him yourself.' He reaches out and touches my arm below the shoulder. 'It's something every man has to do. You're going to have to stand in front of your dad and make some demands. When you do, don't you move until you get what you came for.'

Uncle Jimmy turns and walks away along the hall. I let my breath out and fill my lungs again. I hadn't known that I was holding it in.

Father doesn't talk much at dinner. Nobody does much of anything, other than dip their heads to eat. Aunt Beth tries to keep the mood up. She floats from the table to the kitchen bench to the icebox. Her dress whips the air, pushing around the smells of meat, roast vegetables and sauces.

'Who wants more ham? Jude, you must have some room,' she says.

Father lifts his napkin and wipes his lips and the hair below his nose. 'No, thank you,' he says.

'Oh, come now. You must be able to fit a thin slice.' She lifts some ham with the serving fork. Oil drips on the dish. Father looks at Aunt Beth and then lowers his eyes. She drops the ham on the dish. Father keeps his eyes down. He hasn't looked my way, hasn't spoken to me at all during dinner.

'Give it to Flo,' Uncle Jimmy says.

Flo shakes her head and wraps her arms around her belly. 'I'm too full,' she says. 'I can't.'

'You've barely eaten,' Uncle Jimmy says. 'We're not wasting any of this. I want to see all these plates empty.'

'I can't.'

'Leave her, James,' Aunt Beth says. 'She doesn't want it.'

'She should feel lucky to have it. Plenty of folk won't be eating anything like ham this Christmas.'

Aunt Beth makes a sound. It's a short squeal, air rushing from the smallest space in her. 'We almost didn't with the state of this farm,' she says.

Uncle Jimmy leans forward, elbows resting on the table. 'What's your meaning?'

Aunt Beth smiles and looks around. The skin beside her eyes is tight and straining. 'Nothing, my sweet,' she says. 'Don't pay any mind to me.'

'Tell us. What do you want to say?' Uncle Jimmy has his eyes locked on Aunt Beth.

She waves a hand and smiles. 'I only mean we're lucky, given the way of the world. It's no secret our accounts aren't what they used to be.'

'I'll have the ham,' Lottie says.

'Good girl,' Aunt Beth says.

She moves the ham over to Lottie's plate. Uncle Jimmy leans back. He winks at Lottie. 'That's more like it.'

We keep eating, a silence falling over the table. Flies hover around the last few potatoes. Nobody reaches out to move them away. The sounds of cicadas drift in through an open window.

'Uncle Jude, do you really think that man from the camp killed Catherine?' Flo's question settles over the table. Father sighs and pulls at the hairs on his chin.

'Not this again,' Uncle Jimmy says.

'Did you find out where Will Fletcher was that night? He doesn't treat Mrs Fletcher well at all, you know.'

Father doesn't look up, doesn't answer Flo. He nods slowly, enough to make it known he's heard her.

'Did you know Eamon used to be her sweetheart? He had pictures of her. They used to be sweethearts but he says she ended it. Isn't that odd?'

'That's enough, young lady,' Aunt Beth says, a finger raised and pointing at Flo. 'You shouldn't be asking questions like that. These are people in our town, people we live with.'

Uncle Jimmy's face is the colour of the ham. He's breathing heavy. I can hear it from across the table. 'I've had enough of this talk,' he says.

'I think there are still questions,' Flo says, her voice shaking, straining. She looks past Uncle Jimmy and stares at Father. 'I haven't had enough. I don't think Uncle Jude has either.'

'I've had enough of the overalls,' Uncle Jimmy says, pointing at Flo's clothes. 'On Christmas, of all days. Why can't I have a normal daughter who dresses like a normal girl? A girl who knows her place. I have to end up with a half girl, half boy. Where's that nice dress your mother bought you?'

Aunt Beth rises and picks up one of the serving plates. She takes it to the sink. 'She doesn't like wearing it,' Aunt Beth says.

'And I don't like paying for it, if she's not going to wear it. Maybe I should just give her my old clothes when I'm done with them, if she really wants to be a man.'

Flo sinks into her chair. Her body seems to fold in on itself, getting smaller and smaller in front of us.

'Leave her be,' Father says. 'It's Christmas.'

Father looks at Flo and back at his plate. His face drops, as if it took all his might to say that. This is the man who put countless criminals away in Pentridge. He can't even look his own family in the eye.

'He talks,' Uncle Jimmy says, his voice rising in a song. 'It's Christmas, you say? I thought this was a funeral, the way you've been acting.'

Father shakes his head slowly. The strength has gone out of him. He's a prune, all the life drawn out.

'Why don't we have some dessert?' Aunt Beth says. 'Lottie, come help me serve dessert, dear.'

Lottie joins Aunt Beth at the kitchen counter. They move cutlery and plates around, the sound almost deafening.

'Morris helped with the trifle,' Lottie says. 'Did you hear that?'

Father doesn't look up. He grunts and keeps staring at his plate. I can see him running his tongue across his teeth, under his lips. Maybe he isn't the man people think he is. He won't open his mouth, won't talk, won't smile.

'There's also pudding,' Aunt Beth says. 'Morris helped with the custard. Didn't you, love?'

'Yes,' I say.

Another grunt from Father. Uncle Jimmy rolls his eyes and leans back in his chair, folding his arms. I don't know why he's doing this to us. I don't know why he's doing it to me.

'Who wants pudding?' Aunt Beth asks. 'Any takers?'

Father keeps his eyes down. He can't even hold up his head at Christmas. With all we've been through this year.

'Mother used to like pudding, didn't she?'

Father raises his eyes, two stars burning across the space between us. He shakes his head but his mouth stays closed.

'Or was it trifle?' I ask. 'Maybe she didn't like dessert at all.'

Lottie reaches over and holds my arm. I shake her hand loose.

'I don't know anything about her. She could've hated Christmas for all I know.'

Father is breathing fast. All the words we haven't said are written on his face. The black and grey hairs falling from his chin, the lines reaching across his forehead. They can't hide the words. It makes me tired down to my bones.

'Don't,' he says.

'Nobody ever talks about her,' I say. 'Why don't you ever talk about her? Does anyone remember anything?' My heart is pounding against my ribs. The world narrows to Father's eyes, the two stars firing out light, burning in his face. 'It's like she was never alive. I don't know who she was. She's a ghost and you made her a ghost. She died and you took every bit of her and you hid it away inside yourself. You don't let her out. I don't have anything. You kept it all inside. You kept her for yourself.'

All I can hear is the ringing of the cicadas and the sound of Father's breath. Nobody moves. We could stay this way until the end of the world, until weeds grow through the wooden floorboards, until the trees break through the walls, until the stars blink off in the sky and everything grows dark and close.

And then Father breaks through. Time starts again. He lifts a hand and strikes the table with his palm. Silverware falls to the floor.

'Get out,' he says.

Everything is bright and hot. I'm running, the ground rushing below me, dry grass cracking beneath my feet. I run until a pain opens up my ribs, pushing on them until I feel they could snap.

I stop and turn around. I can't see the big house. I've run so far it's gone, out below the horizon, somewhere under the grass and weeds and trees. I sit on the ground and feel the heat push into me. All the thoughts leak from my mind. Father and Mother and Catherine Fletcher and Ollie and the river. It all leaves my mind and I don't think of anything, only the hot air going in and out of me, and the pain in my lungs. The pain that hides under my ribs, down where nobody can see, a pain that's all mine.

I stay there, looking out at the horizon, and I see shapes climbing over the shimmering edge and moving toward me. I see a dress on one side and overalls on the other. I see the faces of Lottie and Flo. They reach me and sit down on either side of me, facing back the way they came.

'You tell us when you're ready to go back,' Lottie says. 'We'll walk with you.'

We stay there on the yellow grass, the wide blue sky stretching out above us, the moon faint and white and low against the horizon.

33

When we get back to the house, Father is gone. Aunt Beth is cleaning the kitchen, strands of hair falling over her face. We pick up cloths and tea towels. None of us speak. There's only the sound of water sloshing in the sink, of silverware scraping together and glass clinking. When it's done, when the house is back to how it was before dinner, me and Lottie walk down the path to the cottage. The sun is behind the hills and the land is letting go of the heat. There are kangaroos on the edge of the paddock, grazing in the shade cast by the bush. A breeze is blowing from the south. Between the trees, magpies and currawongs fly from branch to branch. We walk into the cottage, into the bedroom, and Lottie opens the window to the wind. We lie on our beds in the dim light and sleep comes to us easily.

When I wake, the room is dark. Lottie is lying still in the bed opposite me, her body rising and falling with her breath. I make my way into the hall, careful not to wake her.

The cottage is empty, no kerosene lights burning. I fumble in the dark until I reach the back door. Moonlight leaks into the kitchen. In the corner of the room, over by a pine cabinet, the brass rings of the telescope shine.

I walk barefoot on the stones of the path, treading lightly. I walk past the big house and out to the paddocks. The air is cool and the chain and white heather around my neck are like water against my skin. I walk across paddock until the light coming from the big house is soft in the distance. I set down the telescope and look into the eyepiece.

I move the telescope and stare at the constellations, all the names Father told me. Above me is Aries, the ram with the golden wool, and Taurus, the white bull that swam into the sea. I can see Orion, the hunter, and Pegasus, the winged horse that carried lightning. On either side of the sky, as far west and as far east as I can see, are Capricornus and Gemini. The gate of the gods, where all the souls of the world pass when they die, and the constellation that gives this town its name. This town where my father and mother were born, where Catherine Fletcher lived and died. I think about the other names for these stars, the ones Father told me came from this land. I think about the paddocks and the streets and the buildings and I imagine what it would be like if people never came over in the ships. The sheep would be gone, the kelpies never coming to be. No horses to tramp down the grass. There'd be no holes in the ground, no scars of tunnels running under the surface. There'd be no Hawthorn or Richmond, no stock exchanges to worry about, no susso to dole out. I imagine what it would be like to scrub away all of that. All the church steeples and dirt-floor cottages and soup bowls and pennies and knives and coal dust. I imagine it all going, wiping away like dust off a windshield.

I think about everything I know vanishing as I look into the eyepiece, my face pointed at the ground but my eyes filled with all the light of the sky.

'What do you see?'

It's Father. He's next to me. I didn't hear him coming. He's standing next to the telescope, his face pale and soft in the moonlight.

I can see him watching me but I can't see his eyes, only a shadow where the light goes in.

'Nothing,' I say.

'Mind if I look?'

I step away from the telescope and Father bends down. Some of his hair comes loose and falls over his forehead. He's still for a long time and then he moves away from the telescope, kneeling in front of me.

'Remember the story of Perseus?'

'Yes,' I say.

'How about Cetus, the sea monster?'

'Killed by Perseus.'

'Very good,' he says, nodding. 'You'll know more than your father soon.'

I grunt. I try to make it sound like the grunts Father let out at Christmas dinner but mine comes out thin and empty. I want to take it back, eat up the sound and draw it back into my body. I don't want him to hear me fail, even at that.

'You used to be frightened by that story,' he says. 'About Cetus, the monster who almost ate the princess. Do you remember? You used to ask me what if Perseus never came to rescue her. It used to frighten you, that part. You were scared by the hand of fate, not the monster itself.'

'I'm not scared anymore,' I say.

I can see Father nodding out of the corner of my eye. I look out over the black land, at the line where the darkness ends and the lights of the sky take over.

'I've got something for you.' He reaches into his coat pocket and takes out a small package. In the moonlight, I can see that it's wrapped in wax paper and tied with twine at the top. 'This is your Christmas present,' he says, holding up the package.

I take the package from Father. He pulls out a lighter and strikes the flint until he gets a flame. I pull on the twine until the paper falls open. Below me, glowing in the flickering light of the flame, is a ribbon. Long and white, the kind women use to tie their hair.

'This ribbon belonged to your mother,' Father says. He clears his throat. 'It belonged to Audrey. I've been carrying it around for many years.'

I reach down and pick up the ribbon, letting the wax paper and twine fall to the ground. The ribbon is soft and silky. I wrap it around my fingers. In my mind, I see the woman in white, ripples in river water, oars shipped to the sides of a rowboat. I see her hair tied with a white ribbon.

'She was wearing it that day on the river,' Father says. 'I can't carry it any longer. It's time you had something of hers to carry with you.'

The boat rocks on the river. The current pulls the bow straight. The ground below me shifts. I bend my knees a little to keep from falling over.

'What happened to her?'

Father gets up off his knees. He places a hand on my shoulder. The ground below me levels out. I'm not shaking anymore.

'Don't you remember?'

'No.'

Father looks at the stars, at the patterns drawn over the sky. 'She left you on the bank of the river, the Yarra, out by the boathouse. You were only little then. She let her boat drift downstream. Let herself go.'

The back of her hair, the ribbon holding the hair above her shoulders. The boat following the current around a shallow bend. I can see her drifting away, getting smaller and smaller, until the trees close in around her and she's gone.

'What happened after that?'

'She drowned, Morris,' Father says. 'She let herself drown downriver. On purpose.'

I see an empty river, the flat surface of the water carved with ripples and eddies. The water is brown, a cloud made of water and clay.

'Why would she do that?'

'She wasn't well,' Father says, squeezing my shoulder. 'She was sick, Morris. Sick in her mind and it was a bad sick that she couldn't heal on her own.'

'Am I sick like her?'

'Do you feel sick?'

'I don't know.'

Father closes the lid on the lighter. He takes hold of both my shoulders and squares me to him. We face each other, out in the darkness of the paddock, under the constellations. I wrap the white ribbon around my fingers. I can just make out Father's eyes in the darkness under his brow.

'If you ever do, you come to me and we'll heal it together.'

'All right,' I say.

Father's hands feel cool on the other side of the cotton covering my shoulders.

'There are parts of life you won't like,' he says. 'I won't pretend otherwise. There are some parts you'll find hard to understand and when you come across them, remember there's also good in the world. It's like the night sky. It's dark and it's cold out there but there are many bright spots if you remember where to look.'

He lets go of my shoulders and picks up the telescope. He pulls the legs of the stand together, clicking them into place, and hitches the telescope over his shoulder.

'Come on,' he says. 'Let's go back now.'

We walk through the paddock until the big house appears, a warm yellow shape getting brighter with every step. I hear Father take a deep breath beside me.

'We're going to talk about her,' he says. 'From now on, we'll do that. Any time you want to talk about her, you say so.'

'All right,' I say.

We keep walking, side by side, the yellow light of the big house shimmering in the distance.

'I should have done it differently. I can see that now,' Father says. 'You know that, don't you?'

'Yes,' I say.

I look to my side, at Father's face bathed in the light of the moon. I look at the bend partway down his nose, at his eyes, wet as the dew.

'All right,' he says. 'All right then.'

We pass the sheds and the big house, and turn down the path to the cottage. The stones of the path are wet under my feet. I change my step so that my feet fall in time with Father's. We walk toward the cottage. The light from the big house fades behind us and I can no longer see our feet rising and falling on the path.

34

The new year comes. The trip around the sun is over. We welcome the new year in one of the paddocks. Uncle Jimmy builds a bonfire with branches that have split and fallen from trees in the storms or the heat. The sun is touching the hills as he lights the kindling at the base of the fire. The flames grow higher as night comes. Father lets us stay as the hours go on, and Aunt Beth warms milk in a small billycan at the edge where the kindling is turning to embers. She pours it into cups and we hold the cups to our lips, our faces lit by the flickering fire. Each of us yawns in turn as the night pushes on.

I look at the stars, at the Milky Way staining the black with light and colour, and I think about all that's changed this past year. The bank runs, the people lining for soup and bread in the streets, the shacks covering every clearing. I think about Phar Lap winning the cup and Iris catching polio and George being stuck indoors. I think about the drive out to Gemini and all that I've seen since Catherine Fletcher was killed. Looking at the constellations, thinking back over this year, it feels the way it does waking from a dream, the pictures hazy, the borders blurred.

Father wraps a blanket around my legs and Uncle Jimmy pulls out his pocket watch. The bonfire is burning down. Low flames skip above the dark red coals.

Father is shaking me. I open my eyes, blinking against the smoke. Aunt Beth strokes Flo's cheek and she wakes, yawning, facing the fire.

'Is it time?' Lottie asks.

'Nearly there,' Uncle Jimmy says, staring at his watch.

Father puts one arm around my shoulder and the other around Lottie's. 'I thought you'd want to see this,' he says. 'Start of a new year. Look over there.' Father lifts his arm from Lottie's shoulder and points at the sky. 'Sirius,' he says. 'The dog star.'

'From Canis Major,' I say.

'It's the brightest star in the sky, the dog star,' Father says. 'Brighter even than Mercury. It reaches its highest point on New Year's Eve, right at the change from one year to the next.'

I follow the line from Father's arm to a star burning bright in the north. Sparks from the fire drift up near the dog star. It outshines them all.

'Here we go,' Uncle Jimmy says. 'Be ready now.' He raises a hand, looking down at his pocket watch.

A few moments pass and then Uncle Jimmy thrusts down his hand. 'Ten,' he says. 'Nine.'

We count down together. I look around the fire at Uncle Jimmy and Aunt Beth and Flo, their faces a dim yellow in the light. I look at Lottie, leaning against Father's side. We count to zero, the fronts of our bodies warmed by the fire, our backs cool against the shadows, and we sing the old song about the days gone by.

241

35

Rain falls in the valley for much of New Year's Day. We dress for tea at the pub. Father has to meet someone about his work and Aunt Beth is feeling unwell, and so Uncle Jimmy is tasked with taking me, Flo and Lottie to tea.

It's a tradition in Gemini, so we're told, to have the first evening meal of the year together. The town gathers to eat side by side, miners and farmers and shopkeepers and nurses and teachers alike. When we get to the pub, it's full to the brim. People are in every booth, every corner. They're raising glasses and patting each other on the backs. They're shouting each other drinks, carrying pints from bar to table. I guess after the past year, the town is keen to make this year a good one. We make our way through the lounge, stepping on the red and gold carpet.

Uncle Jimmy points at the counter. 'Flo, you and Morris set yourselves up there,' he says. 'Order a meal and tell them to put it on my account.'

We climb onto stools. There are bottles stacked high behind the counter, shining in the light coming from the lamps. Brass taps stand in line in front of us.

'Lottie, you come with me. There's someone I want you to meet.'

Uncle Jimmy places a hand on Lottie's back and moves her away. Liam walks over to the taps and leans on a handle, filling a glass with amber liquid. He winks at Flo and talks to us out of the corner of his mouth.

'Your mate Sam is over there,' he says, nodding in the direction of the booths. 'I expect he's been looking for you.'

I see Sam sitting in one of the booths, surrounded by people. It takes a moment for him to look our way and then he's sliding along the seat, weaving past bodies and glasses.

'Thought you'd never make it,' Sam says, climbing onto a stool next to Flo. 'I've been listening to my dad talk about the town budget for an hour. I almost stabbed myself with a fork.'

I look over at the booth and see Art Napier, dressed in his finest, black bow tie and matching waistcoat with silver buttons. He looks around the table as he talks, waves his hands over the drinks. The men around him nod and smile. At the next booth over, I see Mr Cornwell sitting with his family. His wife and three children talk, and Mr Cornwell looks past them over at Mr Napier. Mr Cornwell stares, chewing on his bottom lip.

There's a tapping sound on the bar in front of me.

'Are we eating tonight?' Liam asks.

'Not tonight,' Flo says. 'We're only drinking. Three ales, please.'

'Good try,' Liam says, holding another glass under the taps.

'I've eaten,' Sam says, running a hand over his belly. 'The roast is what you want.'

'Two roast dinners, please,' Flo says. 'On the Turner account.'

Liam sighs and shakes his head.

'I only wish someone would bring in some money tonight. The accounts are filling up faster than the outhouse.'

Liam walks to the other side of the bar, holding two full glasses. I let my eyes wander over the patrons, the tall people and short people, the few moneyed folk in double-breasted suits, the rest in cheap thin ones. The pub is loud with talking and laughing and the sound of glass against glass. At the far end of the bar, Uncle Jimmy nods at a stout woman, who pulls down a bottle of whisky from the shelf behind the bar. She pours the liquid into two short glasses. She hands them to Uncle Jimmy, and he turns and walks to a booth where Lottie is sitting. She's on her own, two empty glasses in front of her. Uncle Jimmy sits in the booth beside Lottie and hands her one of the glasses. He knocks her glass with his and they drink. Lottie's eyes roll back. I wonder what Father would do if he saw this. There's a change in Father when he's near his brother. Something holds him back, holds his tongue. There's a space between the two men, somewhere the words that need to be said drop and fall out of sight.

'Where's your dad, Morris?' Sam asks.

'He's off working,' I say.

'What work's he got to do? The murderer's dead and buried.'

'You think it's solved, do you?' Flo asks.

'You don't?'

Flo folds her arms and shakes her head.

'Have you forgotten about the note we found? That man at the falls. Men don't jump to their deaths without a reason,' Sam says.

'They don't jump if they've been pushed.'

'Pushed? Who pushed him?' Sam asks. 'Morris, what do you think?'

The stout woman walks over to the taps and pulls one of the handles. She stares at us under her brow and looks away.

'I think if my father thinks it's solved, it's solved,' I say, in a whisper.

'You think someone who thinks it's solved goes off to work the case?' Flo asks.

'Maybe he's got paperwork to do,' Sam says.

'Paperwork, at this time?'

'Sure,' Sam says. 'I've seen my dad do paperwork at all hours. Must be a lot of paperwork to do when there are two dead bodies.'

The stout woman looks at us and sniffs, the bottom half of her face rising with the effort. She watches us for a moment before walking away with the glass of beer. I get the sense it's not polite to talk about what happened last year.

I look out across the pub. Will Fletcher walks in through the front door and holds it open. Mary comes in behind, wheeling Ollie. Heads turn. Will Fletcher holds his chin high and his eyes dart around. The heads turn away. Ollie has the blanket over his legs. Mrs Fletcher turns the chair and they disappear behind the mass of bodies.

'Keep your voice down, Sam,' I say.

'Flo brought it up,' Sam says, shrugging. 'I don't care to talk about it. I've had enough of the trouble that comes with it.'

Liam walks over, carrying two plates of food. He places them in front of Flo and me. The steam warms my cheeks.

'Flo, you tell your dad this is the last meal that goes on credit,' he says. 'He's got the biggest account in all Gemini.'

Liam smiles quickly and walks away. Flo stares down at her roast, blinking and frowning, opening and closing her mouth. She looks to be searching for some meaning in the slices of meat, the gravy and the potatoes.

'Smells good,' I say to Flo. 'Don't let it get cold.'

We eat in silence, the sounds of the pub and the people around us filling our ears. The meat and vegetables are tender and warm. The front door opens again and a ghost enters. The man wears his hat low,

245

the shadows cast by the brim barely covering the flood of freckles. Eamon has returned. He takes off his hat and searches the room with his eyes. I push an elbow into Flo's side and she follows my stare out to Eamon. She's off the stool before I can stop her, and I stumble after her as if drawn by rope.

'Where you been hiding?'

Flo stands in front of Eamon, between him and the bar, hands on her hips. Eamon sways, comes to a stop. His jaw hangs loose and I can smell the gin on him over all the smells of the pub.

'Quiet, now, Flo,' Eamon says, his eyes pitching left and right. 'We don't want the whole town hearing us.'

'And why not?'

'Some words can't be taken back. Remember Missus Watson.'

I reach out and take Flo's arm above the elbow, pull her a little closer to me. 'Come on, Flo,' I say. 'Let's get back to our meals.'

Flo shakes her arm free. 'You tell me where you've been and I'll keep it down.'

Eamon rubs the back of his neck. When he lowers his hand, I see the grime on his fingers. 'Not far. Went for a stint of work at another mine, that's all. I'm back now the work has dried up.'

Flo snorts. She looks at me, eyebrows raised. 'You believe that, Morris? Tell him what you think.'

Eamon watches me. The skin under his eyes is loose and puffed. His lips are pale and cracked.

'I think he's back now that the killer is dead and buried,' I say.

'Now that the supposed killer is buried,' Flo says, tapping her boot on the carpet. 'Not that we believe that. We think he left because he was scared of what would happen if his secret got out.'

'And did it?' Eamon's question lingers in the air between us, drowning out the sounds of the chatter and glass and footsteps. Flo shrugs and Eamon smiles, lips peeling back to show the rows of small, yellow-stained teeth. He goes on smiling as he steps past me and Flo but I see something in his eyes as he goes. I see something I know well. There is fear in his eyes.

When we get back to the bar, Sam is looking away, out to where his father is seated.

'Where do you think Eamon went?' Flo asks as we get back on our stools. 'Where's he really been?'

Will Fletcher walks to the bar and calls the stout woman over. I watch Eamon shake a man's hand and then shake another. He's no more than five yards from Fletcher. He could call out to him, talk to him the way he might any other miner. I see Eamon glance at Will Fletcher and turn away, just another man in the crowd of townspeople.

'Either in the bush or down to the city,' I say. 'He looks like he hasn't slept all that much. Father says if you want to disappear, you need to go where nobody is or where everybody is.'

'Seems like the kind who would go to the city,' Flo says. 'Doubt he would've lasted this long in the bush.'

'Can we stop talking about Eamon?' Sam asks, looking back at us.

'I'm wondering if Uncle Jude is chasing down a lead on him,' Flo says. 'Maybe he knows Eamon's back and he thinks it was him all along and that's what he's doing tonight, working the case.'

'It's solved,' Sam says. 'Give it a rest.'

'Sam's right,' I say. 'Eamon's a coward. You said it yourself.'

I reach over and take one of Flo's potatoes. I lift it to my mouth and blow. 'From now on there's a one-potato tax whenever you talk about Catherine Fletcher. Sam, you can get your father to put that on the books, right?'

Sam smiles. He reaches over, takes a potato from Flo's plate and drops it in his mouth. 'Sure I can,' he says. 'I'll forge his signature if I have to.'

'Seeing as you took two potatoes, I've got one more thing to say,' Flo says. 'Either it was Will Fletcher or it was Eamon. Nobody's going to tell me someone who's been in town a minute had reason to kill Catherine. Whoever killed her was someone who knew her.'

There's shouting over at the windows that look out on the street. We turn our heads but I can't see who's doing the shouting. It's two men, I can tell that much, but I can't make out any more other than the name-calling, the animals one man is comparing the other to. I look to the other side of the bar. Will Fletcher and Eamon are missing.

'Come on,' Flo says, dropping her cutlery. 'Let's get closer.'

We push through the crowd, staying close to the wall, until we're near enough to the shouting to see who's doing it. One man has another man pressed to a window, his hand on the man's collar. The man against the window, with one arm raised in surrender and the other arm holding off his attacker, is Will Fletcher.

'It wasn't like that,' Will Fletcher says. 'It only happened the once and not for any reason.'

The other man swings an arm low, losing it in Will Fletcher's belly. Fletcher's knees go weak, legs splitting apart like firewood on the block. The man holds him upright. Two more men rush over to the attacker and try to pull him off, but he shakes them loose.

'I can't see,' I say to Flo. 'Who is it?'

Flo steps back, letting me take the space in front of her. I lean forward, searching for the man's face. It's the cook. Elliot. His face is red and his hair is damp with sweat.

'Don't lie to me,' Elliot says to Fletcher. 'I know it's more than once.'

His fist falls on Will Fletcher's nose. Blood streams down Will Fletcher's face, curling over and around his lips, dripping from his chin. He turns and spits at the window, spraying blood on the glass.

'I had to hear it from the mayor,' the cook says. 'Not even the reverend. The bloody mayor.'

I think back to the night of the festival, of Mr Napier talking to the cook's wife. The way he whispered in her ear, the way she fled from him.

'It won't happen again,' Will Fletcher says. 'I swear it.'

'I know it,' Elliot says. 'You come within ten feet of my wife and I'll put you six feet under. I don't care who sees me do it.'

The men come again to pull the cook away. This time, he lets them. As they drag him off, he kicks at Will Fletcher, boot landing on Fletcher's left knee. Will Fletcher cries out, drops to his haunches, holds his knee. Tears fall down his face, mixing with the blood flowing from his nose. The people gathered around turn away and walk back toward the bar. Mary Fletcher walks against the tide, making for the front doors of the pub, pushing Ollie.

'Mary! Mary, wait!'

Mary Fletcher opens the doors and leaves with Ollie. Will Fletcher hobbles to the door, out of the pub, chasing after his wife. A few men, red-faced and swaying, walk out of the pub as if entering a theatre. We follow.

It's getting dark and the breeze is coming down off the mountains, making a thick fog in the valley. It's a strange sight, the air close and glowing with the light leaking from the windows of the pub. Mary Fletcher is pushing Ollie on to the dirt of the street, wheels carving dark grooves in the damp road. Will Fletcher rushes to her, clings to her shoulder the way a drowning man holds to driftwood.

'Wait, Mary,' he says. 'Will you wait and let me speak?'

Mary Fletcher stops. She stands, holding tight to the handles of the wheelchair. We move away from the light, Flo, Sam and me, over to the shadows outside the cobbler's store. The drunk men lean against the columns of the pub, not hiding, not finding shadows of their own. One of the men laughs, a deep laugh that seems to rise from his belly. Will Fletcher looks over his shoulder at the men.

'Shut your mouth,' he says. 'Get away.'

The men stay where they are. Mary Fletcher turns, the wheels of the chair grinding into the road. Ollie is looking down at his hands, down at his lap. He doesn't look up.

'Go on back,' Mary Fletcher says. 'Go on and face what you've done. Have yourself a drink and see if you can live this down.'

'Mary,' Will Fletcher says. 'It was a mistake, that's all. Nothing more.'

'Your son knows about your mistake now,' she says, her voice high. 'The whole town knows about it.'

Will Fletcher falls to his knees in the dirt. 'You've got to know I didn't mean to,' he says. 'Something took me over. You've got to know that's how it was.'

The men outside the pub laugh. One man lets out a hacking cough.

Mary Fletcher lifts her face, pale skin shining against the fog. She stares at the men. 'Go on,' she says. 'Haven't you seen enough? Go on if you have any decency in you.'

The men turn and walk through the doors, back into the pub. The muffled sound of voices rises and falls as the doors swing open, draw shut. A stillness falls over the street, cut only by the soft sounds of the breeze pushing through the leaves of trees by the river, of the water rushing around rocks.

Mary walks close, stands over her husband. Her shoulders are low, her fingers curled into fists. 'You were with her that night.'

Will Fletcher keeps his head down, facing the dirt. I watch his brown and grey hair, lit by the glow from the pub, watching it for any movement. He's still as a rock. He looks shrunken somehow, as if the cook beat him down to a smaller shape.

'When Catherine died. You were with that woman, weren't you?'

I think about what Ollie said to me, about Will Fletcher getting home when the sun was coming up. Dirt on the knees of his trousers. He must've met the cook's wife somewhere dark and secret where the lights of the town wouldn't find them.

Will Fletcher doesn't speak. His back hunches, head dips lower.

Mary Fletcher lifts one arm and points a pale finger at his head. 'Your daughter was lying out there and you were off with a woman. You're going to have to know that. For the rest of your days, you're going to have to know you were off with a woman on your daughter's last night in the world.'

Mary Fletcher lowers her arm, stands still in the fog. She seems to rise above the street. She looks like a monument. They stay that way for a moment, this family. Mary standing tall, Ollie staring at his lap, Will facing down. We look on from the shadows. And then Mary Fletcher turns and wheels Ollie away, their bodies slipping into the fog. Will Fletcher stays behind, looking for all the world as though he wishes the ground to swallow him whole.

36

There's a sound in the air, deep and hollow like someone hit a barrel. It's coming from Will Fletcher. Out there on his knees in the fog, his body bent close to the dirt, his collar a few inches from the ground. Will Fletcher is making this sound.

Mary and Ollie are long gone. We stay in the shadows, Flo and Sam and me, under the awning of the cobbler's store.

'Should we do something?' I ask, in a whisper.

'For him?' Flo asks. Even in the dark, I can see the top of her nose rise into a mess of wrinkles.

'He didn't do it, Flo,' I say. 'He didn't kill Catherine. You heard Mrs Fletcher. He was off with the cook's wife.'

'He may not have killed her but he did a lot besides,' she says.

I think back to the day we went to the Fletcher house. I remember Will Fletcher's hand rising high above his head like a salute. I remember Ollie in the yard, the way he looked at me, at my face through the gaps in the broken fence. The way he looked at me as I took in all the broken parts of his home.

We stay in the shadows, looking on, and Will Fletcher moves. He lays a palm in the dirt, bends his elbow. It seems to take all his strength to push himself up. He rises to his feet and walks into the fog.

'Where's he going?' Sam asks.

'His house isn't that way,' Flo says.

Fletcher's feet fall hard on the dirt road. The sound gets softer as he moves from the light. The street is wet with the day's rain and the fog, and his footprints are a path leading into the darkness.

'Come on,' I say. 'We can follow his steps.'

We keep some distance between us and Fletcher, following his tracks as he moves along the main street. I see some people in the distance, at the edge of what the fog will show. They're moving into the light, into a doorway. The door to the police station. I can see the outlines of men, caps in hands. They're walking behind someone shorter, an old woman by the pitch of her hips and the curve of her back. A bearded man greets them at the door. Father.

Will Fletcher turns from the main street and we follow as the tracks turn right and the road starts to slope up, climbing to the base of Castor. We get glimpses of Will Fletcher when the breeze clears space in the fog. We see him moving slow, head hanging forward as if in prayer.

'Where's he going?' I ask.

'We shouldn't be doing this,' Sam says. 'We should go back.'

Sam stops walking. His eyes are glassy in the light that shows through the fog. We stop beside him.

'What do you think, Morris?' Flo asks. 'Should we go back?'

I look at the path Will Fletcher left in the dirt, boot prints in the damp. We could go back now and pretend we don't have any more questions. We could keep our doubts inside, keep the words from getting out, let them stack like bricks until there's nothing but walls inside us. Do what I did with Mother, close our eyes and pretend it doesn't bother us. We could walk away or we could walk on, keep looking, keep asking.

'We should keep going,' I say.

Sam takes a step back.

'We should see this out,' I say. 'I don't want to keep it all inside anymore, all the questions. I want to know this time. I want to make my life about knowing.'

Sam and Flo share a look across the veil of fog. I get a feeling that I've said too much. I feel open, a shell cracked down the middle, the parts inside leaking out. It feels strange and new.

Sam steps forward. 'We better catch up with him, then,' he says.

Sam and Flo walk on up the slope, following the marks in the dirt. I push on behind them, the feeling inside me starting to cool, the heat fading without a flame.

There are faint outlines of homes on our left and right, pictures that appear in the fog and then vanish. The homes are quiet. They stop appearing as the road twists and narrows, and sends us up the steep side of the hill. Ghostly trees tower over us. Branches spread into the fog. I can hear Flo and Sam breathing heavily. My breath doesn't come easy either. My legs ache with the effort of climbing and bracing for falls. Then we see it. There's an arch spanning over the path. Inside it, spun around the frame, are words spelled out in thin, rusted iron. Gemini Cemetery.

Everything in me wants to turn and run back to the cottage where it's warm and safe. I want to be away from everything that's on the other side of that iron. My breath is fast and my throat is burning. I feel someone take my hand. It's Flo. She's standing next to me, holding my hand, swinging it like a toy.

'Let's find out what he's doing,' she says.

We walk on past the arch, into the wide opening of the cemetery.

We pass grey tombstones, some newly carved, some covered in the veins of creeper vines. It's still and quiet. I can't hear Will Fletcher's footsteps on the soft mud and flattened clover. I can't hear my own feet as they fall. There's no sound other than the faint shiver of gum leaves whenever a breeze passes over the cemetery.

'Where did he go?' Sam asks, in a whisper. 'I can't see him.'

The paths and stones around us start to make sense to me. It starts to fit like a key sliding into a lock. I know where we are and I know where Will Fletcher will be.

'This way,' I say.

We climb higher and the fog starts to lift. I look at the sky and see Taurus and Eridanus and Orion, guiding us on. I see Gemini, the heads of Castor and Pollux, the two brothers. It's beautiful from up here, high above the town. We move around a bend in the path and I see him. Will Fletcher. He's facing us, looking down at Catherine's grave. I reach out with both hands and catch hold of Flo and Sam, holding tight to their wrists. I pull them to the thick base of a gum tree and we stand behind it, looking around the edge of the bark.

'I should've been better,' Will Fletcher says.

I think back to the day of Catherine Fletcher's funeral. I remember standing in the sun, all the townspeople sweating under black clothes. I remember Will Fletcher standing where he is now, eyes dry and empty.

'I don't know how to do it,' he says. 'I don't know how to be better.'

Here in the dark, the moon taking the place of the sun, Will Fletcher's tears come. They drip from his chin down to the grave. The tears mix with the mud, the way the falling rain soaked the soil near the entrance to Long Tunnel East, the night Catherine Fletcher died.

We watch as he drops to his knees and then to his side. He lies down next to his daughter's grave, pulling his knees to his chest. He curls his neck, bending his head toward his knees. Will Fletcher stays there, silent and as small as I've ever seen a man. We watch him, the stars blinking and shifting above us, and then we turn away.

37

We walk through the dark and empty streets, past the still houses, turning whatever way moves us downhill.

'We have to get back to the pub,' Sam says. 'My dad will be rounding up a search party.'

'They'll all be drunk,' Flo says. 'They'll end up lost themselves.'

'We'll wind up searching for them,' I say. 'It'll go back and forth forever in this fog. Someone getting found and then the next person getting lost.'

'My dad will lose half his votes,' Sam says.

'At least he'll only need to campaign half as hard,' I say.

We laugh, pressing on down the hill toward the light coming from the pub. I can see it out there growing a little brighter with every step. Bobbing out on the ocean of fog. We're still laughing when I hear another laugh in the distance. It's a high and strange laugh, carried on the fog like a siren.

'Did you hear that? There's someone out there,' I say.

We move across the street and into some cleared bush. There's a gap between two houses, and we walk on our toes past the trampled ferns and wide tree stumps, tops cut flat as a table. We stay quiet, stepping carefully around strips of dried bark and mounds of dead gum leaves that have been swept by winds into piles against the low fences. And then I see Lottie, standing against the steel of Uncle Jimmy's truck. She's leaning against the hood, her head rolling to one side. She lets out another laugh, quieter this time.

'What are you doing over there?' Lottie says.

I step forward, about to walk out of the fog, out of the shadows and over to Lottie. Sam grips my wrist and pulls me back.

'Wait,' he says, his voice cold and low. 'Don't you know where we are?'

I look around at the dark houses, faint in the fog. I look at the ferns, at the tree stumps, at the fences. There are gaps in the fence up ahead where the fog leaks through, into a yard that's too dark to make out. Fingers appear at the top of the fence, curling over from the other side. Another hand appears, holding some flowers. Lilies.

'The Fletcher house,' I say.

We drop to a crouch. Flo stays standing. We pull on her arms until she falls to the ground, her eyes wide, mouth open. A body rises into the fog ahead of us, lifting over the fence, one hand still holding the lilies. Uncle Jimmy.

'Quiet,' he says. 'You want to wake the street?'

Uncle Jimmy drops to the ground and walks away from where we are, over to Lottie. She's swaying against the hood of the truck. She looks as though she's dancing in place.

'I don't care,' she says. 'Let them wake up. It's plenty early.'

Uncle Jimmy laughs once. It's a short and sharp sound like a bull panting. 'I picked these for you,' he says. 'You like them?'

He hands the flowers to Lottie. She holds them in front of her eyes, turning them over, watching the petals droop.

'Why do you keep giving me lilies?'

'Every pretty girl deserves flowers,' Uncle Jimmy says. 'These are the best in town.'

Lottie looks around, at the street, at the broken fence, at the dark trees in the distance. Her head rolls. The muscles that hold it stretch out and loosen like the hems on old trousers.

'This is an awful town,' she says.

'Come on,' Uncle Jimmy says, reaching a hand behind Lottie and pulling her away from the hood. 'Let's go someplace.' He pulls her close and Lottie sways in his arms. She turns and moves away. Uncle Jimmy walks behind her, close enough he's almost leaning on her. He pulls open the door of the truck. Lottie lifts one leg and falls in. Uncle Jimmy laughs again, the same animal sound. He walks around the hood, shaking his head, and gets in on the other side. The engine turns over and the truck moves away, falling down the hill to town.

'What was that?' asks Sam.

'I don't know,' I say.

'Why is he giving her flowers from the Fletcher place?'

Sam looks at Flo. I look at Flo. She's staring at the place the truck was parked. She's still, her breath going in and out in short bursts.

'Flo,' Sam says. 'What was that?'

Flo keeps breathing fast through her mouth. Me and Sam stand, but she stays crouching for a time. When she finally stands, her eyes are fixed and hard against the fog.

'It was nothing,' she says.

'Flo,' I say, reaching out and touching her arm. 'That was more than nothing.'

Flo turns her shoulder and moves away from my hand. She looks to be trapped in her thoughts. She's in a cage, pressed against the bars, looking out at what she can't reach. Not looking at what's in there with her.

'It was nothing,' she says. 'He's only taking her home. We should go back. It's a damn fool business standing out here in the fog.'

'I don't think he's taking her home,' Sam says, staring at the rough boards of the fence where Uncle Jimmy climbed over.

The night Catherine Fletcher died, she must have climbed over that fence. I picture her hands appearing over the boards, slim fingers holding on to wood. I picture her head coming into view. Her eyes, her cheeks, her nose. I picture her coming over the boards and I want to tell her to go back, not to come any further, not to drop over this side. Go back to the house, climb back through the window, pull down the sheets and lie in bed. Don't come out in the dark. After these months in Gemini, I know it wouldn't have done any good. She was never going to stay in that house. She was always going over that fence. The problem wasn't her leaving, it was what came to meet her.

'What would you know? He's taking her home,' Flo says, her voice rising. 'He's my father and he's taking her home. Don't you have to be getting back to your folks?'

Flo's words hang in the air, wrapping low around the grey tree stumps and leaves. Someone must have heard her. I look around, waiting for a match to flare in the dark, for a candle to float through the fog toward us.

'Keep your voice down,' I say. 'Mary and Ollie are in there.'

'Let them hear.' Flo looks out at the fog, chews her lip. 'He was away selling lambs when she died. I saw him leave, days before. You saw him come back, Morris. You saw it the day you came here.' Flo looks at me. Her eyes are swept away, lost and flooded.

'Something's going on,' I say. 'We have to follow them.'

'Follow them where? I know where they're going and I'm going there too. I'm going home.'

'He gave her lilies, Flo,' I say. 'Lilies from the Fletcher house.'

'Come back with me, Morris. Please.'

I shake my head. Flo steps back, her boots sliding over the damp ground.

'I'm going home,' she says. 'You can come with me or you can go jump in the river for all I care.'

She turns and walks back the way we came. She starts to fade as she moves into the fog, more hidden with every step. Crows call from the trees around us. Wet drips down the boards of the fence. I look at Sam and I can see his face, pale as a bedsheet.

'Sam,' I say.

'I know,' he says.

38

Two thin lines stretch down the street. The marks left behind by
the truck's tyres, dark as stains of sweat. Me and Sam run beside the
lines, boots slipping on the road. We turn a corner and I see bicycles
lying in the yard of a house, metal wheels shining in the faint light
of the moon. I pull on Sam's shirt and we rush over to them and lift
them gently, careful not to make a sound. We let them roll us away
from the house, waiting until we're forty yards clear before we press
on the pedals.

The lines stretch on through the night, crossing here and there
with the marks left by drays and wagons. Birds pass overhead, wings
like the visions in dreams, coming in and out of view. Lights wink
on and off in the distance. I see a car pass, the metal sleek as a fish
underwater. A man in the front seat, a face I've known all my life.
The beard below the chin, the hook halfway down his nose.

'That's my father,' I say. 'In that car there.'

We call out to him, sending our voices out into the fog. The
lights from Father's car slide further into the fog, they rise and pull
to the left, and then they're gone. Father disappears uphill, off in the
direction of the rail tracks.

We pedal on, following the marks from Uncle Jimmy's truck downhill and then out to the other side of town, over near the slope of Pollux. The marks take us near the river and I can sense where we're going, where Uncle Jimmy has gone. I know it before we get there, before me and Sam see the path. The one that's mostly hidden from the street, the one that leads to Gemini Falls.

We drop the bicycles near the start of the path and step carefully in the places where the mud will hide our sounds, where there are no dead leaves or sticks. When we get near the end of the path, where it opens out to the clearing and the wide part of the river beneath the falls, Sam takes hold of my arm. He leads me into the bush. I say a prayer in my mind, one that I've heard in church, as we step around fallen branches and strips of bark.

Sam crouches behind a gum tree and I settle on my knees beside him. Up ahead, in the clearing, the light from Uncle Jimmy's truck reaches to the bank and the water beyond. The fog is thinner here. The river shines like the barrel of a gun. I can see the ripples from the falls spreading out from the sinking water. In the light, between the truck and the bank, Uncle Jimmy and Lottie are dancing.

'I'm cold,' Lottie says.

Uncle Jimmy pulls Lottie close. His hands slide up and down her back. 'It's all right,' he says. 'It's all right.'

'I'm cold and my head. The trees are spinning.'

'It's all right.' He makes a sound like he's cooing at a baby. His hands move on Lottie's back, over her dress.

'It looks so odd,' Lottie says. 'The world is spinning. Is this what it's like to see the world spinning through space?'

'Of course. It's all right. Everything's all right.' Uncle Jimmy's hand slides low on Lottie's back. His head dips down and his face is lost behind Lottie's hair, down somewhere near Lottie's neck.

'Let go.' She pulls herself free and backs away from Uncle Jimmy. She trips, goes down on one arm. There's a sound like the pigs at the farm make, a high sound that comes from Lottie when she lands on the mud and flattened grass. Uncle Jimmy holds out a hand.

'Here,' he says.

Lottie turns away from Uncle Jimmy. She rises from the ground on her own, up on one knee and then the other, finds her feet. She sways in the light from the truck. 'You're disgusting,' she says.

Uncle Jimmy stares at Lottie, his head as steady as a nail in wood. He rubs his hands together in front of his body. The way he rubs them, it's as though he needs to. He has to keep them busy out there in front of his body to stop him from doing something else with them. I can feel my heart start to speed up. It's a hammer swinging in my body, driving me down into the dirt beside the gum trees. I look over at Sam. His mouth is open. I can see his lips in the faint light, dry even with the fog that wets our hair and sleeves and collars.

'Don't say that,' Uncle Jimmy says.

'You are,' Lottie says, backing away to the truck, her body swaying, dress shading the light from the headlamps. 'You shouldn't touch me that way. I'm your niece.'

Uncle Jimmy looks over at the dark river. 'That's only a word,' he says. 'A word like any other. Don't mean anything.'

'It means something,' Lottie says. 'Everyone knows it means something.'

Uncle Jimmy walks to the water's edge. He picks up a stone and throws it low to the water, skipping it over the steel-blue surface. It bounces three times on the water before dropping and sinking out of sight.

'Can we go home?' Lottie asks.

Uncle Jimmy reaches into the water and picks up another stone. This one is as big as his hand. He holds it in his palm, stares at it, feels the weight of it. Then he pitches it over the water. It falls to the river and splashes out there in the darkness. I remember stones like that, wet stones that slipped from the trousers of Charlie Coates, sinking back to the place he was found.

Uncle Jimmy turns back to face Lottie. 'You know what word we should be thinking about? Leave. That's the word we should be thinking about.'

Lottie lifts her chin and spreads her arms wide, bracing them against the hood of the truck. I can see her head bobbing in the light.

'Leave where?'

'Anywhere,' Uncle Jimmy says, taking a step toward Lottie. 'We could leave this town behind, go far away. Don't you want to go somewhere new, somewhere exciting? We could go away somewhere with lights and music and money flowing in the streets. Where the people are rich and beautiful and free of any troubles.'

'There's nowhere like that.'

'There is,' Uncle Jimmy says, walking closer to Lottie. 'There are boats leaving every day. All we have to do is get tickets. Simple as that. You buy a ticket and end up in a city where a man can really make something of himself. Where he can live a big life instead of settling for a small one.'

'What would we do there?'

'Anything. Everything. People are leaving every day. They're packing a case and walking out the door. It's happening all over this country. People leaving for somewhere better. Right now, this is the time to start again. The way the world is, it's the perfect time to leave.'

Uncle Jimmy kneels and scoops up a handful of dirt. He turns and throws it over the water.

'I hate this town,' he says. 'This isn't what I wanted, it's what got chosen for me.'

'What about Aunt Beth and Flo?'

'They'd get on fine. Just fine. They'd be better, even. They're happy with this place. This is what they want, but I need something more than this life. Don't you see that? This small life. A farm that won't make money, a town that'll never change. A place where the storms roll in and they all cower like dogs. It's pathetic. I refuse to live like that. I need something better.'

Uncle Jimmy walks to Lottie. He walks close and she slides her hips away, along the grille at the front of the truck. He takes her face in his hands and she pulls away.

'You're disgusting.'

Uncle Jimmy raises a hand and brings the back of it down on Lottie's face. She falls to the ground, her dress riding up one leg, white stockings streaked with mud.

'I told you not to say that,' Uncle Jimmy says, standing over Lottie. 'I won't have anyone else talk to me that way. I won't have it.'

My eyes are on Lottie, lying on her back on the wet ground, one arm bent behind her back. She turns onto her side. I feel a heat rising inside me. It starts in my chest and it moves up my neck, settles in my cheeks. My fingers curl into my palms. I rise to my feet but Sam holds tight to my shirt and pulls me down. Uncle Jimmy is walking toward us. He's walking away from Lottie, away from the truck and the light, over to the edge of the bush.

'She had a mouth on her too.'

I can hear his boots crushing the damp leaves and bark. He's no more than eight yards away. His body is a black shape, lit from behind. He doesn't see Sam and me crouching low in the bush, the thick leaves above blocking out the sky.

'I won't have that. I won't have anyone talk to me that way.'

I want to pull all the rocks of these hills down on my uncle's head. I want to bury him under stone and mud. I want to lay him flat to the ground, press him down until he disappears into the earth. Keep piling the hills on him until a new mountain rises above him, rises in sharp slopes to a summit nobody can reach. I want people to see it from miles around, to know that this is the place where he fell.

The light shifts and I see Lottie moving past the headlamps. She's running toward the path, lurching forward like she's reaching for something. Uncle Jimmy turns and chases after her. He reaches her, grabs hold of her hair. Lottie's head pitches back. I see her breath rising above her, mixing with the fog. Uncle Jimmy wraps an arm around her chest and throws her back. She falls, head striking the ground. She lies on her back, moaning.

I touch the heather on the chain around my neck. It's as cold as river water. I look at Uncle Jimmy and I feel my face burn. My blood is a storm. Sticks crack beneath me as I rush out of the bush and into the clearing, the fog going in and out of my lungs. I look over my shoulder and I see Sam coming out of the bush, hair peeling back from his face.

'Morris?'

Uncle Jimmy is standing over Lottie. He sees me run at him. I'm ten yards away when a light floods Uncle Jimmy's face, turns his white shirt bright as the day it was made. The light covers everything. The falls, the river, the bank. It makes the fog above Lottie bright as the air in a picture house. I stop running. Uncle Jimmy lifts a hand to his eyes and squints. There's a car coming up the path, wheels slipping in the soft dirt.

'Get away from her, James.' It's Father. He's walking from the car, moving into the light, one hand held up, palm out, the other low by his side. I can see the pistol at his hip, dark as a snake.

'Here we go,' Uncle Jimmy says. 'What you got there?'

Father glances at me and Sam. He waves an arm like he's paddling water. 'Behind me, boys,' he says.

Uncle Jimmy steps between Father and Lottie. She moans again, a deep sound that rattles in the air.

'You ever use one of those, Jude? Ever needed to? We're no stranger to them out here. Got some much bigger than that. You been away so long you wouldn't remember.'

Father takes another step toward Uncle Jimmy and Lottie. He wraps an arm around Sam and pulls him in behind him. 'I know it all,' Father says. 'There's nothing you can do now.'

'What do you know? Go on, tell me.'

'I heard it from the old woman at the camp. She came to me and told me what she remembers. I've been looking for you all night. This is the end of it now, James. I know you didn't take those lambs to market. I know you went to the camp after you did what you did, that you hid out there and bribed that man, gave him the lambs for his silence.'

Uncle Jimmy clicks his tongue. He squints at Father. 'Is that right? Look at you, then. You got it all figured out, don't you?'

Father walks slowly, inching closer to me. I think back to the time me and Flo helped set traps for rabbits near the camp. I remember the clearing with the bones. Little bones bleached white by the summer sun. A little pile of lambs that were meant for market.

Father keeps walking and Uncle Jimmy reaches a hand into his trouser pocket.

'I wouldn't get too close,' Uncle Jimmy says. He raises his hand and something catches the light. He pulls on it with his thumb and a blade rises above his hand, cool steel slicing into the fog. Father moves a little closer to me.

'I know that man from the camp didn't end up in the river on his own,' Father says. 'He didn't go over those falls. What happened? Did he keep asking for more? Did he tell you he might not keep your secret after all?'

Uncle Jimmy snorts, the sound spreading low around us. He points the blade of the knife at Father.

'You're one to talk. You want to talk about secrets? You told your boy here about why you left Gemini?'

'That's not why we're here.'

Uncle Jimmy takes a step toward Father, blade held out. His breathing is fast. 'It is why we're here. It's why everything's how it is. It's your fault. You leaving made everything happen.'

Lottie shifts behind Uncle Jimmy. She goes up on one elbow, her mouth open, tongue rolling against her lips.

'Did you tell your boy how our father was? How he turned after Ma died?'

Father is a few yards from me. I move a little closer to Lottie. She feels the back of her head with her free hand. The dirt is dark where her head hit.

'Do you even remember? Is that it? You don't remember what he was like? The way he drank whisky like it was water. How it was when his mood turned black. You remember that? Even in all those acres there was nowhere to hide.'

I take another step toward Lottie. Uncle Jimmy doesn't see me move. He's watching Father, his world narrowed to the place where his brother stands.

'You left me there with him. That's what you did. You took off to the city and never came back and I had to take it all. I had to take all the words, all the beatings. It all came down on me. I had to come of age under that man. And when he got sick from all the drink, I had

269

to nurse him. Had to bury him when his liver finally gave out. I did that. All alone.'

I'm close to Lottie. I can see the way her hair shines in the lamplight, the way the loose strands curl above her. I can see the colour on her hand as she pulls it away from the back of her head, the way her eyes roll back when she sees it.

'I got left with a farm that wants to ruin me. No money. No prospects. A family that doesn't respect me. Why shouldn't I want more? Why shouldn't I have a better life like you? I lost my life to that man and those paddocks. When is it my turn? Why shouldn't I start over?'

I'm almost at Lottie. If I lunged forward, I could reach her. I'm almost around the back of Uncle Jimmy. His body trembles in the fog, his shoulders shaking, boots almost tapping in the mud. I see the pistol by Father's side, the way his arm hangs straight as an arrow, pointing to the ground.

'I know it's been hard for you,' Father says. 'I know that.'

'You know, do you? I used to meet her here. Is that one of the things you know?'

Uncle Jimmy waves the knife at the falls. The sound of the rushing water seems to grow when he does it and I remember the way the man with the scar looked when they fished him out of the water. The way his skin looked, the way his clothes seemed to be holding him together.

'She told me she didn't need me. After everything I'd done for her, everything I'd risked for her. I put everything on the line and she wanted to leave on her own. Choose her brother over me. She was going to throw me away like I was worthless. That was too much. Far too much.'

Uncle Jimmy waves the knife over his shoulder.

'I had to drag her through this bush to the mine. That's not something that leaves a man. You don't know what that's like. That's not something you know. I know. I know what it's like.'

I think about the cuts on Catherine Fletcher's legs. They weren't from walking through the bush. They were from being dragged. The dry soil under her body, at the entrance to the tunnel. She bled all the way from here to the mine.

'Did you know she was with child?'

'What?'

'She would've known,' Father says. 'The night she died, she would've known about it.'

I reach down and touch Lottie's shoulder. Her face turns to me, eyes rolling in her head.

'A child,' Uncle Jimmy says, his voice soft.

Lottie reaches out and takes hold of my arm. She pulls me down. I fall over her, letting out a sound as the air is knocked out of me. Uncle Jimmy turns and looks down at us. I lie over Lottie. I hold a palm out at Uncle Jimmy, at the knife, at the rage behind his eyes.

'Get away from her,' I say.

His face seems to fall. The lines above his brow flatten out. His mouth hangs open. He lowers his hand, lowers the knife. He keeps lowering it until it rests by his side, blade pointing at the ground.

'She was with child,' he says.

His eyes are like pearls in the light. His jaw drops lower, his tongue rises to his top teeth. He's about to say something, and then his head kicks back. Father is behind him, pressing into his back, holding on to his arm. I watch the knife shift in the air, forward and back, up and down. I kneel next to Lottie, looking up at Father and Uncle Jimmy. They're joined together. Two brothers. Two stars in a constellation, moving across the sky. They keep moving, the blade shifting and falling, and then the blade is gone. The steel has disappeared. Father backs away from Uncle Jimmy. He walks slowly, each step like a fall. He looks down at his belly. The knife is in him, the blade lost beneath his skin. He goes down on his knees, slowly like in a prayer, staring at his brother. The anger is gone from Uncle Jimmy's face now the blade is gone from his hand. I watch Father and I see no anger in him either. I see nothing but a man with all his mind set on his brother, the man who put the knife in him.

The lights are moving across Father's face before I know Uncle Jimmy is gone. Uncle Jimmy drives the truck along the bank, wheels kicking up mud, spreading it like seed over the ground. He runs the truck along the river and turns toward the bush. The lights from the truck pass once more over Father's face and then they're gone, moving along a path I didn't know was there, one that cuts through the thick gum trees, out in the direction of the mine.

Father stays on his knees in the mud. His shoulders sag and I crawl over to him.

'I can't feel it,' he says. 'I see it but I can't feel it.'

'Sam, go get help,' I say.

Sam is over by Father's car. I can see the side of his face, his mouth hanging open.

'Sam!'

Sam turns and runs along the path, toward the place we left the bicycles. I hear tyres turning the dirt and then the sound fades away. There's only the sound of the falls behind me and Father's breath going in and out in front of me. He's looking down at the knife, sticking out like another limb. I take hold of Father's hand. He turns his face to me.

'You'll be all right,' I say. 'Don't worry. You'll be all right.'

39

They have Father over at the clinic. A small building, thick walls white as chalk and a high-pitched roof that seems to point to the heavens.

Father is one of two patients in the clinic. The other is a man by the name of McAndrews who fell off his horse the night Father arrived. McAndrews has a cast covering his leg. The bone snapped clean in half below his knee and pushed through the skin like a dead tree reaching up through floodwaters.

I learned all this from Aunt Beth, more or less. She's been out to see Father but we're not allowed in yet. Aunt Beth has been careful around me and Lottie these past days. She patched up the cut on Lottie's head, has us sleeping in the big house. Men have been coming in and out every day, talking about Uncle Jimmy, asking questions. Aunt Beth cried a full day after it happened but since then she's been making tea, baking biscuits, scrubbing floors. She's been as busy as an ant, from dawn until dusk, never stopping, never falling idle.

The men that come to the big house want to know about that night at the falls. They ask questions of me and Lottie, drawing out what we know like water from a well. They ask Aunt Beth questions about where he might be hiding, where Uncle Jimmy might be headed. One of the men says he could be halfway to Tasmania, riding above the waves to a quiet place on that island. Another says he could've gone inland, where the soil is red and the sun bakes the flat land. He could've gone bush, sleeping under the thick blanket of leaves, trapping animals for food, tracking streams for water. Going by a different name. Growing whiskers. Plenty of folks moving around these days, says one of the men. What with the hard times, it's near impossible to track any one man down.

When they talk of Uncle Jimmy, I think also of Catherine Fletcher. About how alone she must have felt to go to him. She must've wanted to leave Gemini, to find someone who could take her away, but at the moment she could leave, she found a reason to stay. She chose her brother and it was the last choice she made.

Flo hasn't said a word to me or Lottie, not since that night. She takes her meals in her bedroom. She won't leave it other than to wash or draw water from the well or use the outhouse. I saw her one day sliding her feet across the floorboards of the hall, her eyes cast down as though searching for gold. All those questions she used to ask have dried up, all the questions about Catherine and who killed her. The questions she has now stay locked inside her.

A week has passed since the night at the falls. I'm sitting on the bed, looking out the window at the thin white clouds that drift above the front paddock when Aunt Beth and Lottie walk into the room. Aunt Beth is wearing her wide-brimmed hat. Lottie is messing with the hair by her ears, pulling it free and then curling it and running it back behind her ear.

'Come on, Morris,' Aunt Beth says. 'Your dad's ready to see you.'

We wait on the front porch and watch the dust move toward us over the tops of the trees that line the drive to the farm. The dust draws closer and closer, and a car comes into view between the trees. Aunt Beth waves a handkerchief and the car stops. Mr Napier steps out. He takes off his hat and nods.

'Missus Turner. Children,' he says. 'Please.'

He offers a hand and we walk down the steps. The car smells like an old leather armchair inside, rich and smoky. My head floats with the smell.

We ride in silence. It's not until we're past the church and parked in front of the clinic that Mr Napier turns in his seat. He looks at me and Lottie.

'Your father's a brave man,' he says. 'I expect you know that.'

'Thank you, sir,' Lottie says.

Mr Napier looks at me. I see his eyes searching my face, passing over every inch, washing me clean.

'Watch you grow up like your dad, son,' he says. 'Most boys don't have someone like your dad to steer them clear, and the world turns them the wrong way. We don't need any more men like that. You make sure you grow up the right way. Gentle on the outside and strong on the inside. Listen to me, now. Be good to folks, men and women and children alike, and you make sure others are as good as you. The only way the world changes is if we all choose to act the right way. We have the choice, you understand? Make sure you choose the right way.'

'Yes, sir,' I say.

Mr Napier's eyes search me for a time longer. Aunt Beth watches me too, and then she smiles quickly and looks over at Lottie.

'Well, now. I expect he's keen to see you both. You pass on my love, won't you?'

'Yes,' Lottie says. 'We will.'

Mr Napier gets out of the car and opens the doors for me and Lottie. He climbs back in the car, beside Aunt Beth. They drive away, back toward the farm, the dust rising behind the car, the wind taking it south, away from the church. We turn and face the clinic. Over by the side of the building, near a small rose garden cut with stone paths, Father's car is parked in the shade. Someone drove it over from the falls the night of the fog.

A nurse leads us down a hall, past cabinets filled with white gauze and bandages and small bottles of medicine. She smiles and speaks softly to me and Lottie. This is Eamon's mother, the nurse. She reaches behind me and pushes gently on my back, moving me into a room at the end of the hall. There, sitting on the edge of the bed, dressed in fresh trousers and a clean shirt, is Father. His beard is gone. I see his face, all of it, the skin a mottled pink from the touch of a razor. This is the first time I can remember seeing his chin.

'Here you are,' he says and smiles. 'I thought you'd got lost or maybe you'd grown used to life without your old man.'

Lottie rushes to the bed, wraps her arms around Father. He lifts his chin and rests it on her shoulder. I watch tears fall from Lottie's face onto the bedclothes behind Father.

'I'm sorry,' she says.

Father reaches up and touches Lottie's hair. 'Don't worry, love,' he says. 'It's not your fault.'

Lottie's tears slow. She sits on the bed and I sit on the other side of Father. We stay there a moment, each of us staring out the window at the church steeple and the trees behind it. In the distance, partway up Castor, light shines off the stones in the cemetery.

Father stands, moving slowly, a hand pressed to his side. He looks out the window at the clouds passing over the hill.

'Your mother would be proud of you both,' he says.

I carry Father's hat as we walk down the hall and out the doors of the clinic. The nurses follow, each of them waving as we walk beside the building, over to the garden and Father's car. Inside the car, the air is thick and heavy. Lottie sits beside Father, and I take the back seat. Father stays still, hands gripping the wheel, looking out at the light shining off the white building.

'You can ask me anything,' he says. 'I won't keep anything from you, not anymore. From now on, we talk about everything.'

I take a deep breath. The tips of my fingers feel strange, as if needles are pressing into them. I lean forward in the seat, pressing my fingers into the leather, digging my nails in.

'Who was that man by the bandstand?' I ask. 'The one who was talking to you and Uncle Jimmy that day.'

The roses glow in the sun. Bees pass from flower to flower. Above the rose garden, high on the hill, I can see the path that leads to the cemetery and the sign made of iron, showing between the trees.

'I'll tell you,' Father says. 'I'll tell you all of it but first I want to take you somewhere.'

40

The sun shines on the hood of the car, setting off flares of light that settle in the corners of the windshield. Father has the window down and one arm bent, his elbow in the air. From the back seat, I see the hairs on his arm moving in the wind, shifting like grass in the paddocks. Lottie winds down her window and I do the same. The air rushes in, mixing as it presses in from each window. It's a storm breaking around us, sweeping away the dust that we've picked up in these months in Gemini.

We pass over the railroad tracks. Rust-coated, empty railroad cars line a siding on the track, their insides powdered black with coal. Magpies perch on the edges of the open cars. We keep driving past the edge of town, around the base of Castor. The road grows darker, the dirt a rich, murky colour, and we climb the base of the hill and come down the other side.

There aren't many houses out here, only the odd farm carved out of bush. There are sheep and homesteads set back from the road down narrow paths. We pass over thin streams, each one wrapped with weak timber bridges covered in moss. We drive in silence, Father staring ahead, swinging his arms to move the wheel as the road curves through the bush.

We turn down a path marked out between wattle trees. There's an iron sign nailed into the ground on a spike. A name etched into the face. I see it as we turn onto the path and my breath catches. I turn my head as we go, keeping the sign in sight, until we're past it and it's lost behind the thin leaves of wattle.

Father parks the car fifty yards in front of a low, wide house. There's a porch spanning the front with two rocking chairs, each one holding a large cushion. Even from this far away, I can see a crucifix embroidered on each cushion.

'When your mother and I met, she was engaged to marry another man,' Father says. His hands are on the steering wheel, fingers curled around. He's staring out the windshield at the house. Lottie looks back at me, only for a moment, and then she watches Father as he rolls his knuckles over the wheel.

'She was only young,' he says. 'I was too. We weren't much more than children. Old enough for love but not old enough to know what to do with it. We met at a dance at the town hall. Her parents had two children before her and both of them died young, so they'd kept your mother away from the world, hoping to keep her safe from any sickness. I'd never seen her before that dance and when I did, I couldn't look away. It was as if nobody else was there in the hall. It felt like something in me opened up. There was a space inside me from then on, and it could only be filled by being near her. I spent the night waiting until I found the chance for us to meet and talk, and I felt that space inside me start to fill. We started to meet in secret but she'd been picked out by the son of a prominent family. He'd seen her and proposed marriage, and her parents had accepted. The wedding was coming and we were ill with the thought of it. We spent every moment we could together, walking through the bush and going out to the river, away from our families and away from the gossips of town.'

Father looks away from the house, at Lottie.

'Then she was with child. When we told her parents, they cast her out. The engagement was off, and the boy, the son of that family, he climbed to the top of the falls, climbed up there with all his shame and embarrassment, and he stepped over and washed it away.'

Father looks at me. The lids of his eyes are red along the edge.

'The man you saw that day behind the bandstand was the brother of that boy. Even after all this time, there are people who don't want to see me in Gemini. We left everything behind. My family, your mother's family, the town we were born in. But there are troubles that can follow you wherever you go. And there were troubles that followed your mother. That's the truth of it. She loved you both, you should know that, but there are some troubles that can block out love, the way clouds block out the sun.'

Father turns back to face the house and runs a hand through his hair. He straightens his collar, pulls on his hat. 'Come on,' he says. 'Let's go on up to the house.'

The ground is soft under my boots, dark and thick as wet clay. Father walks ahead of us. He walks with his hands by his sides, shaking them as he goes. We get a few yards from the house and the door opens. Father stops and Lottie and me fall in beside him. An old man and woman come through the door and onto the porch. I've seen them before, at Catherine Fletcher's funeral. The round red nose. The eyeglasses. They're the ones who stared at me at the grave, the ones who watched me and Lottie as Catherine was lowered into the ground.

'Good morning, Dale. Morning, Esther,' he says.

The man, Dale, nods at Father. He seems to be stooping, as if trying to pass under a barrier. Esther's eyes are wet.

'Morris,' Father says. 'Lottie. These are your grandparents, Mister and Missus Edwards.'

Mrs Edwards, my grandmother, walks down the two short, worn steps by the porch. She moves with effort, the way people move through water. She looks as though she might stumble as she reaches the soft ground.

'It's a pleasure to meet you,' Lottie says.

My grandmother stands in front of Lottie. She lifts a hand, almost touching Lottie's face, but her hand falls short, stuck in the air. 'You look like her,' she says. 'Doesn't she, Dale?'

He stays on the porch, shuffling his feet, bearing an invisible weight on his back. He nods his head. My grandmother looks between Lottie, Father and me. She looks at Father, at his side, the place where the knife went in.

'How are you feeling?' she asks.

'I'm fine,' Father says.

My grandmother rubs her hands together, in front of her belly. The skin looks as dry as paper.

'I believe she'd be happy to see us here today,' she says. She walks over and wraps her arms around me. Her wool jumper is soft against my cheek. She smells of biscuits and honey. 'Dale,' she says, letting go of me and turning around. 'Come down and give a proper greeting. Don't stand there all day.'

My grandfather steps off the porch and onto the stairs. His back is an arch, curving toward the ground. He peers up as he walks to Father then stands there a moment, partway to the ground, staring at Father's boots.

Father holds out his hand. 'Dale,' he says.

My grandfather looks up and sees Father's hand. His back starts to straighten and he takes Father's hand and shakes it. 'A lot of words were said. A lot of words before you left,' he says.

'I know,' Father says.

'Not a day goes by I don't think on it.'

'I know,' Father says. 'It's all right now.'

They shake hands for a long time before letting go, then my grandfather walks to me. His face is the colour of toast, baked by the sun and pocked with pale spots.

'Well, then,' he says. 'You best come inside. We'll brew some tea.'

We walk to the house. The door opens and I can see straight through to a window on the other side that looks out on a field of grass. I can almost hear Mother there, through the house and over by the window, telling me to come in.

41

A storm rolls in after the drive back from the other side of the hill. At the cottage, the air cools and the sky darkens. The wind picks up, rushing into every corner. It whistles as it moves, pushing on everything. The tin roof buckles, doors creak and moan.

Me and Lottie help Father move the firewood undercover. We turn over the wheelbarrow and tie down the axe and rake and the other tools. Father throws a rope over the boughs of the trees nearest the cottage. He leans his weight on the rope, testing each of them. His face draws tight when he does it and I see him touch his side.

Father goes off to the big house to help Aunt Beth shore up the windows. When he gets back to the cottage, the wind is shaking the walls, pressing on them like a beast trying to break in. The rain comes down hard, striking high notes on the tin roof. For most of the night, we sit around a kerosene lamp in the kitchen, huddled in close to the table, each of us yawning and nodding off, then waking with a quick pulse whenever a tree cracks and comes down in the bush. Each time it happens, Father touches me and Lottie on our shoulders.

I wake with my head and arms against the kitchen table. The storm has passed. One of my arms stays limp and I hit it to get the blood moving. I hear a noise outside and look through the window to see Father and Lottie walking and crouching. They're picking up sticks and bark, armfuls of litter from the storm. I walk through the back door and Father lifts a hand from his pile. He waves for me to come closer.

'Quite a big one,' he says.

I walk onto the dirt and look around at what the storm has left. There are leaves scattered over the grass and soil. There are long strips of bark like peeled skin hanging from trees. There are saplings lying on their sides, wrecked from top to bottom. I see a few large trees lying flat to the ground or propped at odd angles against other trees.

'What would've happened if one of those came down on the cottage?' I ask.

'Best not to ask that question,' Father says, looking out at the bush. 'Better to face the world we've got than the one that could've been.'

I look at Father's side and see the part of his shirt where the bandage pushes against the cotton. He drops his pile of sticks and bark on a bigger one over by the lean-to. He looks up at the thin streaks of cloud that break up the blue. I lean down and pick up strips of bark longer than my arms and take them over to the pile.

'Why don't you sit down? Me and Lottie can clean,' I say.

Father turns away from the clouds and smiles at me.

'I'm all right, son.'

I go back and join Lottie by the side of the house. We carry more of the storm wood to the pile. Father goes into the house and comes out carrying a cup of tea. He blows and steam rises into the air.

'We'll go home tomorrow,' he says. 'I'm needed back at the station.'

Me and Lottie share a look. Home tomorrow. Away from Gemini. I think about all the miles between here and home, how far we've come and how long it might take for us to return. What we'll leave and what we'll go home to. My mind races ahead and I can feel my heart start to keep pace.

'Do we have to?' Lottie asks.

'You've changed your tune,' Father says and smiles. 'You wanted nothing to do with coming here, remember?'

'It's different now.'

Father blows on his tea, looking over the rim of the cup. 'We don't have a choice, I'm afraid,' he says. 'We have to go.' He turns his eyes to me and stares, then gazes out at the bush and sips on his tea. 'Don't worry,' he says. 'We'll come back.'

When we're done clearing what fell in the storm, we sort out the inside of the cottage. We clean the kitchen and run a mop over the floors. We scoop the ash out of the woodstove and pack our clothes away in cases.

Father leads us down the path to the big house, pulling up fallen branches and ferns as he goes. We spend some time clearing bark and branches from outside the house. I sneak glances at the windows as I hunch over. There's movement inside. I see Aunt Beth and Flo folding clothes, taking pictures off the walls. As I'm leaning over, Aunt Beth stops near the window and looks at one of the walls. She reaches up and wipes her cheek.

We take our lunch outside on the porch. Aunt Beth brings us bread, cheese and tomatoes. She pours us cool lemon water. She doesn't say much, only to thank us when she sees the drive cleared. She looks down at her feet as she speaks, watching her bare toes as if they hold a secret. I don't see Flo. She stays in the house.

Men arrive at the farm in the afternoon. They appear in low-slung wagons hitched to teams of draught horses. I follow Father as he leads them to the sheds and paddocks. They stuff their hands in their trouser pockets as they walk beside the pig pens. They scratch their chins as they look at the udders of the cows. They sniff and nod as they look down at the chickens and they rub their palms together as they count the sheep. One by one, they hand over money to Father and leave with animals. We wave them off, squinting at the sun. After every sale, Father counts the notes and coins then climbs the steps of the big house. When he comes out, he's no longer holding the money.

Late in the day, two men arrive in a horse-drawn wagon. One is older, his forehead halfway back up his head. The other is younger. His son, no doubt. I follow Father and the men out to the stable. There are no more animals on the farm, save for Red and Blue. The horse is the last animal left. The younger man checks the horse's teeth, then he kneels and lifts each hoof. He stands and stares at the horse, running his tongue over his lower lip.

'How much you want for her, then?'

'Whatever you think's fair,' Father says.

The younger man looks at Father's side. He digs a hand into his trouser pocket and pulls out a handful of notes. He gives them to Father and they shake hands.

'It's a strange day,' Father says, staring at the money in his hands. 'More than one life's work building up stock and it's sold off in a few hours.'

The younger man doesn't seem to know where to lay his eyes. He looks around at the stable, at the dirt, at the wooden beams, at the gaps where the caulk has fallen out. His eyes settle on his father. He watches as the older man walks to the horse, touches the hair along its flank and whispers in its ear. It's his property now, this horse that used to belong to Uncle Jimmy. It belongs to him and his son.

'Shame about Jimmy,' the older man says. 'What brings a man to do that, I'll never know. To take a girl away from her family like that and to go at his own brother.' He sniffs and scratches the high part of his forehead.

Father shifts the earth with the heel of his boot. 'I suppose some people need something others can't give them,' Father says. 'When they don't get it, they need to square it away in their mind.'

'I guess we didn't know him,' the old man says. 'Guess he was bad all along.'

'I don't see it that way,' Father says, looking down at the dirt. 'There aren't any good or bad people, not like that. Only good and bad actions. There are choices people make, and James made the wrong choices. He'll have to pay for that.'

The old man scratches at his head, shakes it gently.

'Any news?' the younger man asks. 'About where Jimmy is, I mean.'

'Not yet,' Father says. 'Won't be long. They'll catch up with him soon enough.'

There's a silence, the younger man and his father looking at the horse, me watching Father shift the dirt with his boot. It stays a while, the silence, and then the horse neighs and the bridle chimes. The younger man unwraps the reins from the post and leads the horse out. The older man and Father follow.

I stay behind in the stable. The air is warm where the horse was and light peeks in through cracks in the wall, shining on the wood and the hay. I see something bright in the far corner. Out behind some offcuts of leather and old barrels, something is shining in the light. I walk over and kneel by the barrels. I reach in behind them. It takes the full length of my arm to find what's back there, feeling around until my fingers grip on something. When I pull my hand back and see what it is, I get a feeling like my insides are dropping to the floor. In my hand are some ladies' undergarments and a pair of shoes. The steel buckles on each shoe shine in the light.

'What you got there?'

Father is standing in the doorway, his face and body in shadow, the light behind him. I hold up what I found behind the barrels. All I can do is shake my head.

'What is that?'

I keep shaking my head. I can't get the words to come out of my mouth. Father walks over and holds out his hands, both of them. He takes what I'm holding like he's taking an offering, something sacred. He looks down at the leather and steel and cotton in his hands.

'Where did you get it, Morris?'

I point at the barrels, at the dark space behind them. Father nods. He stands there a long time, looking at the corner of the stable.

'I didn't know,' I say.

'It's all right,' he says.

Father turns them over in his hands and the light catches the steel buckles. The light runs a course across Father's chest as he turns the shoes over in his hands.

'Promise me this,' he says. 'Don't tell your aunt or Florence what you found.'

I think about the words I kept inside, the words I held that joined together into bricks. I remember the weight of them, pressing on my lungs and my stomach. I remember how it felt to keep them secret, keep them from getting out. Father seems to sense what I'm thinking. He moves the hair away from my eyes and runs his thumb over my brow.

'I know I said we're going to say it all from now on, but there are some words that can only hurt. They know the worst of it already. They know what he did. No need to tell them about this.'

I nod.

Father sighs and then he smiles, a weak smile that only seems to make his face tremble. 'Come on,' he says. 'It's getting late.'

I follow Father out of the stable. The last of the sun shines through the tops of the trees. He takes off his hat and covers the shoes and undergarments, keeps them covered until we're past the big house and making our way down the stone path.

We get to the cottage and I think about what Father said about words that can only hurt. Maybe there are some words we have to keep inside, some bricks that we need to carry. Maybe that's why our bodies grow from children into men and women. Why they need to stretch and fill out. Maybe we need to grow so we can carry the words inside. Maybe the world is a place that needs us to be strong, makes us change into a size that helps us hold the words we can't say so we can help each other, keep each other from hurting.

42

There's a knock at the door of the cottage. It's our final night in Gemini. We're sitting at the kitchen table, me and Father and Lottie, finishing off the last of our tea. Father walks down the hall and opens the front door.

'Morris,' he says. 'There's someone here to see you.'

Sam is standing in the doorway next to his father. He's holding his cap in his hands, wringing it like washing.

'Evening, Morris,' he says. 'I was hoping you could show me those stars.'

'The stars?'

'Sure, the stars,' he says. 'Those constellations you can't stop talking about. I was hoping we could have a look with the telescope.'

I look at Father. He smiles.

'Good idea,' he says. 'Art can have a drink with me.'

'Excellent idea,' Mr Napier says, rubbing his hands together. 'Got any sherry?'

'Half a bottle left,' Father says, moving to the side to let Mr Napier in. 'Morris, take a light with you, so you don't lose your way.'

Sam carries the kerosene lamp and I hitch the telescope over my shoulder. The brass is cool against my neck. Sam walks fast on the stone path, his footsteps echoing off the trees in the bush on either side of us, dark and silent in the shadows.

'What's the hurry?'

Sam doesn't answer. He holds the lamp out in front of his body. The flame moves, sending waves of light along Sam's arm.

'The constellations don't tend to run away,' I say. 'No need to rush.'

Sam stays silent. We reach the end of the path and I turn to walk out to the paddocks. Sam makes for the big house.

'Sam,' I say. 'Over here, in the paddock where it's dark.'

Sam climbs the back steps of the big house and knocks on the door. I tighten my grip on the telescope. Sam waits on the steps, spine as straight as a rake. The door opens and I can see Aunt Beth's face in the light. She looks at Sam and then over at me, squinting against the dark.

'Hello, Missus Turner. Can I see Florence, please?' Sam asks.

Aunt Beth draws her dressing-gown tight at her neck. 'It's getting late, Sam,' she says.

'Please, Missus Turner. It won't take long.'

Aunt Beth pulls some hair away from her eyes and tucks it behind one ear. She looks out at me, standing twenty feet away in the dim light. 'I'm not sure she'll want to come,' she says.

Aunt Beth turns and walks into the house. The door stays open. Sam stands on the steps, his body leaned in toward the door. The farm is quiet without the animals. There are no chickens scratching the soil, no pigs snorting, no sheep calling to each other. There's only the low, steady hum of crickets and cicadas filling the dark. After a time, Flo appears in the doorway. She's wearing a thick woollen jumper, and slacks that seem to hang from her. Her face looks tight, the skin like wax paper. She looks the way the men by the river in Melbourne looked, the ones me and George saw. She looks as though she hasn't eaten for days.

'What do you want?'

'Only the pleasure of your company,' Sam says. 'We're going to look at the stars. I've got Morris with me and he's brought the telescope.' Sam waves a hand in my direction.

Flo glances at me and then looks down at her feet. 'I don't think so,' she says. She turns to walk back into the house. Sam takes hold of her arm.

'Come on, Flo,' he says. 'You can't stay in there forever. It's only us and the stars. Nothing to worry about. A quick trip out to the paddock then you can come back.'

Flo leans against the door. A wind passes over the ground, pushing leaves onto the steps, gathering around Sam's feet.

'Let me get my coat,' Flo says.

We walk out to the paddock, Sam in the middle, me on one side and Flo on the other. Sam holds the lamp out in front, the way he did on the walk to the big house. He looks like a man on a ship, holding a lamp out over the water, peering down at the black ocean. Flo keeps quiet.

'Here looks good,' Sam says. He places the lamp on the ground and steps back in line with Flo as I drop the telescope from my shoulder. I set it down and swing it until it's pointing north.

'Who's first?'

'Let Flo have a look,' Sam says.

I take a step away from the telescope and Flo walks over, leans down.

'What do you see?' I ask.

292

I hear her breathing, fast and shallow. She lifts a hand and tilts the telescope. 'I can see Taurus, the bull. I can see Orion,' she says. 'It's clear tonight. You can see them just fine.'

Flo stands and walks away from the telescope. She hangs her head as she goes, walking to a spot a few feet from me. She must have been studying the constellations since we last came out, found a guide in one of her books.

'You know more than you let on,' Sam says. 'My turn.'

We watch Sam tilt and turn the telescope. The way he moves it, it's as though he thinks it's a cricket bat. We watch him swing back and forth.

'He's got no idea what he's doing,' Flo says.

'I heard that,' Sam says, still leaning over the telescope, moving it wildly.

The lamp flickers by Sam's feet. I watch the flame curl and twist, sending light into the darkness. A humble light, fragile and small, pushing against the black of the night.

'I'm sorry about Uncle Jude,' Flo says. Her face is turned away, the skin on her cheek tight and pale. 'I'm sorry my dad did that to yours.'

'It isn't your fault,' I say.

Flo turns and looks at me. She drags the back of her hand under her nose. 'A great detective, I am,' she says. 'I didn't see it. Didn't see it could be him.' Flo wipes her eyes and presses at the swollen skin beneath. 'I heard you and Lottie saying what he said,' she says. 'That night by the falls. I heard you telling the men that came to the house. I suppose I was right about one thing.'

'About what?'

'You remember that day someone attacked the Chinese shop? We were in the back of the truck and I was saying he didn't want to be left behind. You remember? I said he didn't want to be stuck here while she went off and lived a better life. I was saying that about Will Fletcher and I was right, only not about Fletcher.'

Flo looks at the sky and I follow her eyes to the bright lights above us. We stand there, watching the stars while Sam pushes around the telescope.

'Father told me the black next to the stars is just as important as the lights,' I say. 'It's the darkness around the light that helps us know it. He said you can't know about the light without knowing about the dark, and we have to make sense of both of them to really see what's around us.'

Flo nods, eyes still taking in the constellations. I think back to that night on our balcony in Hawthorn, back before we came to Gemini. I remember imagining what the night sky might look like this far from the city. Out here between the mountains, the light from the stars rushing through pure darkness to reach us. I have a strange feeling, as though I'm looking back at myself, looking back on this night. I feel as though I've already left.

I move over close to Flo and I reach out and take hold of her hand. We stay there, staring at the stars. I let my eyes relax until they're a blur, the dark and the light, all of it blending together. No longer sharp, no longer one thing and the other.

43

We pack the car early. Dew covers the grass and ferns beside the stone path, beads shining like jewels in the early light. We walk back and forth along the stones, carrying our bags and cases, odds and ends. Father tells us to wait by the car as he collects the last of our possessions.

Me and Lottie lean against the wheel guards on the car. I look out over the paddocks to the west, the yellow grass reaching out to the horizon. I look at the sheds closer in, the wood sides weathered grey by years of sun and storms, tin roofs rusting at the edges. Red and Blue are lounging near the sheds, legs still, tails limp, now there aren't any sheep to herd.

It seems important to look out over the farm, take it in with my eyes. I wonder if this is how it feels to go back from somewhere. If there's always a time, right before you turn away, when you try to take in everything. I want to paint a picture in my mind with a fine brush, each stroke careful and small. I want to capture every stone, every branch, every blade of grass. I won't leave anything out.

The front door of the big house opens and Aunt Beth walks onto the porch. She wraps a shawl around her shoulders then walks down the steps and onto the ground, feet bare to the dirt. Flo trails behind her. When Aunt Beth reaches us, she tilts back her head and looks at the sky.

'Good day to be travelling,' she says. 'You won't have any trouble on the road.'

Red and Blue come trotting over, legs stiff and slow-moving in the cold. Flo reaches down and scratches Blue behind the ear. Lottie calls Red over and she sits next to her, tail fanning her ankles.

'It's always cold in the morning at the start of a clear and sunny day,' Aunt Beth says. 'A little discomfort early on and then the enjoyment comes later. We're in for a treat of a day, I think.'

Father comes along the path carrying the telescope and a wicker basket. He raises his eyebrows and smiles when he sees Aunt Beth and Flo. Aunt Beth waves, pulls the shawl tight around her neck with her other hand.

'You don't want to leave that behind,' she says. 'Morris here would be lost without the stars. You're a landlocked sailor, aren't you, Morris?'

I smile at Aunt Beth, not sure what to say. She seems to want to fill the air around her with words, piling them into a barrier of easy words that stops the harder words from getting out.

'We've got plenty more stars to stare at back in the city,' Father says. He drops the wicker basket by the car and wraps an arm around my shoulder. 'Won't be the same as out here in the open though.'

'You'll have to come visit us down the coast sometime,' Aunt Beth says. 'Plenty of sky for stargazing down there.'

'You're leaving?' Lottie asks.

'Next week,' Aunt Beth says, nodding. 'There's too much for us here.' She looks around at the bush and the paddocks and the sheds, at the early light touching the tops of the trees and the shadows below. Her shoulders seem to shake as she does, a shudder from the cold or something else, I can't tell. 'We're going down to stay with my sister and her family. They're down Inverloch way, down near the water. We're looking forward to it. Aren't we, Flo?'

Flo keeps her eyes on Blue, smoothing the fur around his snout and running her hand along the length of his back.

Aunt Beth watches her, then she turns to us and smiles, lips pulled back, all her teeth showing. 'We'll be just fine,' she says.

We finish packing the car, the dogs walking loops around our legs as we place everything on the back seat and the boot. Father takes two empty gallon jugs from the boot and goes with Aunt Beth to the well to fill them with water. Me and Lottie take our seats, Lottie up front and me in the back, same way we came into Gemini. Red and Blue line their flanks to the car, and I lean out the open window and let them lick my hands. Flo stays back a few paces, face as low as the sun.

'Flo,' I say. 'When you get to the coast, let us know if you find a case that needs solving. Shipwrecks, sunken treasure, anything. We'll help, won't we, Lottie?'

'As long as we get a piece of the treasure,' Lottie says.

Flo's face lifts, the corners of her mouth turning up, the closest to a smile I've seen on her since before the fog. 'All right,' she says.

Father returns with the jugs of water and takes his place behind the wheel. Aunt Beth and Flo stand back as Father starts the engine. They wave as we pull away from the big house. I turn and look through the back window. They're still waving, and I watch until we pass into a dip in the driveway and they disappear from view.

The town is coming to life as we get to the main street. Shopkeepers run brooms over their front steps and hang signs in the windows.

Horses tied to posts flick their tails at the morning flies. Children chase each other around the legs of their mothers. I see Liam rolling a barrel along the side of the pub.

'I need to stop at the store,' Father says. 'Won't be long.'

Smoke rises from the chimney at the back of the general store. Outside, on the verandah, Ollie is sitting in his wheelchair, facing the river.

'Let's stretch our legs, Morris,' Father says. 'We've got a long drive ahead.'

I follow Father as he moves to the verandah. When he reaches the stairs, he stops and turns. 'Stay out here,' he says.

Father opens the door and enters the store. The bell above the door rings. Ollie looks at me and then quickly looks away, back to the river. I watch the dark water flow.

'The stairs again.'

I look at Ollie but he's still facing the river, eyes fixed on the water.

'Did you say something?' I ask.

'The stairs,' he says, still looking away. 'They stop me every time.'

He looks at me now and I think about how I saw Ollie when we came to Gemini. The way I pitied him. The boy I could have been, if polio had found me. The small body, the thin legs, the pale skin. He is more than that, stronger is some ways than a man.

'I can go give the stairs a kick if you like,' I say.

He makes a sound through his nose. It's not a laugh but it's not a whole lot less than that. 'Maybe another time,' he says.

I smile and look out at the river. I think back to the last time I spoke to Ollie, about the rocks and the current and his clothes steaming in the sun.

'I'm sorry about what happened that day.'

I look over at Ollie and he's looking at me from under his brow.

'What did I tell you about saying sorry? I don't want to have to scream this early in the morning.'

A horse and cart pass in the road, the driver hunched over against the cool morning air, gripping tight to the reins. There are crates in the cart filled with glass bottles of milk. The driver waves to us as he passes and then lifts the reins to his mouth and blows on his hands. We watch the cart go on up the road, the glass chiming.

'Are you all right?' I ask.

Ollie shrugs. 'I'm fine,' he says. 'Dad is staying with another miner, out in a cottage on the edge of town. He's been there since the new year. He says sorry more than you these days. I'm not sure if Ma has heard him yet or if she even wants to. She says he'll bring his earnings over and that's that for now.'

We watch the street. The sun rises over the hill and long shadows stretch from each tree and wall and post. Over by the thick grass on the riverbank, I see a rabbit move from behind a fallen tree trunk and into the clear.

My mind goes back to the camp, to the people skinning and boiling rabbits by the open fire. I wonder how long they'll be out there, travelling from place to place, working when they can, catching whatever will feed them. I think about the man warming the little girl's hands by the fire. Somebody should help them, make sure they don't have to live like that. They should give them a place to call home that isn't patched-together scrap where the wind and rain get in. More than anything, after what I've seen these past few months, I want that.

'I heard Ma say they're leaving town, Missus Turner and Flo,' Ollie says. 'Are they?'

'Next week,' I say. 'They sold off all the animals. There's only the dogs left now.'

'What will happen to the farm?'

'I don't know. They'll sell it sometime, I suppose. I guess it'll be empty for a while.'

'I suppose someone will have to come back here now and then. If only to keep it tidy.'

'I suppose so,' I say.

'Good,' Ollie says. 'That's good.'

The bell rings and Father walks onto the verandah. He's carrying two brown paper parcels tied around with twine. He puts the parcels under one arm and lifts his hat with his other hand. 'Good morning, Ollie,' he says.

'Morning, Mister Turner.'

Father looks between me and Ollie. He takes a step away from us. 'Come on over to the car soon, Morris. We have to set off. I saw your mother in there, Ollie. She'll be out before long.'

Ollie nods and Father walks out into the street and over to the car.

'Goodbye, Ollie,' I say.

'Goodbye, Morris.'

I walk to the edge of the verandah before my legs stop moving. I walk back to Ollie and I lean down and wrap my arms around him.

44

A cool wind blows in from over the bay. We turn into our street, Father pulling on the steering wheel, leaning on it as if steadying himself. The light flickers inside the car as we pass the trees and electricity poles. I see our neighbours going about their afternoon. I see Mr Greene, out in front of his house, polishing the headlamps on his car. I see Mrs Clayton tilting a watering can over her roses, Fish and Chips hugged against her ankles.

It feels as though we never left. All the time in Gemini, the cottage, the mine, the people, the falls. It could be a dream brought on by heat or fever. A season lived in a single night, fast asleep in bed. Nothing in this street has changed, but we have. Father and Lottie and me, we're coming home different.

We park outside our house. Mrs Clayton raises her head above her roses and waves. Fish and Chips bark, muzzles pointing to the sky. I get out of the car and straighten my spine until I hear the bones crack. I look to my right and see Lottie doing the same.

'You look like two newborn foals,' Mrs Clayton says. 'Just born and learning how to use those limbs.'

'It feels that way,' Lottie says. 'I need to learn to walk again.'

Lottie moves, stiff-legged, over to Father, who is pulling bags from the boot. She takes one from his arms and hitches it over her shoulder. Father watches her walk along the path, and then he takes a light bag and carries it past me. He tips his hat to Mrs Clayton.

'Afternoon, Ethel,' he says.

Mrs Clayton's lips come together. I can see her eyes move over Father's belly. She stays watching him, looking at the middle of him, and then her lips turn up into a smile. 'Welcome home,' she says.

I walk to the fence and put my hand through the iron bars. Fish and Chips lick my fingers. I run my hand over their ears and then I stand across from Mrs Clayton. She takes off a glove and places a palm on my cheek.

'It's good to have you back, Master Turner,' she says. 'It's not been the same here without you.'

From here, the street looks small. I can see the chimneys of houses stretching down toward town and I can hear the sounds of the city. The engines of cars, the sliding of trams in their rails, the hum of factories in the distance. It seems so big, this country. An endless place of plains and valleys and mountains. It seems as though there should be a spot for everyone here.

'Tell your father you can all come to mine for tea,' Mrs Clayton says. 'I've a big stew on. You tell him I won't take no for an answer. No use exhausting yourselves after such a long journey.'

'This is yours,' I say.

I reach under my shirt and pull out the chain Mrs Clayton gave me. The heather shines with the last of the sunlight. I unclasp the chain and pull it from around my neck.

'That's yours,' Mrs Clayton says. 'I don't mind if you keep it.'

'Thank you,' I say. I hold the chain over the fence and drop it into Mrs Clayton's hand. 'I don't want to need it. I want to try without it.'

Mrs Clayton looks down at the chain in her hand. She stays looking at it for a long time. I know that she's thinking about her boy. I know what she's feeling now, this sadness mixed with joy. The way you can hurt to think of someone who's gone and still want to remember them. It's the way I feel about Mother now. I can see that this is a way to live, holding the sadness and joy together.

'I'm glad to hear it,' Mrs Clayton says.

On the other side of the street, up the slope, I hear my name being called. It's George, kicking up his heels and running over to us. When he reaches our gate, he's panting like a dog.

'Turner,' he says. 'How long you been back?'

'We only just pulled up,' I say.

'You ought to have called ahead. We'd have put up a banner or formed lines for a parade. Wouldn't we, Missus Clayton?'

Father and Lottie come out of the house and make for the car. Father nods at George.

'Come on,' I say. 'Let's go down to the water.'

George blinks, surprised. I look at Father. He takes off his hat and hangs it over one of the iron posts on the gate.

'Go on,' he says. 'Lottie and I can finish up.'

Lottie lays her hands on her hips and rolls her eyes. 'Well, that went back to normal fast,' she says. 'I'll be sure to unpack for you too, your majesty.'

She shakes her head but there's no anger in her eyes. She smiles as I back away from the gate and lead George down the street.

Our feet fall into a rhythm. We walk along the bluestone gutter, balancing on the rough path. At the end of the street, we cross over to the high grass, passing small bushes covered in vines, and further to the tree line of the riverbank.

'You made the newspaper, Turner,' George says.

We sit on the soft clay bank and let our legs hang over the side, above the muddy brown water. The water goes on south, down to the edge of Hawthorn, where it'll turn west toward town. George picks up a stone and throws it into the river.

'You're famous,' he says. 'We all saw it. I tried to cut the story out of the paper. Mother told me I shouldn't be saving something so awful and did we all really need reminding? I told her if my friend Morris is in the newspaper, I'm cutting it out even if it's about him bursting into flames. She took the scissors off me after that. You wouldn't believe it, Morris. She's kept me inside most of the summer, what with Iris catching polio, long after other mothers let their children out. Said it won't be long until it's back. Now she's got to have her hand in everything. Can't even let me alone to save a newspaper story.'

'I saw it,' I say. 'They get papers out that way, same as here.'

George raises his eyebrows.

'Do they and all? The things you learn when your old friend comes back from solving crimes in the country. You a detective now?'

I pick up a stone and throw it over the water. It falls to the river and disappears below the surface.

'Hardly,' I say.

George clears his throat. He rubs his knees and looks out over the water, blinking.

'Sorry about your uncle,' he says. 'And your father too. He looks all right though. Good thing he's tougher than my father. Mine would've given up his life at the sight of a knife.'

I nod. George goes on rubbing his knees and then he picks up a stone and pitches it far over the water. It lands near the opposite bank, splashing at the surface and setting off a cormorant. The bird spreads its wings and soars above the water.

'I met my grandparents,' I say. 'Two of them, anyway. It's odd but I didn't know any family before this. Strange how someone losing their daughter could bring me to my family.'

George nods and throws another stone. It falls short, water splashing high above the river's surface.

Looking out over the water, I think of the night, months ago, when Father took that telephone call. Late at night in the hall, the kerosene lamp burning beside him. About how I learned of Catherine Fletcher. How I wanted to know more. What I know now is that I can't know Catherine Fletcher. If I didn't know her before, I can't know her now. You can't know a person by the way they left this world. A murder is like a planet forming, making us circle around and around the end of a life, but that doesn't get us any closer to the person. You can't know someone by finding who took them away. When someone goes, all that they were is left behind in the people who remember them. It's the shadow left when an eclipse passes over the sun. The sun is still there behind the shadow. It's that way with Mother and it's that way with Catherine Fletcher.

Wind blows over the water, picking at the surface, making small ripples that push against the bank. George wraps his arms around his knees. I let the wind pass through me, let it dig in under my shirt and cool my skin.

Something happened to me out there, at that town near the falls. I went through my own fall. All of Gemini, every one of us went through a fall and when we came up, we weren't the same.

The sky between the trees is a pale grey colour that stretches as far as I can see. Down low, near the horizon, I can see the first star of the evening. A faint light, easy to miss. It's only clear if you try hard to look at it, to keep it in front of you, keep it in sight. Finding out about the world is like watching the first star. I can see that now.

It's about not letting it get lost against the colours, the parts around the star that might hide it. You have to hold on to it, watch it until it starts to shine brighter and gets easier to track.

I lean back against the cool bank. Tomorrow is my birthday. I'll be fourteen years old. I keep staring at the star, soft and dim against the sky, and I rest my head against the dirt.

Author's note

Let me start by saying thank you so much for reading my book. It's a great pleasure to have written a novel that is being picked up by readers like you.

It's a curious thing, this relationship between the writer, and you, the reader of fiction. It's a slow-moving dance between expression and perception. The writer offers a tale that, hopefully, shows their commitment to honing their craft and training their eye, and to capturing truth and beauty. And then you come along. You give your time, exercise your patience and create the world of the story inside the little cinema of your mind, in response to the marks on the page. A novel doesn't really exist without the reader, so thank you for giving me your time and patience, and for screening my story in your own little cinema. I hope you feel it was worthwhile.

I started out, around twenty years ago, writing short stories before moving on to scripts for plays. I wrote four full-length scripts before trying my hand at a novel. Writing plays was, in many ways, a perfect way to learn how to tell a complete story from beginning to end. All you have are characters and the ways they relate to each other through dialogue and action. It's like learning how to boil down a bunch of ingredients until you have a rich stock that you can add to other meals. Writing plays helped me understand what stories, at their best, can do for people.

Stories are, to me, a safe space where we can explore the difficult and tragic and joyful and hopeful parts of life. And we do that by showing how characters and relationships transform through conflict. When telling stories, I want to entertain and delight (as I have been by so many stories I've encountered), but I really hope that I can move readers so that they feel something as these characters and relationships change. I think we get a deeper understanding of the themes inside works of fiction when we're moved in that way. If I didn't hit that mark for you with this book, I can only hope that you'll give me another chance with the next one.

So, it's probably time I explained why I set this coming-of-age story in the early years of the Great Depression. It was, in part, because of the stories I heard about my grandparents' childhoods. I come from a long line of working-class people. During the Depression, my pop was one of thirteen children growing up in inner-city Perth, trapping rabbits to help feed the family. On the other side, my nanna grew up with an alcoholic mother and shellshocked father in interwar Manchester. She was, by the accounts I've heard, raised by her sister. My granddad and his sister were abandoned by their mother in a village market in Greater Manchester. I can understand why, when war came around in the late thirties, it must have seemed, in some ways, like a path out of hardship. I can understand why my pop lied about his age to join up at seventeen. These are the stories I heard about my grandparents' lives, but I only knew them as warm, generous, loving people. I wanted to explore how a person could go through all of that and come out good on the other side.

There's also a strong tradition of using the past to make a point about the present. Miller did that with *The Crucible* at the height of McCarthyism, and it goes back at least as far as Shakespeare, with *Julius Caesar* and the late-Elizabethan threat of civil war. Exploring contemporary themes through the echoes of history gives us some distance, and that distance can be valuable.

At first glance, a small Depression-era town may not be an obvious setting to explore our predicament as we approach the mid-2020s. But I hope, now that you've made it to the end of the story, you'll agree that the broad-strokes colours of the Great Depression have more than a passing similarity to those in today's picture. There are the issues that have modified but have never left: power, violence, xenophobia, problematic masculinity, strict gender norms. The list, unfortunately, goes on. Other issues improved somewhat after the Depression, at least for a cohort, but are now returning. You could say that the world was sleepwalking toward the Great Depression from the start of the industrial revolution. You could also make a case that, since the 1970s, with the rise of neoliberalism and increasing inequality, we've been sleepwalking toward our own crisis. In the 1930s, as now, there were people being displaced; inadequate housing; weak labour rights and temporary gigs; a rising interest in far-right ideology; populist politicians using tensions to divide people and gain power; and charities and community groups having to step in to fill the gap in government interventions.

It's one thing to want to show all that, but I had to set up a scenario that would help me explore the themes of this book. There needed to be a catalyst to bring the Turner family to Gemini and dial up the pressure on the town. And so, Catherine Fletcher. Murder is the most tragic and confronting action, especially in a small town like Gemini. It sends ripples of fear through a community and rocks the stability of the society. I think that's why we're so interested in stories that involve murder and why I was so interested in writing one. We want to understand the outer edges of human experience so that we know what's possible in this world and can build our courage to protect what's important.

That's the heavy stuff in the book. It's important to pay attention to that, but we can't lose sight of the good. As Morris says, you can't know about the light without knowing about the dark, and we have to make sense of both of them. I hope you took some pleasure in the love, friendship and wonder in this story. I certainly did when writing it. In particular, getting lost in ancient stories about the stars and constellations was a joy.

As a kid, growing up in the fringe suburbs of Perth, I would have struggled to believe you if you said I would one day write a novel, never mind being invited by my publisher to add a message to you in this Author's Note. That wasn't part of my world. I would have thought myself more likely to travel to outer space than to have my name on a book. In a way, with *Gemini Falls* and with your help, I've been lucky enough to do both.

Acknowledgements

To Kat for the unwavering support, the early reading and for being a willing participant in my Odysseus pacts.

To my family, Kat's family and my friends for all the support and enthusiasm.

To Martin Hughes, Keiran Rogers and all the team at Affirm Press. Publishers take a big swing when they sign a debut author and I'm grateful that they went for the ball when they saw it coming.

To my agent, Lyn Tranter, for the belief and backing.

To Martin and Ruby Ashby-Orr for their expertise and patience in editing this book.

To Laura McNicol Smith, Grace Breen and Bonnie van Dorp for paving the way for this book in the world.

To the Redmond Barry Reading Room, the La Trobe Reading Room and the Queen's Hall, where I wrote parts of this book, and the staff of the State Library of Victoria.

To my adoptive home of Victoria and the traditional custodians of this land. It is a privilege to live in and write about this ancient, beautiful setting.